THE THIRD
Snoopypuss
MYSTERY

The CASE of the EX WHO Plotted Revenge

Georgann Prochaska

outskirts press

The Case of the Ex Who Plotted Revenge
The Third Snoopypuss Mystery
All Rights Reserved.
Copyright © 2017 Georgann Prochaska
v3.0

3 1350 00362 9385

Cover Photo © 2017 thinkstockphotos.com. All rights reserved - used with permission.

Outskirts Press, Inc.
http://www.outskirtspress.com

Paperback ISBN: 978-1-4787-8852-2
Hardback ISBN: 978-1-4787-8897-3

Library of Congress Control Number: 2017906030

Outskirts Press and the "OP" logo are trademarks belonging to Outskirts Press, Inc.

PRINTED IN THE UNITED STATES OF AMERICA

For Nancy Arnier

List of Characters

Whittle Residents:
    Phil Greer, his brother Griff, niece Taylor

Limekiln Residents:
    Alice Tricklebank and her bloodhound Audrey
    Lena Vincenti
    Julian Mueller
    Neda Zug, and her son Stephen, owners of Bait and Books
    Roger Zug
    Lt. Robert Unzicker "Bobby"
    Officers Briar and Jinn
    Mrs. Gina Pickler, cafeteria lady
    Trisha Parker and her mother Emily, father John
    Rooney Santoro, former student, home on leave
    Crystal Butterman, once housekeeper to Flossy Grueber
    Gretchen Kluski, Alice's next-door neighbor
    Gary Tuchman, historian
    Claude Grouper, retired historian
    Scott Stringini, neighbor

Guests from Bottom Ridge
    Silvie Jakubowski
    Gladys Wax
    Virgil Deke

Resident from Wisconsin
    Zadie Vanek

Chapter 1

November, 2013

Phil Greer walked out the prison door with all the swagger a man in his sixties could call up and saluted the guard. He shielded his eyes as if a Midwest November day had a bright sun, and frowned at his lumbering older brother who struggled out of the car and stood beyond the gate, next to his beat-up, old Chevy.

Griff had gotten heavier than Phil remembered, his face lined with tired, soft wrinkles. Phil imagined Griff's early morning as Angela probably nagged him about which car to drive into the desolate prison neighborhood. *Do you have to go pick him up? Can't he take the bus? Why does he have to stay with us?*

Griff was always one to do his duty. That's why he ended up running Pop's bicycle shop where hard work earned you dimes, not big bucks. His plain-faced kids picked up on Griff's small town notion of hard work, never lived anywhere but in Whittle.

Phil ran his hand over his short, gray hair buzzed close to the scalp. He walked toward his brother. His bones ached from sleeping in prison beds for forty months. The pale shadow on the ground told him his walk had changed to leaning forward with a catch in his hips.

Someone needs to pay for my years of missed opportunities.

Griff gave a small wave although he was standing in front of Phil and said, "Good to see you Philly." He didn't step forward with a hug or even a handshake. Instead he stood there like a big oaf in his worn winter jacket.

"Need a long-tabled, buffet lunch," Phil said. "Some place with spice and pie."

Griff had those weepy eyes, not out of emotion for reclaiming his brother but because of age. He patted Phil on the back as if testing their sibling relationship, and said, "Then I'm buying. Know just the place. Connie's on the highway. Remember Connie's?"

Phil thought Connie's was a dump, but he nodded anyway and got into the car. They talked of football until Griff parked in Connie's lot.

"This time, things will be different, Philly," said Griff. "You'll come home to the shop. Pop left it to you as much as me. You'll see. Be different."

"You can put kids' bikes together, not me," said Phil.

Griff pulled back from the steering wheel, his face colored. "Pop made a good living at the bike shop."

"When Pop was alive, I told him and I told you, I'm not giving away my time smiling at snot-nosed kids. Where'd it get him?"

"Or me?" suggested Griff, but seemingly tempered his anger with a stiff grin. "Angela and I want you home. Prison makes looking for a job tough. I know you don't like bikes, but for a short time . . . 'Til you get your head straight. 'Til you find work that suits you."

Inside Connie's neither spoke until a bored waitress escorted them to a table and brought two mugs of steaming coffee. Miniature plastic cups of non-dairy cream sat in a bowl on the table. Phil tore off the tops of each and poured the contents into his water glass. Griff frowned at the waste, but said nothing.

"I have big plans," said Phil, his jaw setting.

"And where'd your big plans get you last time?" asked Griff looking up from his coffee.

Phil didn't speak of his plan until he had eaten plates of food and asked for a cherry pie, whole.

"A whole pie?" asked the waitress.

"What I said, *Honey*."

The two looked at each other. Griff figured she had known difficult customers before. When the pie came, Phil shook his head, eyes mean. Raising his hand like a claw above the pie, Phil eyed Griff, before plunging his hand through the crust and into the thick baked cherries, slamming and squashing. As he pulled his hand out, his fingers crushed the filling and crust, working destruction until all that remained was red mush. Griff blinked his watery eyes and stared at the mess, horrified.

The waitress shook her head, straightened her shoulders, and muttered something before she spoke. "I'll get a wet towel."

Phil emptied the napkin holder, wiped his hands, and created a mound of debris. With a hateful look, he reached over and wiped the last red sticky off his thumb and onto his brother's shirt.

"Philly?" Griff asked, looking more alarmed than angry.

"This is how it's gonna go. I ain't going back to Pop's bicycle shop." Phil's voice rose in volume as if challenging everyone in the restaurant. "Not wasting days putting tricycles together for pampered kids. Let their fat-assed fathers do it."

The waitress slapped a wet towel down without cleaning the mess. Phil watched her walk away.

"You see the disrespect, Griff?" Phil pushed the sticky, wadded napkins to the floor.

"Okay," said Griff. "Not the shop, but you need a job. How you gonna live?"

"Trouble with you, Griff, you think skinny. Me? I'm going back to Limekiln. It's payback time. Got an old partner to see."

"Philly, no. Richie'll call the cops. He'll tell them you're back. He testified against you." Griff paused seeing his words carried no weight. Softly he added, "They'll all expect trouble."

"Richie gave me up to save his own skin. Gotta let him know what that means. Consequences." Phil rubbed his chin, newly shaved and itchy. "And, Lena."

"She's not your wife anymore."

"We had a priest, Griff. Eyes of the church, still married. She should have backed my story. Didn't. We all gotta face consequences."

"This is dangerous. You'll go back to prison. Come home with me."

"Been thinking about this a long time. Richie, Lena, and that busy-body friend of hers."

"Limekiln police'll arrest you for just walking down the street. People there are afraid of you." With more edgy emphasis Griff added, "You got no friends there."

"You're wrong," snapped Phil. "Got me one friend." Phil rubbed his chin, again. "Paid my debt to society. As a citizen, I get to go where I want. Got a daughter who's getting married. I think a good papa should walk her down the aisle."

"You don't *have* a daughter," said Griff, his voice pitching higher. "Lena never gave you any kids."

"Don't have to be married to have babies," said Phil. "Imagine Emily Parker's embarrassment when I claim Trisha as mine." His eyes looked out the window, and a wicked grin spread over his face. "Unless Emily chooses to play ball."

"You haven't learned a thing," said Griff, finally claiming the wet towel to clean his shirt. "You're my little brother, and I came here to help, but looks like you want to go back to prison life."

"Not prison. Got a plan," Phil leaned back in the chair, rubbing his palms together. "Richie, Lena, and Alice, always messing in my business. And others. . . whole lot of others. Griff, fun's a-coming. I can smell it. I can taste it. That Internet is a mighty good thing. I'll make them all sorry."

Chapter 2

From Milkweed Slough on the cold walk home with Audrey, her black and tan bloodhound, Alice removed her gloves to read two text messages. Neda Zug asked Alice to pick up her Christmas book order as soon as possible from Bait and Books on Corncrib Road. The second message came from a stranger asking for afternoon time to talk about Limekiln. Alice went through her normal routine of cleaning Audrey's paws of winter slop, followed by a snuggle on the leather couch, followed by the dog's breakfast.

Audrey was a messy eating machine. Her mouth dripped water while drinking, and her powerful shoulder shake sent streams smack against cabinets. Wiping the kitchen cabinets and floor after Audrey's energetic slurping, Alice once again filled the bowl with fresh water. While smaller dogs resembled vacuum-cleaners scooping up fallen crumbs, Audrey couldn't be bothered. Her focus was puppy enough to spot a stray sock she wanted to chew and, God forbid, swallow. Alice became hyper-vigilant at minding whatever her one-hundred-pound dog spied.

Winding a scarf over a woolly blue shirt covering her turtleneck, Alice harnessed her dog and drove to Bait and Books. Neda, the owner, loved books, but her income in the small town of Limekiln depended on also selling bait, lures, hooks and lines, even rods and waders.

On a crisp gray day with melting snow, the Limekiln village square offered a snapshot of another time. One end had a World War II tank that enticed boys to climb on top in warm weather, making pretend firing sounds - *pew pew pew* - followed by *pah-ting*. At the other end of the square stood the brick clock tower, built in the 1920s. The hourly chime was tinny and usually off by five minutes. Garden beds in winter slumber sat between the two attractions, a nativity scene nestled among decorated Christmas trees.

At one time when the economy slowed, Alice worried the town might deteriorate. A family-owned drug store closed, but the Joyce brothers opened a pizza restaurant in the building, and a bar specializing in craft beers opened two doors down. Both drew a younger crowd determined to party on Friday night.

As she drove across town, Alice saw a fire truck slowing, returning to the station. She waved, and the men gave a nonchalant wave back. One fire fighter, an ex-student, now so much taller and muscular, hardly resembled the freshman boy she once taught. Audrey smeared her slobber greeting on the passenger window.

Near the high school, a cluster of women snapped pictures of themselves in front of the sign for the Limekiln High School Fighting Claymores. Alice beeped her horn and waved at the women, remembering them as girls. With Christmas and Trisha Parker's wedding a week away, many former students, now in their thirties, returned to celebrate the marriage of a favorite cheerleader and to reunite with memories of being teenagers.

"You'll like Trisha," Alice said to her hound. "She's marrying a lovely man. You and I will be hosting three elderly people from Bottom Ridge. Trisha's wedding has booked all the available rooms near the interstate, but still . . . not enough rooms for all guests."

Audrey's head swiveled toward her as if she understood every word. "I suspect our three guests don't drive much anymore," said Alice. "Before you came to live with me, I did some searching in

Bottom Ridge. Don't recommend the town, but our visitors are pretty nice. They all have *dogs*," Alice said, pretending to impress her hound. "They won't mind slobber."

Alice petted her dog who went back to watching people walk on the sidewalk. "Gee, I hope they don't mind slobber," she said, shaking her loopy gray curls and blinking with wide owl-like eyes. "I never asked."

As Alice parked her pickup near Bait and Books, the cool air smelled of burning fireplaces. Neda's son Stephen loaded boxes of books from the shop onto his truck bed. At twenty-eight he was a handsome man, tall with sandy hair in a casual style. Somehow, he maintained a day's growth of beard. It crossed Alice's mind Stephen could be a dark, moody model for an outdoor magazine. He wore jeans, a collared shirt, and a rugged dark brown barn coat. She thought his sturdy boots resembled those of lumberjacks.

"What's going on?" Alice called as she and Audrey exited the truck.

"Don't ask, Mrs. T., Ma's inside." Stephen didn't make eye contact, and his right shoulder slumped with the weight of the boxes he carried. His left arm, shorter by at least six inches, only helped to balance the load.

Alice remembered him as a boy before his accident, bright, energetic, not the least bit dour.

In the shop Neda wore a stocking cap covering her ears and brown straight hair and a black puffy winter coat. With the coldness of the bookstore, Neda's glasses fogged and cleared as the front door closed and opened. A harsh chill lingered among the stacks of books. Both Alice and her hound noticed an unpleasant earthy smell, musty, moldy, spoiled. Normally, Neda burned cinnamon candles to cover the smell of old paper and night crawlers. Today, working in fits and starts, Neda packed up books in front of the shop. Alice heard someone in the back doing the same.

"Neda, what happened?"

"Everything is ruined or about to be ruined. Basement flood, no electricity . . . we're removing all the books and magazines before the dampness and odor gets to them." Her hand pushed the thought away long enough to suppress a sob. "Who's gonna buy waders slimed with mud and feed?" She jammed more books into a box. "Stephen's carrying boxes out of here as fast as he can. That's why I called you to grab your Christmas order." Neda looked around the shop, hundreds of books yet to rescue. "Everything in the basement is ruined." She started to weep.

"Let me help," said Alice as she slipped Audrey's leash on a door knob. "I can at least shuttle boxes to Stephen, and we can load up my pickup." At six feet tall, Alice took a deep breath, feeling claustrophobic in a book shop normally tightly organized with books, but also baskets of bookmarks, notepads, T-shirts, hats, and book games - now all disturbed with the haste of packing. Alice relayed filled boxes and bags to the door.

"I don't know what happened," said Neda, looking strangely lost. "Somehow the outdoor hose was left on full blast and water gushed in through the open bulkhead doors of the basement. Wind couldn't have blown the doors open." Neda rapidly blinked. "By the amount of water down there, the flood had to happen maybe Friday night or early Saturday. Neither Stephen nor I was here on the weekend. We had a book fest in Gray Rock." Taking a breath, her eyebrows drawn together, she began to talk rapidly. "We don't keep a lot of live bait in December, but we have some – had some. Poor little crickets. Our lizard owners will have to drive thirty miles to the nearest pet store for crickets. Oh, who knows if they'll think to gut-load before they feed the lizards." Her voice slowed over the crickets as if she were having a difficult time weighing their loss.

Still, Alice had to ask, "Gut-load?"

"Crickets have special nutrients that must be fed to them before they become a lizard's dinner. We use Cricket Chow." Neda's tone sounded like her information was common knowledge.

Alice wanted to hug her friend who stood barricaded behind a counter near the cash register where boxes of books fenced her in.

Neda packed, Alice shuttled, Stephen balanced boxes on trips to the truck, and Audrey's nose twitched and worked in the air filled with new smells. The hound's eyes moved back and forth, following Alice's every move. Her tail gave an occasional wag as her owner slipped her a chicken hotdog treat.

"Everything in the basement's destroyed," said Neda breaking her silence, "and the electrician and plumber can't get here until this afternoon. The water shorted out the electricity, so even my frozen bait . . . stinky. Good thing we didn't have a fire. The heat lamp for the crickets, sizzled."

"Heat lamp?" asked Alice

"Poor little things can't tolerate cold temperatures," answered Neda. Alice nodded at this new knowledge. Neda stopped working and sat on a stool, shoulders slumping. Her fingers collected bookmarks, fanning them like a deck of cards. "It'll take us weeks to clean this up. If you have time, you can help by taking this bag of romances to Lena." She straightened her spine. "What's done is done. If you don't mind, can you drop off these other six bags to customers? They all live near you. Everything is labeled."

Alice grabbed several bags of books and offered to stay a while longer to help Stephen load the truck.

For the first time, Neda smiled. "Thank you, Alice. A book delivery is more helpful in clearing out, making room. I called Gina Pickler who's in the back, and a couple college girls home for break should arrive any second."

"Hi, Mrs. Pickler," called Alice. "School vacation already?" Gina peeked out from the book stacks way in back of the shop, waved, and smiled.

She was in her fifties, a bit younger than Alice, but had the look of a happy, tired workhorse. Since Alice first met her, Gina had always held two jobs - one as a beloved, high school cafeteria lady who knew when to give a student an extra scoop of comfort food and another temporary job as a cleaning lady for the warehouse offices at night.

"Hey, Mrs. Tricklebank. First day of break and don't we have a job here? But don't you worry, Mrs. Zug. We'll have this right in a jiffy."

As often as Alice begged Gina to call her *Alice*, the shorter woman refused, keeping to formality. Alice and most of the other people in town spoke of her as Gina, but everyone addressed the cafeteria lady as Mrs. Pickler.

"Mrs. Zug," said Gina, "I'll be off on the northern run with bags of books." Her beige coat, two sizes too small, was frayed and soiled at the collar and cuffs.

Alice thought Gina had an American, apple-pie kind of face that with a smile assured others that everything would be all right.

"Mrs. Tricklebank, you say hello to Miss Jess and Mr. Peter for me."

"I will. Thank you for remembering my children." Alice shook her head at Gina's old-school concepts of respect. "Stay warm, Mrs. Pickler."

"Me? I'm always warm as toast." Gina steadied three shopping bags of books in each hand.

Seeing it was time to leave, Alice reached across the counter and squeezed Neda's hands. "You need more help, give me a call. Even if it's bringing you dinner or coffee. Today will wear you out."

Neda thanked Alice and said her sister was driving in to help, dinner and a stiff drink on the agenda.

After delivering bags of books to her neighbors, Alice drove to Lena's house on the southern edge of Limekiln, just down the street from her own home. Besides telling her dear friend about Neda's shop, Alice also wanted to share her questions about the fire trucks and police cars she saw, moving as if they were leaving the scene of a crime. A knock on Lena's front door told her no one was home. Alice and Audrey tried the back door. It was locked.

Alice didn't think it odd that her friend wasn't home. Since Julian, the potential fifth husband, entered the life of her best friend, Lena's days were given over to impulsive shopping or the lure of spying on her daughter's Smart Treats Cafe which belonged to Lena until she retired. Of course, as the wedding cake queen, Lena might be in last-minute strategy mode with Trisha Parker, firming decisions of frostings, fillings, and decorations for the wedding cakes. Everyone in Limekiln was abuzz about *the wedding* to be held on Christmas Eve. The mother of the bride had orchestrated an extravaganza - at least really big for the size of rural Limekiln.

"Why do you think Lena locked her backdoor?" Alice asked Audrey. "No one in Limekiln locks a backdoor."

Feeling uneasy, Alice left Lena's and drove into her own driveway. Alice kept a firm hand on the leash. Somewhere her hound managed to pick up a strip of sticky packing tape, winding it around her paw, causing her to limp. Audrey's brow furrowed, making her look both puzzled and annoyed.

"Try not to allow any twigs to stick to the tape." Alice said to her dog. "I'll remove the sticky in the house. Promise not to pull your fur. Okay? I *know* how sensitive your toes can be."

Audrey rounded the corner to the backyard and gave a muscular tug, jolting Alice's shoulder and causing her head to snap backward. Leaning in the opposite direction to allow her own weight to help restrain her hound, Alice looked toward a spot in her yard that drew her dog's immediate attention.

"What is that red thing? A ball?" asked Alice. Something lay in the wet grass ten feet away from her backdoor. "Audrey, you're way too interested in whatever that is."

She pushed the hound into the house but only closed the screen door in spite of the winter cold. Old gouges in the wooden backdoor, made by hard dog toenails, proved Audrey had no tolerance for being shut into the house. Alice adapted by allowing her dog to watch through the screen. Still, Audrey barked almost immediately, peeved at being denied the backyard treat.

Alice hurried, not wanting her hundred-pound dog to throw her bulk against the old screen door, or worse, knock it off its hinges. In the grass, she expected to find a dead bird or a piece of rabbit left by a coyote or dropped by a hawk, but instead Alice found a fist-size meatball of raw ground meat laced with small greenish blue pellets. Alice recognized the shape and color, sending a chill up her spine.

"Rat poison!"

She reached into a back pocket of her jeans for the latex gloves and a plastic bag she kept for unexpected dog business. With gloves on, she picked up the poisoned meat, cold to her touch, and put it in the bag. She looked toward the kitchen door. "The police need to know about this. So do our neighbors and the newspaper."

Who'd do such a thing? Is this a random act?

Pulling her cell phone out of her pocket, Alice called her next-door neighbor Gretchen Kluski and told her of the find. Gretchen's cat spent part of her day outdoors even in the winter, and although her cat had no taste for beef, Gretchen planned to be on watch.

"You take care of the police," said Gretchen. "I'll call Neighborhood Watch and check my backyard. This is an outrage."

In the house, Alice fussed over Audrey although she was angry. "I don't know anyone who would do such a heinous act. Not in Limekiln. Not anymore," said Alice to her dog.

Audrey's droopy eyes followed Alice's hands.

Alice pushed aside old memories of cruelties and chose to picture someone young and foolish, not attuned to the severity of his action, pitching a dog's death into a backyard. But who?

In her heart, Alice knew no one in Limekiln was that stupid. Her hands trembled at the thought of Audrey being the target.

"Who hates us that much?"

Chapter 3

When Alice entered the police station, comforting wafts of coffee and sugary treats hit her nose, reminding her of Limekiln High School days where clusters of her past colleagues absentmindedly ate donuts and pastry while preparing for classes. Audrey's nose also rose into the air, her eyes hopeful. Two officers, Briar and Jinn moved about; another sat at a desk, placing phone calls. None of them were disturbed by Audrey. Alice nodded at the men and women she knew and nimbly threaded between desks to stand outside Lieutenant Robert Unzicker's office. He gave her a big smile, left his desk, and greeted her at the door.

Lieutenant Unzicker, who Alice called Bobby, had been a lanky senior in Alice's English class. He grew into a fine police officer earning the title of lieutenant. Strong and serious, he made decisions with both his head and heart. Alice thought back to last summer when Bobby and his two sons played football in her backyard. His boys inherited their father's dark hair and dark eyes. Despite Bobby being dressed in tan slacks, blue sport coat, and tie, Alice thought she smelled smoke.

"Of course, you're here," said Bobby. "Lena called you."

"No," said Alice a bit confused as she gave him a quick hug in the doorway of his office and unwound her wool scarf. "Lena's not home. I haven't talked to her since yesterday. I'm here about this meatball." She held up the plastic bag, keeping it high above Audrey's head. The hound stretched her neck and her nose twitched, but her real interest dialed her nose into Bobby's crotch.

"Whoa, I forgot how assertive you can be," said Bobby to the hound as he pulled back, a white smear of slobber stuck to his pants. Alice pulled another bag with a damp towel out of her shoulder bag and handed it to Bobby.

"Sorry. A little over a year and a half old and still a puppy." Alice petted her dog, working to turn Audrey's head to a new direction as she wiped away slobber still on her dog's lips. "The meatball took my attention away from her."

"I'm assuming the half-pounder is not my lunch," said Bobby with a crooked smile as he moved to stand behind his desk.

"You wouldn't want this. The little green/blue pellets look like rat poison. I found it in my backyard." As she spoke, Alice felt her face reddening with anger. Her breathing became quick but shallow, talking difficult. She had enough worry about Audrey's health since bloodhounds were prone to bloat.

Poison was nasty for dogs, but at least she'd have time to get to a vet. But if this poison caused distress, bloat could follow. Kennedy, her dog trainer, once warned she might have less than an hour to save her dog's life. *That's because a dog's stomach fills with gas or fluid, knotting it, pinching the blood supply to organs, making it difficult for the dog to breathe.*

Friends thought her caution was crazy, but Alice worked every day to keep her dog happy, calm, and healthy. Privately, she linked the stray hound to her husband's spirit. She lost Baer, but wasn't about to lose Audrey. Alice gladly catered to Audrey's separation anxiety. Now the need to search her own yard every morning before Audrey went out? Most distressing.

"This character who threw the meatball is dangerous," said Alice. "Need to catch him fast."

"This was thrown into your yard?" asked Bobby.

"My backyard." Alice's voice weakened as she kept back tears.

"Someone had to stand outside the fence and pitch it in. The question is: is Audrey the only target or are other dogs in danger? This amount surely could kill any dog."

"You do have a knack of hitting upon a mess." Bobby shook his head and got serious. "I'm glad you brought this in. Acts like this often escalate. Remember the Jensen kid?" Sitting behind his desk, he leaned forward. "BB gunned birds, then cats and windows. Shot friends in the ankles before shooting his little brother with a rifle."

Alice nodded at the memory. "No one wants to see a child harmed."

"I'll send this to the lab for testing. Want to learn exactly what it is," said Bobby. "In the meantime, we'll operate as if this is poison."

"Thank you." Alice let out a sigh and sat.

Audrey leaned into Alice, her big head covered her owner's lap, sad eyes searching her owner's face.

"It may take a few days," said Bobby. "We've had a hectic morning."

"You mentioned Lena?" said Alice, feeling slow to pick up Bobby's earlier comment.

"You don't know?" asked Bobby, his face registering surprise. "There was a fire early this morning, about four, at the Smart Treats Cafe. It started outside in the garbage bins. Fire trucks got there in time so the structure is mostly okay."

Of course, thought Alice. *The fire trucks driving back to the station. Lena not home. The smell of smoke on Bobby.*

Alice knew of Lena's plans to bake Trisha's wedding cake in the ovens of the cafe. "What's the damage?"

"Mostly smoke," said Bobby. "The construction should only take a week. A section of the wall needs to be replaced along with a small part of the roof. It's the cleaning of soot that will be time consuming. All the electrical work has to be wiped or replaced. Everything inside the cafe has to be cleaned. But none of that can start until the insurance company does its analysis. Lena and Cheryl are looking at a month or two before the cafe will be up and running. Cheryl's already called her insurance company." Bobby eyed Alice, and she wondered what he wasn't saying. "Lena took the fire hard, became hysterical."

Alice sat back, dropping her hands onto Audrey's head. "This is terrible. Lena will have to find a new kitchen."

Bobby tapped a pen on his desk. "When I spoke to Lena this morning, she blamed Cheryl for dumping coals from a barbeque grill into the dumpster." He paused.

Alice asked, "What did Cheryl say?"

"That she hasn't grilled outside in weeks." Bobby looked pointedly at Alice. "The fire may not be an accident, Alice. We'll investigate but so will insurance. Lena should probably keep her accusations to herself until we know if this is arson. Why are you giving me that look?"

"Odd coincidences, don't you think?" Alice cocked her head, tilting it back and forth as if weighing choices. "My grandmother used to say tragedy comes in threes. One: the cafe has a fire. Two: I get a meatball maybe laced with poison. And three: Neda's basement at Bait and Books floods destroying her bait in a chemical soup."

"I hadn't heard about Neda's shop. How'd it flood?"

"The outside hose with the water turned on full blast into open bulkhead doors of the basement. Neda figures it happened Friday or Saturday."

"You think we have a bad guy in town?" asked Bobby, his pen tapped faster.

"Maybe. With so many visitors coming in for the wedding, no one would look twice at a stranger or a local who's been set off by . . . something."

"I'll let my men know about a possible problem." Bobby's face turned all-business as he rose and called Jinn to send the hunk of meat to the county lab.

Once Audrey was outside, she energetically shook fresh cold air into her fur, causing another cord of slobber to fly toward a street light. Alice paid no attention. Her stomach was tight with foreboding.

From the police station Alice and Audrey rushed back to Lena's house. This time Julian met them at the front door. "You better come in. We have company," he said as he placed his hand on Alice's back and gave her a gentle push.

A familiar looking woman in her early thirties sat next to Lena, and held her hand. She had a stocky body and prominent freckled cheekbones. She wore jeans and a black hooded sweatshirt jacket over another shirt. A logo on her jacket was a spoked wheel with the words *Schwinn Again*. Alice liked the woman's attention to Lena whose face was puffy with crying, her eyes mere slits.

Alice guessed Lena had rushed to dress when she heard the call about the fire. Nothing she wore matched. She shirt looked more like it belonged to Julian and her long blonde hair, normally curled to perfection, hung in a ponytail at the nape of her neck, held by an ordinary rubber band. Lena wore no makeup, or perhaps it washed away with tears and blotting tissues.

"I heard about the fire. Lena, I'm so sorry."

Alice pulled a chair closer to her friend. Noting Audrey's concern, Alice touched her dog's neck, preventing Audrey from disturbing Lena.

Lena blew her nose and reached for the tissue box. The younger woman patted Lena's arm.

"Hi, Mrs. Tricklebank," said the younger woman softly. "I'm Taylor Greer. Remember me? I'm Lena's niece from Whittle." Taylor turned to look at Lena as if for confirmation, and Lena picked up the story, her voice thick with emotion.

"This is Griff's daughter, Phil's niece." Lena wrapped her arms around Taylor. "And, yes, you are my niece. Just because I divorced Phil doesn't mean I divorced you or your family."

"We feel the same, Auntie Lena," said Taylor.

Alice unwound her scarf and made light conversation of long ago shopping sprees with Lena to buy birthday presents for Griff's children.

Lena didn't join in the rambling discussion of toys and birthday cards. She sat with her eyes lowered, only occasionally glancing at Julian.

Guessing Lena had private thoughts to share with her later, Alice rose to leave. Her heart broke for her best friend. She could tell the morning fire had wounded Lena deeply. Smart Treats was once Lena's bakery called Sweet's Treats, a business she and her second husband Charlie built, a business that supported Lena and her children after Charlie died, a business that sustained Lena even after divorcing two more husbands.

Audrey balked when Alice attempted to leave. The hound usually had an agenda of her own and still had not been allowed to sniff Taylor. She gave a power pull toward this new specimen of smells. Taylor welcomed the dog by grabbing her face with both hands, going into baby talk about what a *good girl* the dog was.

Standing behind Alice, Julian whispered, "You better stay. You'll want to hear this." He poured a cup of black coffee and set it down for Alice. She had been so caught up with Lena's distress, she had missed Julian's anger. Every muscle was taut, his eyes threatening. She sat down, wondering what disturbed him.

"Okay, what's going on?" asked Alice softly.

"Let me," said Taylor once again taking Lena's hand. "Last month Dad picked up Uncle Phil from prison. He served his time for fraud, assault, and theft."

Lena's body went rigid with her head bowed while she stared at the floor.

"Dad offered him a job at our bicycle shop," said Taylor with a tightness in her jaw. "Uncle Phil said the work of putting together bicycles is demeaning. He refused to work. He did, however, claim one of our best bikes." Taylor cleared her throat and looked at the blood-hound as if hiding embarrassment. "I don't know if this is real, but . . . well, Phil said he wants to get even with people in Limekiln."

Alice, who had been concentrating on Lena, switched her attention to Taylor. The younger woman bit her bottom lip and squeezed Lena's hand. Their shared grasp whitened each other's knuckles."

Julian glared at Alice in a way that frightened her. "Tell her all of it."

"He blames Lena for rejecting him and for not lying to the police to keep him out of jail," said Taylor. "Ridiculous, but Phil believes they're still married because a priest married them." Turning to face Alice, Taylor said, "He thinks you broke them up."

"Me?" asked Alice.

True, she and Lena had lengthy conversations as Lena worked out her frustrations of losing husbands – divorce, death, divorce, followed by one more divorce. As Lena dealt with the grief of ending her marriage to Phil, Alice had supported her friend by listening. Discussions led to both women forking Lena's apple dumplings, chomping on oatmeal raisin cookies, and spooning ice-cream covered peach slices with almond paste. Wonderful baked treats added pounds to each woman.

"Phil's crazy," said Lena. "Of course, he blames you. When he and I were married, he blamed all of my friends. Said they interfered." Lena's voice cracked. Alice caught Julian's sneer.

"I don't remember," asked Alice, "when you were married to Phil, were you close friends with Neda Zug at Bait and Books?"

The question seemed to confuse Lena. "She went through her divorce shortly after I divorced Phil, and I gave her advice. I buy books from her now. We're friendly, but I can't say we're close. Why are you bringing up Neda?"

"Could Phil have any grudge against her?" asked Alice.

"I can't imagine," said Lena. "No, I don't think so, other than when Phil hinted that he was the person who broke Stephen's arm for being rude, but that had nothing to do with Neda. And, anyway, they should be angry with Phil, not the other way around."

Alice explained the flood at Bait and Books. She watched as the details crushed Lena, making her seem smaller.

"Phil ever mention Neda Zug?" asked Alice of Taylor.

"Not that I ever heard, but the water damage sounds suspiciously like something Uncle Phil might do." Taylor then explained the incident of crushing a pie within the first hour of freedom. "Phil wiped his fingers on Dad's shirt. He is *such* a jerk."

"Gross," said Lena with contempt. "So like Phil. Never had appreciation of food or for the people who labor to make it." Lena's response was more abbreviated than Alice expected. In the past Lena strung together many expletives to describe Phil's behavior.

The hound went to Lena and sat at attention in front of her as if expecting a homemade treat.

"What about Richie Mills?" asked Alice enticing her dog away from Lena's knees with a chicken hot dog treat. "He testified against Phil. If Phil is angry, it should be at Richie. Did he say anything about him?"

Taylor's eyes dropped, a hunched tension struck her shoulders. "Dad said to talk to him first. I tried to find Richie before seeing Auntie Lena," she said softly. Her eyes recorded fear and failure. "He wasn't home. A neighbor told me Richie's truck was in the driveway so he can't be far. Said maybe he went to the corner for a beer, but I looked. He wasn't there."

"Maybe he went to a different tavern?" said Lena.

"Three others are open before breakfast," said Julian. "Serve the night crews from the warehouses."

Alice felt a chill. Richie Mills worked security at nights at one warehouse along the interstate. Early in the day, he should be home sleeping. Alice reached for her cell phone.

"We have to tell Bobby, uh, Lieutenant Unzicker," said Alice, "about Phil being out of prison. This morning your cafe had a fire, Neda's basement flooded, and I found a poisoned meatball the size of a man's fist, lying in my backyard. The police should check if Richie is okay."

The two women sitting together gasped, and Julian let out a grunt. Taylor paled as her face filled with contempt. "You think Phil . . .?"

"Can't hurt for them to check." Alice dialed the police station.

Julian went to Lena, placing his hand on her shoulder while Alice explained to Bobby this new information about Phil. While the three waited for the police to do a wellness check on Richie, they diverted fears by discussing the upcoming wedding. Taylor recalled childhood memories of Lena's fancy cupcakes. "Do you still have cream puff ads on a pink van?"

"Not the same van you remember," said Lena, "but pink. Still have cream puffs, maybe even bigger than you remember."

When Bobby called back, he explained the disarray of Richie's attic apartment in the old bungalow-style house. "Since you mentioned Phil might be back in town, I think it's time for Audrey to sniff out what happened. . . if anything happened. . ."

Chapter 4

Alice parked her pickup behind two squad cars in front of the brown, brick bungalow. Down the drive, Lieutenant Unzicker stood with Officers Briar and Jinn in front of a single garage, door down. A wreck of a battered pickup sat next to the garage, backed into place. They waited for Alice to secure Audrey for the search. A cold wind and spits of snow came early for December. Alice watched as her hound danced in the wet grass, not with excitement but with impatience at having cold, wet feet while being restricted in one spot as the officers limited information to skinny details of the mess they found in the apartment.

"Sorry, Sweetie." Alice patted her dog's side. "You're supposed to be an all-weather dog for searches. We'll move soon."

"We're not seeing any evidence of where Richie might be," said Bobby. "Looks like a small scuffle inside, but maybe it's just bad housekeeping."

"He go to Tori's for a beer?" asked Alice, knowing Richie's beer-drinking reputation.

With a nod from Bobby, Officer Briar finally said, "Checked the tavern. Not there. His truck's here. Neighbors next door said they saw him yesterday. Said he was a little drunk." Briar flipped open a small notebook, eyes alert. "Mrs. Kennan lives downstairs. She believes Richie wasn't home last night. Didn't hear anything. Said a woman knocked on his door earlier this morning and left." Briar's chin rose as if waiting for instructions.

"Taylor Greer," said Alice to Briar and Jinn. "She's Phil Greer's niece. Taylor came to warn Richie, then Lena and then me."

Bobby took a breath, Briar put his notebook away, and Jinn's expression tightened as he crossed his arms across his chest.

Alice knew Richie, but not well enough to detail his entire routine. Richie was in his fifties, carried soft, belly fat, and droopy bloodshot eyes. He was a quiet man, usually agreeable, some said gullible. Phil easily drew him into schemes, bilking the elderly out of money for house repairs that never happened. Richie received probation after testifying against Phil, the brains behind the plan.

Audrey gave a tug and a rolling gurgle came from her throat. "I know," said Alice. "You don't like standing still in a driveway with nothing to do." The bloodhound danced, shifting from foot to foot. "Just you wait," said Alice, "winter will be colder. I have boots for you to keep your paws from freezing. Don't care what your trainer thinks. Ready for stairs?" With a twitching nose, the hound looked up at her. "Yes, I'm the silly one. Of course, you're ready."

The bungalow had a pitched roof line with no dormers to expand the attic standing space. Two windows, one in front and another in back allowed natural light. Exposed to weather, the steep, rickety wooden stairs in back led to the attic apartment.

"Are you sure you want to take Audrey up there?" asked Bobby, "We can bring something down for her to sniff."

"No. She'll be fine," answered Alice as she turned to her dog. "Up."

Having a piece of Richie's clothing brought down would be just as useful for the search, but Alice had her own snoopy reason to see Richie's apartment. All three officers at the scene were men, trained in criminal observation of precise detail. Alice thought, however, women had an eye for important trivia. Maybe it was her own nosy interest, but Alice wanted to see the apartment for herself.

Audrey was used to climbing stairs, but the ice layer had thinned as police feet climbed and the day warmed, leaving a gloss of ice that shattered underfoot, returning to water. The hound liked when snow or mud squished between toes, but moving became awkward for the big dog on this slick, cracking ice. As a kid might move to prove strenuous effort, Audrey exaggerated each step, her brow furrowing at each snapping sound below her paws.

The apartment was as Alice expected: the slanted ceiling made standing tall difficult. The furniture was grouped at least two feet away from the slanted walls. An unmade double bed sat close to the door, a willy-nilly scattering of papers formed a heap that extended under the bed.

"Racing sheets, sports sections from newspapers, girly magazines as my dad used to call them," said Alice absently.

"Is it important?" asked Jinn.

The question drew Briar's attention, and he pulled his notebook and flipped it open.

"No. I'm just noticing what's in the pile," said Alice.

At the far end of the room near the front window stood a small table covered with cracked oil-cloth. Two chairs, a small dresser and refrigerator, all well-used and battered. On top of a three-shelf wooden bookcase, a hot plate left charred markings along with a river of dried spills of soup down the side. Boxes piled up where floor met ceiling.

"Odd the way the apartment is set up." Alice caught the expressions of the younger officers and quickly added, "Just noticing."

Bobby's right, thought Alice. *Housekeeping isn't Richie's strength.* At least Richie hung one shirt over the back of a chair. All other worn clothing bundled and tangled on the floor next to a saggy couch.

"Is this a closet?" Alice opened the door and pulled the chain to light the inside, only to find a bathroom. The builder had created a bathroom using wood paneling for the walls. In the taller part of the space stood a shower, the shorter part, a toilet but no sink.

"No sink? Who builds a bathroom with no sink?" asked Alice.

The men didn't answer.

Walking around the outside of the make-shift bathroom, Alice found a sink backing up to the shower wall.

"One sink," said Alice absently, "servicing both the kitchen for washing up and the bathroom as well. Huh."

"Is that important?" asked Jinn. His tone sounded weary of Alice's musings.

No . . . no," said Alice scanning the room, seeing the trash filled with empty beer cans.

"Might have to mention this construction to the village," said Bobby with distinct criticism in his voice.

The room smelled of stale sweat and burnt bacon fat. Audrey sneezed, sending a spray of dog snot.

Bobby smiled. "I won't tell Richie about Audrey. I don't think he'll notice a little more goo."

"Probably not," said Alice, forcing a smile. If she had to guess, Richie hadn't been here for hours. There was something about the coldness of the room that felt like abandonment.

"See. Hard to tell if there was a scuffle," said Bobby. "Officer Briar thought the way those loose newspapers were strewn across the floor seems suspicious."

"Probably kicked out of the way," guessed Alice, "but probably not through anger or an accident."

"Why do you say that?" asked Briar.

"Something my son would have done as a teen when I told him to clean his room." Alice again checked out the disarray. "Looks like an intentional scooping as if the newspapers were swept together by a kicking foot."

In spite of his partnership with Phil, Alice liked Richie, a polite man who always said hello. Yet, she thought him shy the way his head dipped to prevent eye contact, and his fingertips hid in his pockets.

Once he complained to Alice about chronic headaches and said, "Don't have money for doctors."

Alice pulled on latex gloves. "I need a piece of clothing that's been worn. Audrey's partial to pajamas, but I don't see any. How about that T-shirt from the pile?"

Bobby nodded, and with gloved hands, Alice placed the shirt in a big zippered bag.

"Why don't you just let Audrey sniff the shirt?" asked Officer Briar, not keeping judgment back as he looked to Jinn for agreement. The shorter officer nodded and glanced at his watch.

"I could," said Alice. "Hounds take years to mature. Audrey still has enough puppy in her that she might chew on the shirt. She's in that stage of testing objects to see if they're food. Smelly's good in her world, for a hunt or a meal."

Alice crouched down and pulled an excited face. "Okay, girl, here we go. We have a hunt. Time to sniff." Alice held the bag open, and the hound plunged her nose inside, filling the bag. The dog's eyes closed. Alice imagined the thrill of odors and swore Audrey's body gave a shudder of delight. "Audrey, find!"

The dog's nose dropped to the floor. The loose skin of her face fell forward virtually covering her eyes, and her long ears dragged on the floor, sweeping odor and dust toward the hound's nose. Audrey's head darted back and forth, backtracked across the room, lunging forward as if a brighter smell caught her attention. Finally, she gave a tug toward the door.

"We're off," said Alice to the policemen. "She's found the most recent or most interesting scent."

"How can you tell she found the right one?" asked Officer Jinn.

Alice shrugged and called back over her shoulder, "Just seems true." She followed the hound down the wet stairs. Rather than pulling toward town as Alice expected, her dog tugged down a side street. With Bobby and Briar following at a distance in cars, Jinn clipped along behind Alice.

"Richie has to be on these streets several times a day," said Jinn. "How does your dog know which trail to follow?"

"No idea," said Alice turning her head to yell back at Jinn. "We all shed skin cells, hair, sweat. If anything happened to Richie, Audrey might be picking up fear sweat."

Audrey's pace picked up, along with eagerness in her shoulders. Alice struggled to keep up, not anxious for a full-out run. Her dog always impressed with her ability. Here was Audrey following a scent that was at least a day old, a scent diluted by light snow and rain. Yet, Audrey hustled over wet ground as if Richie stood in front of her, waving her ahead.

"It's winter. How much sweat can hit the ground?" puffed Jinn trying to catch up.

Following Audrey had its own stamina. The pace of trailing wasn't like the rhythm of a foot race. Audrey stopped and bounded forward, each stop allowed a heartbeat to catch up, each surge kicked a follower's heart to beat faster. In her sixties, Alice was used to the pattern. Jinn, in his late twenties with weightlifting shoulders, not so much.

"If Richie is afraid, fear sweat is stinky," called Alice.

The hound's muscles rippled as she pulled Alice down the side street to Cemetery Road. Passing six houses, Audrey turned into the drive of the Grueber Mansion, which wasn't a mansion by modern standards but quite dramatic when it was built in the late 1800s.

To Alice, the Grueber house was a hodgepodge of asymmetrical paneled rooms, towers and nooks, a wide porch covered the front, several balconies projected from the second floor -- all of it covered with fancy fish-scale shingles and extensive turned woodwork. It was a crazy quilt of architectural detail.

Audrey's nose went to the air, and her pace increased. The hound moved in an easy lope, and Alice added a couple skips to her power walking, barely keeping up with her dog. They moved to the back steps of the mansion where Audrey barked and pawed the backdoor, insistent and probably annoyed with the barrier denying her access.

No one had lived in the Grueber Mansion for the last five years. Alice's son Peter once considered buying the old house to establish a bed and breakfast. After Flossy Grueber moved out to live in Oklahoma with her elderly daughter, Peter toured the house. His heart sank. Seven tiny bedrooms and only one bathroom refocused Peter's desire for a B & B in Limekiln. Instead, Peter decided to buy a house in New England where renovations wouldn't be as extensive. No current buyer was interested in taking on the Grueber Beast.

Out of habit, Bobby put his hand on Alice's arm and pushed her behind him. Officer Briar tried the back door, finding it unlocked. Bobby hand-signaled directions to Briar and Jinn. He and Briar then entered the house with guns drawn. Jinn grabbed Alice's elbow and held her back.

Knowing Audrey would keep barking if not allowed to enter, Alice pulled her dog close and whispered to Jinn her request to enter the enclosed back porch. He listened to the silence and waited before nodding his agreement. Together Audrey, Alice, and Jinn stepped into a mud room fitted with hooks on the wall, benches, and an old concrete utility sink. Alice played with Audrey's loose skin to silence her and popped a chicken hot dog treat into her mouth.

"I thought hot dogs are bad for dogs," whispered Jinn. "Too much fat."

"These are specially made by the Tran family at their chicken farm," said Alice keeping her voice soft. Engle Tran's working on a marketing strategy: hot dogs for pets." Alice and Jinn froze at the sound of a door closing.

"Quiet, Audrey," whispered Alice, "Be a good girl. You brought us here and now we're done." Alice knelt and tapped her own shoulder, and Audrey responded with a vigorous placement of both wet paws on her owner's shoulders, a signal she understood the search was over.

The move, however, knocked a kneeling Alice to the floor. Out of the corner of her eye, Alice caught Jinn's surprise and covered her own embarrassment by saying, "Such a big girl. Doesn't know her own strength. I wonder who's feeding you?" She pulled three more chicken hot dog treats. Each slipped easily down Audrey's throat.

"Why are you sitting on the floor?" asked Bobby as he stood in the doorway into the house. He motioned Jinn inside. "You all right?" He offered Alice his hand, but she shook her head and stayed on the floor. In her tumble she happened to see pale footprints as if they had been made by dirty water now dried. *Small feet*, noted Alice.

"I'm keeping Audrey occupied," said Alice as her fingers caressed the ears of her sitting dog. "Did you notice these shoe prints?" Alice pointed to the dried footprints next to her hip. "No telling how long they've been here, but interesting all the same."

"I'll have Jinn take pictures."

"Find anyone inside?" asked Alice, unable to stop her curiosity.

"Time for you to leave," ordered Bobby. Then in a softer tone, "We found Richie."

None of the officers scurried about, so Alice guessed the answer before she asked. "Is he hurt?"

Bobby looked over his shoulder and in a low voice said, "Richie's been shot, twice in the chest. You know to keep this quiet, but you might mention his death to Lena. If this is Phil's doing, we can use pertinent information of where we might find him."

Phil got to Richie after all, thought Alice. Sadness took over followed by fear. Who was next?

"Lena was upset when I left her," said Alice. "I'll wait a couple hours before telling her about Richie. Does he have family?"

"We'll look into it. At the moment, I have no idea. Time to go."

With one hand, Bobby opened the porch backdoor for Alice to leave. Alice gave Audrey a jingle with the leash, and her dog rose to move outside. Slow-stepping toward the driveway, Alice's ears picked up Bobby's orders to his men about interviewing neighbors and friends plus his request for an evidence team from the county. Through the window her eye caught Bobby's free hand shooing her along. His mouth formed the word *Go*.

Alice and Audrey walked back to the pickup parked on the quiet street in front of Richie's apartment. For all the excitement of trailing, Alice felt the shattering truth. Murder had returned to Limekiln.

Chapter 5

"This isn't going as promised," said Alice to her dog as they drove home from the search. "I wasn't ever going to involve you with anymore dead people, but here we are." The bloodhound sat on the bench seat of the pickup with her classic ha-ha-ha face, eyes droopy, mouth open, tongue lolling to one side. "I know you're thrilled with searching," continued Alice, "but you and I need to think about Richie so I can figure out what to tell Lena. How do I tell her Phil's a murderer?"

Years of Richie and Phil stories flashed through her mind. Richie was almost as short as Phil, but where Phil had bravado, Richie's kid-like gentleness made him easily swayed by a con man like Phil. The police also found it simple to convince Richie to turn against his old partner in crime and testify in court.

Returning home with Audrey, Alice didn't recognize the woman inside a car parked in front of her neighbor Gretchen's house. She pulled into her own driveway and checked the backyard.

"Any meatballs?" asked Alice. "Nope. Looks like you're safe to play until we go inside."

The young woman from the car, probably in her early twenties, followed Alice to the back of the house. She was petite with a narrow face, her eyes wide-set, cheekbones and nose freckled, hair a mess of brown ringlets. She wasn't pretty, but attractive in a quiet way. The word *settled* came to Alice's mind. Or *resigned*. She wore black tights and a short black skirt bunched around her thighs by the elastic hem of her winter coat. She wore no scarf, and Alice could see blushing mottled the young woman's throat. *She's nervous*, concluded Alice.

"Mrs. Tricklebank?" Alice nodded. "Mrs. Tricklebank, you don't know me. I texted you this morning about setting up a time to meet?"

"I'm sorry," said Alice remembering the second text of that morning. "I got busy and forgot. So many things . . . Please come in." Alice opened the backdoor, "If you don't mind, a very friendly bloodhound at some point will sniff your crotch."

With the door open, Audrey powered her way past Alice to be the first inside, then turned as if she stood as the official greeter.

The young woman's nose wrinkled and one eyebrow rose. "That's okay," she said. "She's partly why I'm here."

"You texted you had questions about Limekiln. How can I help?"

Once in the house, the women removed coats, scarves, and gloves. Audrey snuffled all the important smells of a new guest and left only a slight white streak of slobber behind. Alice handed the woman a damp towel.

Clearing her throat, the woman said, "I'm Zadie Vanek, but I was born Deirdre Hart, named apparently after my birth mother." Zadie's voice rose at the end of her sentence, making a statement sound like question. "I'm looking for her and thought you'd be able to help me."

A school teacher for over thirty years, Alice knew many residents in Limekiln, but try as she might, the name *Hart* didn't ring a bell.

"Off the top of my head, I don't recall anyone named Hart. Do you know details about her?"

Zadie explained her past. Born in Iowa in 1990, she had been adopted and raised by older parents in Wisconsin. They'd waited a long time for a child and gave her the family name of Zadie. Because she recently met the love of her life and talked of marriage and children, one haunting question consumed her: Why did her birth parents give her up?

"I sent for my birth certificate. I expected my birth mother to be maybe fifteen or sixteen because . . . well, you know. Sometimes a girl . . ." Zadie looked down at her hands and began to chew her lower lip as the blotching on her neck deepened in color. "My birth mother turned out to be thirty-five when I was born." Zadie's overly bright eyes scanned the room. Still she bit her lip as if waiting for Alice to fill in the gaps and reveal terrible forgotten information.

"I hate to disappoint you," said Alice as softly as she could, "I've lived in Limekiln for well over thirty years, but I don't recall anyone with the name Hart. That doesn't mean she didn't live here. Maybe someone else in town can help. I have a friend who owned a cafe and also works on genealogy. She's a whiz with Google and newspaper archives. Maybe if we get our heads together . . ."

Zadie dropped her chin with a small tolerant smile. "I've Googled every Deirdre Hart in existence, including Heart, Hartmann, Heartstone. You wouldn't believe how many Deirdre Harts exist in all fifty states."

"Well," said Alice as possible leads crashed together in her mind. "Let's look at this from a different angle." Audrey came to attention before dropping to the floor near Alice's feet. "First, what led you to me or even to Limekiln, and second, when did your mother live here?"

"That's just it. I don't know if she ever did live here," said Zadie. Her fingers knotted together. "But three things pointed me to you and Limekiln. Internet has information about how you helped a doll sales-woman search for a little girl. Your pictures are on Pinterest. Also, you and Audrey found a lost man."

Alice remembered the annoying woman who sold dolls on eBay and brazened her way into Alice and Lena's investigation of a lost girl, all for her doll company to gain online publicity. And last summer, when an old man with dementia wandered off, his granddaughter called for help. Since young people record everything in pictures, the granddaughter snapped photos for posting online.

"I understand, but none of those things point to Limekiln," said Alice.

"The real reason I wanted to find you," continued Zadie, "is in the blog of Flossy Grueber's cards and letters."

Mentioning Flossy Grueber stunned Alice. She sat back in her chair. Audrey sat up and pawed at Alice's knee. Not sure how to respond, Alice patted her dog's head. Flossy had passed a few years ago, leaving her house empty.

What are the chances Audrey and I'd return home to a young woman who read Flossy Grueber's blog post?

Not one to ignore a juicy coincidence, Alice asked, "Really?"

Zadie nodded.

"I knew Flossy very well," said Alice. "She's gone. Can't be a blog by the same woman."

"Yes," insisted Zadie, "it is. The postings are by her great-grand-niece, Trulee Metto. Flossy willed the letters to her niece. Trulee said she has thousands and thinks they're historical. Since September, she's posted almost three hundred letters."

"Wow!" said Alice, imagining old, personal letters being shared with the world. *Will they produce embarrassment or awaken ghosts?*

"When I Googled Deirdre, I found the blog," said Zadie. "The index listed a letter addressed to Deirdre Hart. In that letter, Flossy also mentioned you."

Alice had nothing to say and shook her head as if to rattle something loose. Audrey rose to place her paws on her owner's shoulders. "I'm okay," said Alice after their hug. Her dog went back to lying on the floor.

"Anyone can read the blog?" asked Alice.

Zadie nodded and pulled her phone. In seconds, a picture of Flossy appeared on the screen.

Alice's mind raced over what she knew of Flossy's personal correspondence to the town's residents. Surely most letters were filled with gratitude and encouragement. But she felt that chill of the unknown. This intrusion into private conversations wasn't right.

"Flossy wrote that Deirdre's decision was painful," said Zadie. "Mentioned a gift she sent. Hoped the new baby was well." Zadie's forehead frowned as she blinked control of tears. "I'm sure the baby was me."

Alice offered a tissue and wondered who in town gave up a child.

"Flossy was a lovely woman," said Alice as a flood of memories returned. "She supported the high school band and regularly bought uniforms for the football team. I have fond memories of the school emptying for a parade down Cemetery Road to the Grueber Mansion. Every year neighbors lined the road with lawn chairs. But the special celebration came when Flossy turned one-hundred."

Flag girls and cheerleaders led off the parade, followed by the football team in full uniform. The tap of snare drums drowned out the soft click of cleated feet on pavement. The band marched in taking position directly in front of Flossy's house. High school students filled front yards across from the Mansion.

That last year the drum major blew his whistle for the serenade to begin. Horns blasted for attention. Neighbors stood as the band played the *National Anthem*. In all, the band played six songs, ending the concert with an unexpected choice: the Rolling Stones hit *Satisfaction*. The audience gasped, but a few friends like Alice knew the song was one of Flossy's favorites although she didn't understand why. Everyone watched as the elderly woman sat in her wheel chair on the porch, both of her arms waving wildly. Later she told a reporter she danced on her birthday. Tears pooled in Alice's eyes, remembering her lost friend.

"In Flossy's letter," said Zadie, eyes narrowing, "she wrote she was sure you and the other teachers allowed the senior girls to win the softball game. The way she wrote it led me to Limekiln and you. Maybe you don't know Deirdre," said Zadie with doubt in her voice, "but she knew you."

"I want to help, really," said Alice. "Let me chew on this awhile. So sorry. Just not recalling anyone named Hart or Deirdre."

"Some possibility, I guess," said Zadie taking a deep breath, "Deirdre listed a maiden name or changed her name through marriage. Or maybe the person who filled out my birth certificate got it wrong."

The young woman twisted in her chair, tilting her head from side to side before rolling her shoulders. When she put the heel of her hand on her chin and gave a push, Zadie's neck popped with the forced stretch. "My neck gets stiff," she said.

Alice had seen the maneuver many times with high school athletes, but the pop alerted Audrey who sat up, looked at Alice, and gurgled a whine in her throat. Alice shushed her dog.

"You said Flossy mentioned your mother by name?"

"She did," said Zadie with a nod.

"So, really, there can't be a mistake in recording your birth." Alice frowned and said, "I can't imagine your birth mother gave a false identity because why not create a different name for you? Curious. She named you after herself before giving you up for adoption."

"Exactly!" Zadie's hands fluttered in front of her as if pulling threads together. "I understand a teenager hiding her identity, but a woman of thirty-five? Do you think Deirdre was a nun?"

"A nun?" sputtered Alice, shocked at Zadie's conclusion, not one she'd have ever drawn. "Limekiln, of course, did have a few nuns assigned here, but Flossy was Lutheran so I don't see her being close enough with the Sisters to send a gift for a new baby. Anyway, I remember the nuns being way too old for childbirth."

"If *you* can't help, I don't know what to do next." said Zadie chewing her lip again. "I've exhausted every Internet site. I wrote to Trulee to see if she also had envelopes with return addresses, but she doesn't. And no address books, either." Zadie looked downcast. Her eyes blinked as she looked at a blank wall, working at control. "Maybe this search is hopeless."

Alice felt sympathy for the girl who was so determined to find her birth mother.

"We have a researcher in town who maintains the Historical Museum," offered Alice. "Gary Tuchman keeps newspapers, phone books, even church bulletins."

"Won't all that be online?"

Alice shifted in her chair, stopping a chuckle. Zadie's tone reflected the doubt young people had in the Internet skills of the older population. Almost launching a defense for keeping hard copies of church bulletins with who participated in what, Alice stopped. In this case, Zadie was quite right. Alice had little notion of the depth of historical material online. For that information, Alice depended on Lena. At any other time, Lena stood ready to dive into a search, but with Phil in town, Alice wasn't so sure.

"I don't really know what our library or historical society keeps online," said Alice. "But it's worth asking Gary. He's in his *thirties* and, odd as it may seem, collects even the smallest detail. He might surprise you."

Zadie's mouth twisted to the side of her face. Alice thought the young woman's expression reflected impatience.

"Can a bloodhound smell DNA?" asked Zadie as she sat taller with this new idea. "Maybe your dog can sniff me and find my mother based on that?"

So many people had the wrong impression of a bloodhound's ability. Maybe Audrey could smell DNA, but a find was dependent on the communication between handler and dog. Her hound liked a challenge of a physical hunt but was stubborn. Once at the police station, Alice gave her dog the identifying smell in a plastic bag and expected Audrey to slobber on the suspected drug dealer in a lineup. Audrey's eyes looked insulted, and Alice imagined her dog's reply. *Sorry, not worth my time. He's standing right there with the other men. If you don't believe me, bring in a drug sniffing shepherd. That's his job.*

"I wish Audrey could identify DNA," said Alice to Zadie. "The truth is *I* don't know how to present that to her. On hunts, I supply her with a specific scent and she searches. DNA, however, is too abstract, too tricky for me to communicate to her what we want."

After they exchanged contact information and Zadie left, Alice picked up her cell phone to search online for Flossy's blog. She found two thank you notes of the many letters Flossy wrote to her. Deirdre Hart's letter, also an easy find. Alice scanned a few other letters, finding examples of small town simple life - the fish fry at the VFW and a spaghetti dinner for the father/son soccer team. Curiosity forced Alice's fingers to type *Richie Mills*. Sure enough, one letter to Richie popped up. Alice didn't recognize Flossy's harsh tone. The letter commended Richie for "doing the right thing for the second time in your life by testifying against Phil."

Alice sat back. "Pretty severe," she said to her dog. "Not like her to be cruel."

Gathering her thoughts, Alice set up her mental white board with what she knew about the time of Zadie's birth. In 1990 Deirdre Hart, the birth mother, was thirty-five. Alice and Lena were forty. All three of them knew Flossy. True, Limekiln had nearly a thousand people in town, not including farm families. Alice knew of families with children in high school, her fellow churchgoers, her children's friends and families, shopkeepers, people who appeared in newspaper articles, but not everyone in town. Regularly young professionals with small children moved into and out of the new neighborhood developed close to the interstate. Perhaps upwardly mobile couples found a quiet rural life too boring. Alice's knowledge of residents was more town oriented.

But, Zadie had prompted an itch.

"Audrey, how unlikely is it that Phil is out of jail, Richie is found dead in the Grueber Mansion, and a young woman appears, looking for her birth mother who knew Flossy Grueber."

The big hound awkwardly climbed onto the leather couch and stretched out before flipping onto her back.

"Okay, you take a nap. But, don't let your imagination wander."

Was it a simple coincidence in 1990 Zadie was born and Lena divorced Phil Greer who had been unfaithful to her with many women?

Chapter 6

Julian met Alice at the door, his shoulders hunched, jaw tight, with usual grumpy demeanor.

"Been ordered to pick up butter pecan ice cream," he said, pulling on a trucker's cap and zipping his jacket. "Glad you called. Maybe you can talk sense into Magpie on this Phil thing. It's like talking to a wall." With that he pushed past Alice, ready to leave.

Oh, boy, thought Alice. She welcomed Julian's change of nicknames for Lena, always sensitive about her weight. Once Alice told Julian she'd like to hit him over the head every time he called Lena *Fatty*. *Magpie* was cuter, but this new nickname was still a jab since it referred to Lena's obsession with many collections of chickens and roosters, cookbooks, kitchen tools, bowls, dolls and doll house furniture. Because of Christmas, Julian's past as a truck driver inspired Lena to drag out all of her sons' Tonka trucks, decorating them with ribbon and small pine cones. With limited space for displays, Lena charged ahead setting out twelve motion-sensitive dancing Santas. The swaying hips drew Audrey's attention, and she barked back a warning.

"Is Taylor still here?" called Alice over her shoulder to Julian.

"Nah. Officer Briar called," said Julian. "Wanted to see her right away. She went to call her old man before going into the station. Magpie's in the back. Maybe she'll talk to you."

Pulling Audrey close to her thigh, they threaded past the delicate

Christmas decorations. Alice kept an eye on Audrey's whip-like tail, very able to send a display crashing to the floor. The hound continued to bark as music played for Santas with gyrating hips or Santas who ho-ho-ho'ed.

Lena sat in the sunroom thumbing through November/December magazines, bending corners, to remember pages. When Alice entered the room, Lena didn't look up. It had been hours since Alice talked to Lena and Taylor. Her best friend still hadn't styled her blonde hair into long curls. Delaying grooming, not unusual for Alice, but this was Lena who was all about glitz and glam. Alice wondered how long Lena cried. Her eyes were bloodshot, cheeks red and shiny as if newly scrubbed.

"Finished with your lieutenant?" Lena asked, everything about her tight, bottled up except for a tremor in her hands.

"Yes. You want to hear what happened?" Alice kept her voice soft. *Something is wrong.*

"Not particularly interested," said Lena taking a deep breath, "more crazy mischief?"

Watching Lena's hands, Audrey moved to the patio door. Her brow wrinkled as she turned to look at Lena. The hound's twitching nose probably concluded there were no special homemade treats available.

"It's concerning Richie." Alice waited for Lena's curiosity to ignite, for interest to relax her shoulders and brighten her eyes. Lena, however, flipped more pages.

"I'm rethinking my wedding cake design for Trisha's wedding." Lena's tone was flat as if Alice intruded into her personal time. "She wants blush roses both real and in sugar for the cakes, but a collection of small frosted green leaves will provide a nice framing contrast. What'd ya think?"

Alice leaned forward to view the collection of pictures Lena had assembled.

"Lena, why are you thinking about cake design now? The wedding's eight days away."

Audrey sniffed the coffee table, leaving a streak of slobber. Her movement activated a small train to run around a track beneath the table, tooting. The hound woofed three warning baritone protests. Alice ran her calming hand down Audrey's back and wished she knew what could alleviate Lena's guarded posture.

"Lena, what's really wrong?"

"I told you. I made forty cake layers for the twenty layer cakes. All now ruined in the fire. I thought they were protected from the heat and smoke because they were frozen. But . . . " Lena shook her head, one hand turning palm up.

"They were in the freezer?" asked Alice.

"Yes, Alice, that's what you do with wedding cakes," snapped Lena. "Make the cake, wrap it in layers of plastic wrap, and freeze." Then softening her voice, Lena added, "Putting on the crumb coat is so much easier and faster after the cake defrosts yet is still cold."

"I don't remember ever putting on a crumb coat," admitted Alice in a small voice.

Lena looked incredulous. "How many years have we been friends? Do you even know what a crumb coat is?" Alice blinked with big owl eyes, and Lena shook her head. "It's that thin coat of frosting you put on a cake to hold the crumbs down away from the final coating of frosting. Do you at least crown the cake before you ice it?" Lena paused, her tone that of a regal cake superior. "Remove the rising bump when it bakes? Y'know, create a *flat* surface?"

"Seems a waste of good cake," said Alice. "I just frost a cake, mostly when it's still warm." She pictured dripping frosting and edited out a comment of her family not being fussy. "We're gobblers."

"Good thing your son became a chef . . . not you." Lena rolled her eyes, but their banter managed to pull a smile to Lena's lips.

"What happens now?" asked Alice.

"Throw it all away. Start over," said Lena, a shiver tossing her head. "The firemen didn't allow me into the bakery kitchen early this morning because they were still checking for fire in the walls. Cheryl called to say the electricity cut out during the fire and with all the smoke and turmoil of fire-fighting, the freezer doors opened. It's all gone."

"I wish I could be of help."

Lena's face registered a bemused no-thank-you. "I have time to bake the cakes again, but where? All my aluminum pans, cake stands, frosting bags, spatulas for the crumb coat . . ." Lena looked over her reading glasses at Alice. "All gone. Where do I find the equipment, the space, the ovens?"

"Cheryl will help."

"I don't need help. I need a big oven. The fire throws off my schedule." Lena still pretended to concentrate on the magazine, wrinkling pages as she flipped them. "Trisha expects twenty wedding layer cakes as part of the twenty table decorations and one small wedding cake for her and Nick. Counting tomorrow, I have seven days. As Julian says, 'I'm skunked.'"

Alice decided to change the topic. "Want to hear about Richie?" asked Alice.

"Okay. What?" Her small voice was sarcastic. "Phil drink all his beer? Or did they break into the hard stuff?"

The hound rubbed against Lena's thigh, her nose almost on Lena's chest. Alice saw her dog's face full of expectation. *Treat?*

Any other day Lena often tossed homemade dog bones in Audrey's direction. Lena's recipe included oatmeal, cottage cheese and carrots. Instead, she pushed Audrey's face away.

"Lena, Richie was shot. He's dead."

Alice knew her tone was too heavy. If she expected Lena's sympathy to take over, she was wrong. For any tragedy, even squirrel road-kill, Lena offered sobs, but not for Richie.

"You think Phil did it?" Her voice remained edgy.

"*Maybe* Phil shot him," said Alice keeping judgment out of her voice. "The police are investigating."

"You taking on Phil as a case?" Her question sounded like an accusation.

Alice heard the warning. The hurt of the morning's devastation morphed into exploding anger. Even an insistent whine from Audrey didn't break Lena's dark mood.

Alice wasn't a detective, but sometimes she snooped into situations when people wanted to share what they knew but feared causing needless trouble for a neighbor.

"No one asked me to look into all these troubles," said Alice. "Bobby's in charge. He'll handle it."

"Good!" Lena's voice, loud, startled the hound who backed away and hid behind a chair. "If anyone asks for help, don't include me."

"I know you don't have time because of the cakes."

Lena looked up, her anger flashing. "I want Phil in jail for all the bad things he's done and people let slide. Let the police arrest him for arson or trying to kill your dog, but I'm *not* going to help prove he's not guilty of murder."

"You think he's innocent?" Alice couldn't believe Lena still trusted Phil. No wonder Julian was angry.

"I *know* Phil Greer," sputtered Lena. "Let me remind you that he's a genius - a *genius* - at spotting weakness. The shenanigan of throwing a meatball filled with poison into your yard was done because somehow he knows Audrey is your weakness. She's the tripwire that will hurt you the most . . . for the longest period of time."

"With Bait and Books," said Alice, her knee jumped with fear, "he went after the business not to destroy but to cause pain."

Lena nodded. "He burned the cafe partly because Cheryl's now the owner. When she was a kid and I wasn't around, he was mean to her." With a fierceness, Lena added, "And she hated him."

"What do you think he had against Neda Zug?"

Lena shook her head. "Don't know. Years ago, he viciously hurt Stephen. We *all* knew it. Of course, no one could prove it. Probably a warning. Why did he go after them again? Don't know."

"You think the target could be Roger," repeated Alice.

"The pig farmer?" asked Lena. "Can't imagine. Roger stayed on his farm until he and Neda divorced. No, I think Phil is getting even with Neda or he wants something from her."

"If you're right about Phil wanting to cause pain," said Alice, but with the look on Lena's face she quickly added, "and I'm sure you are, why would he kill Richie?"

"That's what I'm trying to say. To Phil, lingering pain is more important. It's a warning: if you don't do *exactly* as I say, something worse will follow. If he killed Richie, murder spoils his usual plan."

Alice remembered the time years ago when Lena became secretive and held her hand behind her back, hiding a broken finger. Unable to stop herself, Alice intruded into Lena's privacy and called Phil on it. He responded with eyes elated with power, "Discipline, for my girl." Yet even that confession didn't convince Lena to press charges or leave him. With the splint off, Lena went back to the game of pleasing Phil, complete with giggles. Alice hated that time in their lives as Lena see-sawed between welcoming a contrite Phil to her bed and tossing his butt out.

"Phil's violent and cruel," Alice said absently, piecing together details of the morning.

"Don't I know it." Fire entered Lena's eyes. "Learned it the hard way. He manipulates weakness. Worked at my stupidity until . . . until no self was left. Poor Richie never had a chance." Tears finally filled Lena's eyes.

Alice reached over to squeeze Lena's hand, and as she did, her action cued the Santas who ho-ho-ho-ed and danced to Christmas music. Audrey came out of hiding, a low grumble in her throat as she eyed Alice first and then the menacing Santas. Two big woofs did little to stop the festive men in red.

"Well, I'm done with Phil," said Lena, oblivious to the room's noise. "He's Bobby's problem." She threw down the magazine, pages tearing as it landed, and another round of Santas played out.

Alice took a deep breath to calm her thinking. "In a few hours, stories will circulate about Richie. Because of your marriage to Phil, you need to be prepared for questions. Richie was killed in the Grueber Mansion. I'm guessing he walked there for an appointment. Maybe Phil - maybe not," said Alice carefully, aware of Lena's sensitivity. "Big empty house."

"And you think what? Phil lived there, hiding out?"

"This morning the police didn't let me inside to know," said Alice. "But, it's a good place to kill someone. Huge piece of land, overgrown landscaping, big rundown house. Anyone might assume a gunshot wouldn't be heard or that Richie wouldn't be found right away."

"Does it have heat?" asked Lena

"I was only allowed in the mudroom."

Lena shook her head. "Waiting in a cold house, probably without furniture? Phil? Not wanting the body to be found right away? No way! Not Phil's style. If he wanted someone dead, he'd stage it to look like something else. Make the police guess at motive . . . or method." Tears again entered Lena's eyes, but Alice didn't know what her friend was remembering.

"You really don't believe Phil killed Richie?" Alice cautiously asked.

"Alice, it makes no sense," Lena tilted her head, breaking all eye contact. "What's his motive? For Phil to murder someone, that person had to be in his way. A major hindrance. Know what I mean?" When Lena looked up, her eyes held fear.

"Not simple revenge?" offered Alice.

"Nothing is ever simple with that man." Her voice softened as if remembering defeat. "He doesn't make mistakes."

"He went to *jail*," said Alice, trying to bolster Lena's hope.

Lena crossed her arms and pulled herself taller. "Look how he manipulated Richie all those years. Phil distracted a home owner's attention outside while Richie entered the house through the back and took what Phil told him to steal."

Lena rose, rummaged in a decorative box on a shelf, and removed a gold wedding band. "Phil was too smart." She sat down, rolling the ring in her fingers. "If Phil hadn't lost his temper that one time and hit the old man with a hammer, he wouldn't have spent three years locked up."

Newspaper stories reported the elderly veteran recognized Phil's two-man heist scam. As he charged into his home for his gun, Phil grabbed and spun him around. The old man's arm and shoulder caught the first blow of Phil's hammer. According to the article, Richie saved the man's life, wrestling the hammer from Phil's hand.

"What's with the ring?" asked Alice.

"A wedding ring."

"Yours?"

Lena held up the ring. "I gave it to the police to check if it's stolen. No record. They gave it back. So, is it mine?" Lena's face held doubt.

"Let it go," demanded Alice, feeling the chill of Lena's complicated bond with her ex. "Donate it. Sell it."

"I can't," said Lena, gripping the ring in her fist. "But I'm not snooping with you if it involves Phil."

"You still have feelings for him."

"Of course, I have feelings. I hate him." Lena's body withered. "Alice, I don't have the emotional energy. Call me a coward, but I don't want any more pain." Lena's chin dropped to her chest. "Case closed."

Alice understood how the events in town had upset Lena, first the fire at the cafe she nurtured and handed off to her daughter and then learning her ex-husband was out of jail and back in town. Even the delight of baking wedding cakes for Trisha's wedding was scarred by the need for borrowed ovens and baking equipment. Alice decided to change the topic, once again.

"Will you listen to another case? One we've been invited into?"

"What is it?" Lena's voice was suspicious, her eyes curious.

"Remember anyone in Limekiln named Deirdre Hart?"

"No. Who is she?"

Alice told the story of Zadie Vanek's search for her birth mother and Flossy Grueber's letters posted online in a blog. Alice expected Lena to be amused at a blog about Limekiln residents.

"Who knew Flossy copied letters to us for a history?" said Alice, a lightness in her voice. "And why would she? No wonder she remembered conversations and so much daily detail. I always thought she had a phenomenal memory, not an FBI file on each of us."

"What are you saying?" asked Lena, an echo of fear in her voice. "Surely, not all the letters?"

"I don't know, but boxes of them. The great-grandniece inherited the letters and plans to post them for the purpose of recording Flossy's history in Limekiln." Lena's face paled as Alice continued. "I've only learned of the letters today. A few of mine are already posted - just thank you notes, but Flossy wrote many to me and my children. That was just her way."

"The niece can't post mine," said Lena, her body stiffening again. "Those are private."

Julian walked into the house and called out, "Got a half gallon of butter brickle. No butter pecan." Neither woman answered. "Putting it in the fridge."

Alice whispered to Lena, "Julian on edge?"

"Mad at me. Thinks I'm defending Phil." Lena picked up her magazine from the floor and straightened the coffee table before the ring went back to the box.

Julian stood in the doorway of the sunroom, sour-faced. "That crazy-assed ex of yours dumped a whole, big bag of fertilizer on the front lawn of the guy down the street. You know the one with the stupid animated deer on his lawn. Stringini? Lawn'll be dead in days. He'll be planting a whole new lawn in the spring. You still forgiving Phil?"

Alice wanted to ask how Julian knew Phil was behind the damage, but she kept quiet.

"It's not that I'm forgiving," said Lena, "but not helping. Alice and I are trying to find a young woman's mother. We've decided the police can throw Phil's butt into prison all by themselves. I'm on a different case." Alice saw Lena's enthusiasm rise. "We're all working to find Deirdre Hart. You, too. Final answer."

After a long day, Alice settled on the couch to watch *It's a Wonderful Life* on television, Audrey joined her, throwing her shoulder into Alice's hip and allowing her face to drop on her owner's thigh.

"Deirdre Hart. Don't know anyone with that name, Audrey, but it's haunting." Alice's fingers made light, lazy circles in her dog's fur. "Anyone can read Flossy's blog. Even Phil." Alice felt a chill and adjusted an afghan to cape her shoulders as she repeated, "Even Phil."

As her eyes become heavy, she blinked rapidly, trying to stay awake long enough to watch the end of the black and white movie. After George Bailey found ZuZu's flower petals in his pocket, Alice nodded into a twilight sleep. A chubby smiling angel with a naughty smile slipped into her dream, ringing a school bell. "Time to wake up. Really, Alice, wake up."

With her heart hammering, Alice awoke to remember the nagging question from Richie's apartment that only just took shape. The make-do construction placed the only sink in the kitchen. So why wasn't Richie's toothbrush sitting next to the dish soap?

Chapter 7

Audrey's morning walk was gray but not cold for December. Low hanging clouds promised a snow shower before lunch, but the weather report predicted rain followed by bright sun in the afternoon.

The hound loped along in her yellow light coat with her nose to the ground of a new route toward Milkweed Slough for her peaceful morning squat-down. Alice changed their normal path when the Stringini family decorated their yard with animated Christmas deer. Lit with twinkling lights, deer heads glided left and right, causing Audrey to bark. Her brow wrinkled more than usual. Alice considered her hound a good listener, but no amount of explanation made a difference to her dog's snit fit. Apparently, in the hound's mind, those deer had to go.

In the air was the smell of the fertilizer dump. *Poor Scott*, thought Alice, *so particular about his lawn and now this.* Not knowing Scott's history with Phil, Alice wondered, *Why?*

Skirting the Stringini house, Alice directed Audrey around the block, cut through a park, and hopped a ditch to avoid the bad deer. Audrey's paws became a little dirtier, but what was new? At home, Alice had warm water and towels ready for cleaning toes that squished in mud.

"You have to be on your best behavior today," Alice said to her hound. "We're invited to the country club. Trisha's mother insisted we both attend, but it's not like we have a role in the actual wedding or reception." Alice smiled as she mused, "Having you as a flower girl could have added interest." Alice wiped a piece of gunk from the fur around Audrey's eyes. "Try not to push your nose into crotches, okay? These will be ladies, well-dressed, not crazy about slobber on their clothing."

Alice thought, *the wedding is only seven days away.*

Audrey's face registered ha-ha-ha.

Before she left for the country club, Alice received a text from a former colleague. Something was up with the bride's mother, Emily. Instructions in the text asked Alice to read Flossy's blog, particularly focusing on Emily Parker.

Country Club always sounded exclusive, but Alice remembered it as the farm it had been before G&G bought it, turning corn fields into fairways and roughs, the barn into a clubhouse restaurant, and remote fields into a gun range. For some residents, Golf and Guns took the edge off being rural. The barn tripled in size to accommodate large gatherings for shooting tournaments and receptions but maintained the traditional red-barn design. Most days the residents who lunched at the restaurant or golfed the back nine heard the distant cracking of gunfire.

The invitation to a rehearsal lunch (to prepare for the rehearsal and eventually the actual wedding), ordered everyone with any responsibility to attend. Alice tried to beg off by using Audrey as an excuse. No country club, even one that resembled a big red barn, wanted a bloodhound slinging slobber at a buffet, but Emily Parker was not a woman easily moved to change her plan.

"I personally will bring you food," said Emily over the phone. "You and Audrey will eat in the welcoming entrance next to coat check so you can hear my wedding instructions."

As Alice and Audrey entered the restaurant, Emily glanced at them with a scowl. Alice tugged at her roomy belted jacket with bulging patch pockets and wondered if her dog's treats were too noticeable.

"Ladies," called Emily and clapped three times. A nod of Emily's head sent Alice to a chair at a small table in the entrance. As a football coach might address an assembly of players, Emily reviewed the iron-clad schedule. Alice guessed for many, this was the third telling. The first was a letter, second, the phone conversation, third, the rehearsal for the rehearsal. As a host of three elderly people from the groom's home in Bottom Ridge, Alice's responsibility was to know Emily's schedule and see to it that Silvie Jakubowski, Gladys Wax, and Virgil Deke were dressed and in church pews on time. "Like clockwork," finished Emily.

The bride's mother was the epitome of spit and polish. Her blonde hair was teased into a smooth helmet, perfect makeup highlighted eyes, brows, and lips, her silk suit the color of Christmas berries.

Alice kneeled and petted Audrey, often whispering in her dog's ear, and worked to keep Audrey occupied as Emily spoke, but the country club servers brought trays and hot dishes to the long buffet tables. Audrey's nose twitched at wafts of meat, with eyes that seemed to evaluate which tray she'd attack first. Alice stood and wound the leash around her arm and hoped one hundred pounds of dog didn't dash for the table, dragging her owner behind like a freshly chopped Christmas tree.

Emily handed out a timeline sheet to the silent women in the audience. Audrey sat, stood, and sat during the presentation with a whining gurgle in her throat. Finally, Emily went into a pep talk, "doing this for Trisha!" The younger women clapped and stood. Guests in the dining room grabbed plates, and began sharing stories, playing catch-up.

Alice watched, shifted from foot to foot, and finally decided her dog had calmed. It was safe to sit in a chair as Emily instructed.

"This is like in the spring when the birds return. Bird chatter," whispered Alice into Audrey's ear as they both observed dining room activity from afar. "Some of these women haven't seen each other since high school."

The food line clogged with chicken or vegetarian indecision or was it something else? A few eyes drifted to Emily. Young women covered their mouths and talked behind their hands.

Alice waved to former students who gave hand signals they would call. Young adults first left Limekiln for college with a second, more permanent leaving for careers. Alice's own children found new exciting lives: Jess in California, Peter in New Hampshire. An unexpected feeling of loneliness crept across Alice's eyes.

How was Lena doing that morning? When Alice had called her best friend, Julian answered, grunting about "things going on," and "might not make it to the doin's."

In full nervous-bride mode, Trisha seemed more than frazzled, standing near the food line while hugging friends, her voice high pitched. Alice heard Trisha's dilemma as the young woman second-guessed her decisions for a perfect wedding.

"I'm in my thirties! Is the film *White Christmas* the wrong theme for a gray December wedding?"

To a large group of her friends, Trisha described the end of the movie in great detail: the red and white coloring, the large barn doors opening to gentle, big flakes of snow. The singing of *White Christmas* before the dancing started was a dream she wanted for her own wedding.

"You have no idea how hard it was to find white fur muffs." Her friends nodded.

Alice knew the *White Christmas* scene of women in bright red dresses, covering hands with muffs, but, just the same, she pictured ear muffs and stifled a giggle.

"The weather prediction is for more gray days," announced Tricia, "with wet snow, rain, and more slop."

Trisha allowed her mother to talk her into a lace jacket to cover her strapless shoulders for the church ceremony. Did her friends think it should have been a white velvet cape over the silk ball gown? Should her long hair be up or down? She planned for up, but maybe curly and long would be better. Friends in their early thirties knew their role; they bounced and squealed like teens, assuring Trisha she was beautiful.

"I promise we'll leave as soon as we eat," said Alice to her hound. "No one will notice us."

When guests with food plates sat, they punched apps to show pictures of their own little children. Emily brought a plate of food for Alice and a paper plate with chicken for Audrey. Alice observed the young women standing behind the bride's mother, their body language and eyes telling secrets. Alice concluded Emily's secret was definitely out and spreading.

"The kitchen staff washed off the gravy and cut up pieces for your dog," said Emily. "No chicken bones as you requested."

Alice placed the plate with plain chicken on the floor before Audrey's impatient paw could strike it from her hand. The hound loved chicken.

"We have to talk before you leave," whispered Emily. "I'm being blackmailed." That said and with a nervous pat to her hair, Emily walked back to the dining room. Alice was left speechless.

Blackmailed?

"Is this something different?" whispered Alice close to her dog's ear. "Maybe she doesn't know about the blog."

"Hey, Mrs. Tricklebank," called a soft voice, just entering the clubhouse through doors behind Alice. "Remember me?"

"Rooney!" said Alice as she stood and hugged the young woman with one arm while keeping a tight hold on Audrey. "When did you get home? Your mom and dad have to be so pleased."

Rooney Santoro looked down at the hound who licked the now empty paper plate. "Got back yesterday. On leave for the holidays and, of course, Trisha's wedding."

Rooney was in the military, although Alice wasn't sure if it was Army or Marines. The last time she saw her former student, Rooney's brown hair was closely shaved, her muscles definition cut. Now her hair length was about two inches of un-styled softness. She wore camouflage pants with a black sweater and a light-weight black jacket. At twenty-eight she wore no makeup. Her eyes moved unsettled, uneasy. From the dining room, Emily glanced at the two of them, shaking her head, disapproval tightening her lips. Rooney raised her hand in a slight wave.

"Hey, Mrs. Parker." To Alice she said with a sly grin, "My clothes don't meet her approval."

"You look great to me. Trisha's mother is determined her daughter will have the perfect storybook wedding, or rather movie-set wedding," said Alice, "as if perfect is ever possible. I'm not sure she approves of my trusty black pants and clodhopper jacket. Maybe to her I look like a tired tent. But everything's washable and probably a good thing with a dog who every three seconds needs a hanky for slobber and treat crumbs. That's an exaggeration, of course. But, Audrey and I have been banished to this hallway."

"Nice dog," said Rooney. "Big."

Audrey looked up as if knowing the talk was of her before dropping her nose back to the empty paper plate, her eyes expressing hope for more chicken to appear.

"Perfect table manners," said Alice, and they both laughed. "It's good to have you back."

"Thanks," said Rooney, her fingers touching the crepe wedding decorations hanging near the door. "After wearing combat boots, all this frosting of a wedding? I don't know." The young woman hunched her shoulders, eye brows pulling together in a frown of rejection. "Don't feel like I belong here."

"I'm hosting out-of-town guests," said Alice hoping her voice reflected being overwhelmed. "What's your job at the wedding?"

"Mrs. Parker wants a guest book." Softening her stance, Rooney rolled her eyes, "I had to come. Mom and Mrs. Parker are good friends. Trisha's older than me. I was closer in age to her brother Brad."

"I'm glad you're safe." Alice squeezed Rooney's hand.

Rooney gave Alice a haunted look that said it all. She wasn't out of harm's way. Places like Limekiln with doting parents were now foreign.

"Maybe, I'm back," said Rooney. "Got to find a job if I become a civilian."

"What did you do in the military?"

Rooney's eyes had a faraway gloss as she looked toward the dining room. "You know, housekeeping. I guess somebody has to clean up."

Alice thought Rooney sounded sad. "I thought the military would recognize your skills."

"What *my dad* called my Annie Oakley skills?" For a moment, Rooney looked pleased with the memory. "Shooting made my dad happy. Dad wasn't exactly one for Indian Princesses."

"We were so proud when you won the junior rifle competition." Alice smiled.

"That was a long time ago. Someday women in the military will be allowed into the sharpshooting school, but not with today's standards. Men have more upper body strength with bursts of energy. The powers-that-be will one day recognize women have great stamina, but I'll be gone before rules change." Alice recognized the discontent that came with rejection.

"As much as I like to see women advance," said Alice, "I'm not sure I want *you* in danger."

"You sound like my mom," said Rooney with another eye-roll.

Alice smiled, but Rooney's eyes were sad and hard. *She's having trouble transitioning her thinking to a civilian life filled with lace, silk ruffles, and happily-ever-afters*, thought Alice.

Audrey's nose became restless and pushed forward, wanting

attention from the woman standing in front of her. Rooney's toughness softened as she kneeled and rubbed the dog's face and ears. "You like that. You're a big girl. You could be a guard dog on base. Scare away the bad guys."

The hound's body shimmied and leaned into Rooney, draping her head over the young woman's shoulder.

"I'm afraid she's not a guard dog," said Alice while pulling Audrey back and checking her mouth for slobber. "More for welcoming and licking approval. You ever work with dogs in the military?"

"No. At home, we had them as pets. I like dogs. Sometimes better than people." Rooney grinned while continuing to pet Audrey whose back suddenly became flexible before flopping on her side.

"Ah, belly," said Rooney her fingers found the dog's exposed chest an invitation. Audrey stretched pleasure with this new scratching.

"A friend of mine, James Kennedy, has five bloodhounds of his own and recently took on two rescued hounds for training." Alice tried out her plan of dog therapy to help Rooney adjust to home life. After serving in Vietnam, Kennedy's dogs helped him transition, and Audrey definitely helped Alice cope with grief. "The new hounds need a lot of practice, learning to be good dogs," said Alice. "While you're home, if you're interested, he'd appreciate help. Providing you don't mind slobber or dogs who can be physical, arrogant, stubborn, yet give great wet kisses."

"Sounds like basic . . . minus the kisses."

A chubby young woman spotted Rooney and ran to her side. As Rooney stood, the woman grabbed her and spun her around in a hug before pulling her into the dining room, while apologizing to Alice for leaving her former teacher alone. With a watchful eye, Emily slipped Rooney two hand-wipes as she passed. Alice whispered to Audrey, "Don't take it personally. Emily's a civilian when it comes to dogs."

"I know being away from the crowd isn't much fun for you," said Emily to Alice, "but I need to talk to you." Emily took Alice's arm and steered her to an open office. As she pushed Alice and Audrey through the door, locking it behind her, she said, "I'm in trouble."

"You said blackmail?" asked Alice, fearing Emily's secret was out and rapidly spreading.

"Yes, blackmailed. You know Phil Greer's back in town?" Alice nodded. "Everyone's talking about these vile things he's done. I wish the police would catch him." Her eyes grew big with fear. "He texted me. Plans to show up at Trisha's wedding to announce *he's* her father." Emily paused to let the horror of the threat sink in.

"But Emily," said Alice. "No one can look at Trisha's face and believe Phil is her father. She has John's eyes, his jaw, even his square shoulders. No one will believe him."

Emily shook her head, her hand dismissed Alice's defense. "For me to stop him, Phil asked for a real estate list of houses up for sale that are less likely to have clients looking to buy."

So Phil plans to hide out in real estate for sale, thought Alice. "You have to tell the police."

"Not on your life," squealed Emily. "I sent him the list. I'm not taking any chances of ruining the wedding."

"But Emily . . . "

"No," said Emily with force.

"Then after the wedding."

"Not even after the wedding. I'm being blackmailed. Remember?"

"I don't understand," said Alice.

"You settle things for other people. Now it's my turn. I regard you as one of those Lego artists. Give you a pile of colorful misdeeds you hatch a plot to catch a murderer. I'm hoping *you* can take care of Phil and leave me out of it. Phil can't think I cooperated any way."

"But Emily, people know about Phil," continued Alice. "If they didn't, the last several hours have proven how despicable he is. When he's caught and if people learn he planned to embarrass you, everyone will be sympathetic."

Alice remembered the young women gossiping in the dining room. Zadie told her of the blog only yesterday. And then it dawned on her. She had sent Zadie to Gary Tuchman, town historian. Alice guessed he posted the newsy blog link to the historical website. Shortly the whole town would read about Emily's night of splendor.

"You don't understand," said Emily looking away. "Phil says he has proof . . . of . . . an indiscretion. That bastard has *proof*." Any confidence Emily once had evaporated. Her shoulders slumped.

Alice allowed Emily to marshal usual poise.

Emily pulled Alice into a corner, away from the door. "Can I trust you to keep quiet?"

"Of course, but . . . "

Emily ignored Alice's attempt of a warning.

"When my daughter was almost two, John and I had a hard time dealing with . . . John was out of town all the time. Circumstances took other family members away. I ended up alone, miserable, no help. No one to talk to. One *neighbor* was kind. One night we . . . *one night*. After . . . everything went back to normal. Family came back into place. John home. The neighbor and his wife moved. *No one* knew." Emily grabbed Alice's arm. "So how did Phil, of all people, learn about my one weak moment?"

"He knows," stated Alice picturing Phil at a prison computer laughing. *If Zadie easily found the blog, so did Phil.*

"He has details." Emily looked away in pain. "If I go to the police and tell where he may be, Phil will reveal my secret to John."

"Did your neighbor possibly mention details to Flossy Grueber?"

"No!" Emily's face paled. "Why would he do that? He loved his wife. We both wanted to put our fling behind us."

"Did you tell Flossy?" asked Alice. Emily's drooping body language announced her confession.

"It can't matter," said Emily. "She would never tell secrets."

"Emily, Phil *knows*," repeated Alice.

The shock of realization finally hit Emily. "Flossy? Why would Flossy tell Phil?"

"She didn't," said Alice, feeling direct truth was best. "Flossy made copies of all the letters she wrote to us. Her great-grandniece inherited the boxes of letters and is posting them to a blog online. So far maybe three hundred letters. Every day she adds ten to twenty more. Anyone can read them."

Emily's hands covered her mouth as she stifled a small scream. Her body shuddered. "I hadn't heard. *Anyone* can see the letters Flossy wrote to me?"

"One of your letters is there. Most of Flossy's posted letters are thank-you's and congratulations, but some offer encouragement to friends going through tough times."

"Do people in town know about the blog?"

"I'm afraid so," said Alice. "Gary may have posted the link to the historical website. Emily, the only way to handle this is to tell John what's coming. And tell Trisha so she's not blindsided with rumors."

Emily closed her eyes and shook her head. "I can't. Who's the niece?"

"Trulee Metto," said Alice. "She lives in Oklahoma."

"I have to stop her. Make her take the letters down."

"Emily, think. More than likely Phil read that letter online, maybe even in prison. You have to face he downloaded a copy as proof. Asking Trulee to remove the letter isn't an option."

Alice placed her hand on Emily's shoulder.

"I have to try," said Emily as if she knew the fight were already lost. "I gave Phil access to real estate lock boxes to keep him from telling what he knows. He has the freedom of any empty house he wants to use." Emily turned. Her fingernails bit into Alice's arm. "*We* have to stop him. Please help me."

Driving home, Alice shared an explanation with Audrey. "I'm guessing Phil kept up with Limekiln news while in prison and when he lived with his brother's family. That's probably how he learned about you. You're a celebrity with pictures on Facebook of people you've found. And all Phil had to do was Google a person's name and the search gave up Flossy's blog. The same way Zadie ran across the letter to Deirdre Hart."

A shiver ran up Alice's spine. Audrey sat on the bench seat of the pickup, her wet feet leaving paw prints, her wet mouth smears on the window, breath fogging the glass.

"I wish you could talk. I could use your help," said Alice, feeling annoyed with coincidences. "Zadie is searching for her birth mother. Phil threatens to claim Trisha as a daughter. Emily had a fling. Lena's also afraid of Flossy's letters. Audrey, there are still pieces to put together, but when we do, will answers make people happy? Isn't truth better?"

Audrey snorted and Alice rubbed her dog's neck.

"Yeah, I know, we should be more like dogs. Sniff butts and don't judge."

Audrey turned back to the window and saw a woman and dog on the sidewalk. Several deep woofs followed.

"That's you talking, but I wish I understood," said Alice with a sigh.

Back at home, Audrey found her special toy secured under a throw pillow and held it in her mouth for her afternoon nap. Alice called Bobby and left a message. "Just a thought: since Richie was killed in an abandoned piece of real estate, maybe Phil is living in an unoccupied house - one that's up for sale?"

After she hung up, Alice said to no one, "That may give Emily cover. Or not."

Chapter 8

"Alice, Gary Tuchman calling. Thanks for sending Miss Vanek to me." Gary's voice mail stunned Alice. "I checked everything we have. I'm afraid I can't help her with info on her mother, but Flossy's blog. Yowzer! Have you seen the latest posts? Glad my kids are too young to explore this. Did you know Emily Parker had an affair? Where did Vicky Deutcher get the money to bring Avery home after he ran off to Hawaii with the pharmacy saleswoman? I sent a special blast out to historical society members and posted Flossy's blog site. Facebook and Twitter picked it up. My phone's been ringing. People curious. We need to talk soon."

After her brief nap, Audrey wanted out to play in the warmth of the sun. Cardinals flitted through trees stubbornly holding leaves, and the hound's nose went to the ground rediscovering exotic smells. On the street, neighborhood boys on skateboards enjoyed the warmth of the afternoon, chasing down the middle of the street. Audrey stood with her front paws on the wooden fence, barking her desire to join them. As she pulled away in excitement, she picked up a hose Alice hadn't put away for winter and ran with it, tossing it in the air and letting it drop. Turning on the water and holding the hose, Alice watched as her dog challenged the water spray, biting at the stream, allowing the water to flush over her tongue while she sang with a guttural voice. Fluffy towels sat ready inside the backdoor to dry Audrey the explorer.

Could it be possible the flood at Bait and Books was a silly accident? questioned Alice, running through all the blaming of Phil.

After drying off her dog's face, shoulders, and feet, Alice led Audrey into the house and snapped back to the problems in Limekiln with another waiting voice mail.

"How many of Flossy's letters will be posted to the blog?" asked Gretchen Kluski, her neighbor. "Have been reading for an hour. Can't stop. Did you know the piano teacher put herself through college as a stripper? My *son* took piano lessons from her. I keep picturing Elliot sitting next to her on that bench, only now in my mind's eye, she's naked. Do you think Father Ed confessed he was once married in a previous life? And poor Emily Parker. Poor Trisha! Of course, Everyone knew the mayor had breast implants, but to see it stated in print online . . . Oh, Alice, this is better than a soap opera."

An actual phone call came from Julian. "Magpie talked the lieutenant into interviewing Taylor here at the house rather than at the motel where she's staying. She don't like to talk about it, but Magpie's nervous about Phil's activities since he got out of jail. she's afraid the lieutenant might think we're in cahoots. You should probably be here. Don't know if I can keep Magpie away from the interview."

Alice couldn't imagine Bobby agreeing to an interview at Lena's house, but recent events had messed with the town. She worried about the gossipy reception Flossy's blog produced, tickling the town.

"Audrey, why does seamy and sensational always have to trump support and accomplishments?"

Lena stood with her arm around Taylor's waist, whispering how she wasn't to be nervous. Reminding Lena she had already talked to an officer the day before, Taylor looked more composed than Lena gave her credit.

Taylor wore jeans, chunky shoes, an unzipped, hooded jacket over a T-shirt adorned with gold lettering, *Vintage American Flyer*.

"Tell Lieutenant Unzicker everything you know," said Lena as if talking to a child. "He's not going to hold it against you that Phil's your uncle. We'll be waiting in the sunroom." Lena shot a glance at Bobby. "Unless you want me to stay with her." Bobby shook his head and ran his hand through his dark hair.

Probably tolerating Lena's motherly hoopla, thought Alice.

Taylor smiled and rolled her eyes.

"I made African spice bread this morning," said Lena, "so we have open faced sandwiches. Fontina cheese and sliced apples drizzled with honey. The green pitcher has iced tea. The thermos hot coffee." She turned to Julian. "Am I forgetting anything?"

"We'll be fine Auntie Lena," said Taylor. She sat with her forearms on the dining room table, and hooked her ankles around the chair's legs as a child might. With amusement, she added, "I'm not afraid of the big, bad policeman." Taylor took a plate and lifted a sandwich. Coerced, Bobby also helped himself. As the sticky honey ran off the apple slices toward the bread crust, his face tightened.

No sticky for this policeman, concluded Alice.

Lena's inviting smile disappeared. Alice knew her best friend often chose baking to outrun her problems. She wished she could steal Lena to another room and discuss what was beneath her fears before another surprise shook their bones.

With his eyes crinkled as if in pain, Julian placed his hands on Lena's shoulders and steered her toward the back sunroom. Lena peeped back as if she wanted to whip up more sandwiches or potato salad or maybe a lasagna.

Alice and Audrey followed, weaving through more Christmas finery. Small dangling glass ornaments decorated bare red branches standing in old-fashioned milk bottles. Alice's hand caught Audrey's tail long enough to keep the happy dog from doing damage as they passed.

"You sit there," directed Lena pointing to a chair closest to the door, "better for you to listen. I'll sit over here so I can watch them."

Alice wished she too could watch. Maybe to squeeze in a chair next to Lena? But Lena sat between a Norfolk pine tree decorated with Disney ornaments and a tablescape of family pictures. No room existed for another chair and definitely, no room for Audrey's tail.

After switching off all the noise from the dancing Santas, Julian lowered his chin and folded his arms. "I need a beer." But he stayed put, carefully out of dining room earshot and watched Lena. "Magpie, he only wants information about Phil. Not about *you* and Phil."

"I know. I know." Her eyes never left the dining room scene.

Audrey flattened her body to the floor, with eyes tilting upward watching Lena's every move. She wasn't about to miss a chance for a homemade treat.

In the dining room, Bobby sighed. "As you know, we're trying to find Phil. Has anything occurred to you since yesterday that might help us?" His voice almost pleaded for information.

"Not really," said Taylor. "He has some cash. When he left us, Mom and Dad gave him money, but Phil also took one of our expensive bikes. I can't imagine him riding from Whittle to Limekiln. Too far for a man of his age. Maybe he sold it. Worth several hundred bucks."

Maybe he's riding the bike around at night, thought Alice. *Quiet-like. Slipping into places unseen.*

"When he left prison, did he go directly to your dad's house?" asked Bobby.

"Yes. He mooched for a couple weeks then left."

"Did he ever speak of other destinations?"

"Not that I heard," said Taylor. "But I don't live at my parents' house. I don't think Uncle Phil told Dad he was leaving. Just left. I'm guessing he took the bus. I can't imagine anyone giving him a lift. I talked to Dad yesterday. Told him what happened to Richie. As far as we know, no one has heard from Phil."

"You told Officer Jinn you don't have a current picture of Phil," stated Bobby. "We need a description. What does he look like? How was he dressed?"

"Well, as I told the other officer, Phil's short, maybe 5' 4". A little stooped or bent. Old. Gray hair in need of a haircut. Something of a limp, but also a swagger like he's better than us." Alice heard the anger in Taylor's voice.

"What sets him off?"

"Why is he cruel?" asked Taylor.

Alice imagined Bobby nodding.

"Dad said he was always mean. Said as a child Phil liked to play Made-You-Blink. But instead of flicking his fingers in front of someone's face, he actually poked at a person's eyes. Dad said he poked their grandmother in the eye. And dogs. Even babies. Laughed and said, 'Made ya blink,'"

Silence followed.

"When he came home from prison, he tried the game on Mom when she was carrying a pot of hot soup. Both dad and I warned him to back off. Lieutenant, Phil's a . . . a . . ."

"Asshole!" yelled Lena from the sunroom. "He's an asshole."

Julian rubbed her back and said, "It's okay."

Alice looked around the corner from where she sat to see both Taylor and Bobby looking shocked. Bobby cleared his throat.

"Let's move on to what kind of clothing Phil has?" asked Bobby.

"Regular-looking shirts," answered Taylor. "He owns a dark green quilted jacket with a corduroy collar." Taylor's voice brightened. "He bought new jeans. The kind that have a loop on the side. He wanted to carry a hammer in that loop as he did in the old days."

"Like a holster," said Bobby, his voice serious.

"Exactly."

Across from Alice, Lena flinched at the mention of a hammer and her eyes widened.

"Any visitors while he was in Whittle?" asked Bobby.

"Other than neighbors?" asked Taylor. "Only a couple guys visited, and they're friends of Dad."

"Phil have a phone?"

"Yes. When he talked to anyone, he stood outside, so . . ."

Phil was her father's brother yet Taylor knew little about him. Alice felt the same limits, not able to engage Lena in a real search.

"Mail?" asked Bobby.

"Not that Dad ever said." Taylor paused. The only sound in the house was the furnace kicking on. "I think no, Lieutenant. I was glad when Uncle Phil left. He didn't put in any work at the shop. Of course, if he had, he'd probably steal from the cash register or palm someone's credit card," she said with disgust. "I could tell Mom was afraid. She told Dad to give the bloodsucker money if it encouraged him to leave."

"What did he do when the family was together? For dinner?" Bobby's voice was soft.

"Drank, complained about everyone and everything, and looked up stuff on his cell phone."

"You told Alice and Lena he wanted to hurt people in Limekiln."

"Yes. That's why Dad sent me down here. After Phil left, Dad waited because he thought Phil'd be back. When he wasn't, Dad said we had to tell everyone." Alice imagined the sound she heard was Taylor's hand hitting the table harder than she intended. "Sorry. Lieutenant, my dad's embarrassed and afraid of what will happen. I told Auntie Lena . . . " Taylor's voice softened, and Alice saw Lena move to the edge of her chair. "He wanted to hurt Lena and Richie and Alice. I didn't really pay attention to the others on his list. I think one of them was a kid with a deformity. Phil didn't like him or maybe it was his dad."

Alice straightened. Rumor said Phil was the reason Stephen Zug's arm didn't grow properly. Phil told the story of teaching Stephen a lesson for being disrespectful, but he fell short of identifying himself as the person who wrenched Stephen's arm out of the socket and shattering the knobby bits of bone near his elbow. Alice guessed the at-tack with a hammer arrested the growth of Stephen's arm and caused nerve damage.

But why would Phil flood Bait and Books. Why now? To revenge what? Alice reached down to scratch Audrey's head.

"Any idea what he looked up on the computer?" asked Bobby.

"Porn probably. But, one time, he laughed kinda mean as he read the screen."

Alice heard Bobby take a deep breath. Taylor gave her home contact information and told Bobby she planned to leave within hours.

"Dad should hear specifics of Richie from me personally rather than in a phone call." Taylor's voice reflected old anger. "I'll come back if you need me, but I don't want to see Uncle Phil again. As far as I'm concerned lock him up. Throw away the key. He is *not* my uncle."

After they all said good-byes and sandwich-thank-you's, Bobby took Alice's elbow. "Walk you home?"

"It will be a slow walk," said Alice flicking her scarf around her neck. Audrey will be checking her p-mail she left on her walk here."

At the end of Lena's driveway, Audrey made a sharp turn, fol-lowing the road home. Within ten steps the hound stopped, nose to ground, as if reading a new message left behind on a bush by a friend.

"I tried to question Lena," said Bobby. "She's not exactly protecting Phil, but she's not helping. What's she hiding?"

"All I have are guesses," said Alice.

"What do you think?"

"In the first place, with Phil out of jail, Lena's reminded of a past cluttered with her bad decisions. She's embarrassed about ever allow-ing Phil into her life," posed Alice. "Now that Julian's here . . . timing is bad to have Phil back. Lena likes to appear confident and a little wild as if she doesn't care what people think, but she cares very much. And she's frightened about what's in Flossy's blog."

"What's worse than being married to Phil?" asked Bobby.

"Don't know. She won't say." Alice too shook her head and watched Audrey plunge her head into a bush only to draw it back, startled when a bird flew away.

Both Alice and Bobby yielded the roadside as an aggressive, yapping Jack Russell walked past with his owner. Audrey looked curious yet offended by the loudmouth dog.

"Do you recall anyone Phil ran with besides Richie?" asked Bobby.

"Nope. I can't recall Lena mentioning any regular drinking buddies either. He did have affairs while married to Lena and after the divorce. Maybe a woman is helping him."

"Who were the women?"

"I can name two," said Alice, "and both have moved out of town. A young widow who had five small children and a young waitress whose mother had passed away."

"Does Lena have names?"

"May not be accurate. She confessed Phil liked to taunt her with names of conquests, but with Phil, truth is tricky." Alice had never asked her friend to list the identities of other women. "He may have invented stories to wound her."

"Lena was a widow when she married Phil, wasn't she?" asked Bobby.

"Yes," said Alice as she swallowed hard. "I'm fairly sure Phil's courting went on when Charlie Sweet was still alive. If true, that's a load of guilt for Lena to carry after Charlie's death in a car accident."

"Phil's a collector of trophies," said Bobby. Their walk stopped again as Audrey flipped onto her back and rolled in the grass. "No guesses of other women who may still be in town?

"No rumor of substance. One of your men, however, should follow Flossy's blog. Lots of secrets being posted online." Audrey rose with a sneeze, resuming her pull toward home, and Alice said, "Excuse, me, but I need to check for meatballs."

"Have you found anymore?" Alice shook her head. "Maybe, Phil only wanted to frighten you. Get you to back off."

Alice shrugged, "A small possibility he's not done with me." She checked out the backyard, and released Audrey to run free of a leash.

"Don't guess I can ask you to stop following ghosts. Let us handle this?"

"Nope," answered Alice standing tall like a sentry.

"Thanks for the tip on the houses," said Bobby. "Officer Jinn found evidence someone's been in two of them. One had inside destruction made by a hammer. Smashed the sheet rock walls. The other house had a slice of pizza in the refrigerator."

"Store bought or homemade?" asked Alice, suddenly very interested.

"Homemade," said Bobby, and together both said, "He has an accomplice."

"The lab can test for DNA," said Alice as if inspired.

"Sure," said Bobby. "By the time the report comes back and we match it to an accomplice, I'll be ready to retire. Not enough county lab techs, and this case isn't at the head of the line. Yet."

Bobby's grimace drew attention to his dark eyes and straight nose. "Let me know if you think of anyone we should interview."

Alice agreed and before she could say farewell, Audrey lunged at Gretchen's cat whose paws were springs taking her to the top of the fence. A series of woofs broke from the hound, capturing the sound of indignation.

"Audrey's getting stronger," said Bobby with a big grin. "Should I be worried about you being knocked around?"

Alice barely heard him over her dog's baritone barking at the cat who walked away, tail up.

Chapter 9

"Alice, my dog Bianca is missing. I put her in the little fenced area about four o'clock this afternoon and now she's gone. I've looked and called, but she's nowhere. Can your dog find her?"

Alice recognized Crystal Butterman's even voice wrapped in panic. She wasn't a woman usually given to hysteria.

"We'll try. Audrey and I will be right there."

Before Alice could hang up, Crystal added, "I've heard stories about Phil Greer back in town. Is it true he's done those terrible things?" she gulped while breathing hard. "Could he have lured Bianca away?"

"Can't say. Check for holes along the fencing in case she's dug her way out. If Bianca wandered off, Audrey will find her."

The West Highland Terrier wouldn't be the first lost dog Audrey found. Of course, Alice didn't explain how in the spirit of dog adventures, two other family pets wandered down toward Milkweed Slough where coyotes found a small meadow to feast on geese, sometimes seeing small pets as a challenge to their meal. Whenever Audrey found canine bones, her shoulders sagged as if to respect a dog's passing.

"Crystal," said Alice, "before we arrive, I want you to find an item with your dog's scent. Maybe an old collar or a blanket she sleeps on?"

"A toy?"

Alice thought of Audrey's puppy love of toys which might cause her to claim Bianca's toy as her own. "Not a toy. Maybe a towel or a fabric leash?"

"Okay. Alice, I'm glad we have you to help us. I didn't know who else to call." Her voice caught with a sob. "Even after five years on my own, I miss working for Flossy. Bianca helps me fill my day. I can't lose her."

Crystal had been Flossy Grueber's housekeeper, a quiet woman, a hard worker. When Flossy moved away, the Gruber family gave Crystal a trailer and a small pension.

"I'll be right there," stressed Alice.

The late afternoon warmed to the low thirties, but picked up a biting wind. Alice dressed Audrey in the bright green jacket emblazoned with *Rescue Dog* and attached the leash to the harness. She checked the duffle to assure it was up to date and pulled a stocking cap and Baer's big woolly shirt for her own protection against the weather, all the while telling her dog about Crystal and Flossy.

"Crystal lives on the north side of town closer to the interstate. Don't see her much. These days I wave to Crystal in town or have a quick chat, but when Flossy was alive . . ." Alice stopped to picture Flossy and her housekeeper playing Dominos on the big front porch of the Mansion. "I used to know Crystal very well."

Flossy's housekeeper wasn't as old as Alice, maybe ten years younger, but she had cared for Flossy for over twenty-five years.

"I like you in uniform, very smart," said Alice to the hound. "I worry when you're far out in front of me that a driver won't see you. But now with your new acid green jacket, no one can possibly miss seeing you."

The dog moved with authority, nose up, and pulled toward the pickup.

Crystal's trailer wasn't hard to find in the community on the edge of town. Strings of Christmas lights framed her windows, and a small potted evergreen near her door sported cranberries and popcorn for birds. Crystal stood outside, anxious and waiting. Her feet marched in place, fighting the cold. She held a soiled pink dog collar.

Crystal had always been spindly and angular like a windmill built with Tinker Toys, all sticks and knobs. Her cheek bones projected from her face, hands claw-like, but Alice was stunned at how Crystal had thinned even more. Her shoulders looked more coat-hanger-like as she stood in front of her trailer wrapped in a springtime gray jacket.

"This is Bianca's fenced yard," said Crystal, using baby gates to form an enclosure near her front door. The plastic fencing was high enough to keep a small dog in place, but a human or Audrey could easily straddle the barrier.

"Bianca's a Westie, a notorious digger, but I don't see any evidence of her tunneling," said Crystal wiggling the fencing, testing the stability. "The fence slats are close, not enough space for her to squeeze through." Raising her face to Alice, Crystal asked, "Why would Phil target my dog?"

"Crystal, we don't know he has. Dogs can be slippery. Like Houdini. Let's see what Audrey finds."

Alice placed the collar into a plastic bag, and Audrey plunged her nose inside for a whiff. With the command to find, the hound instantly pulled toward a neighboring trailer with a green stripe before making a hairpin turn down the street. The two women followed Audrey's lead crisscrossing streets, following as if Bianca were a dog on an adventure. Alice felt lucky to have a path to follow. If Phil Greer had spirited the dog away, at least it wasn't to a car, to drive to a desolate spot and abandon the poor thing. But it would only take a second to plop Bianca outside the fencing to explore the world on her own.

Crystal had a hard time keeping up with Audrey as the three cut through backyards and squeezed between bushes. The hound's nose stayed to the ground, alerting Alice the Westie still wasn't near. Along the way a few town residents saw the search and followed, creating a threadlike parade of the curious. Cell phones snapped pictures. Alice heard mumbles of Phil Greer, the poisonous meatball, and now a missing dog. Limekiln was gearing up in a way Alice didn't like. Even careful people were rushing to blame.

Snuffling past a truckers' lunch spot, Audrey's nose rose into the air. Her shoulders rolled in that confident way she had, a small happy gurgle erupted into a series of dramatic deep barks.

"We found her somewhere ahead," said Alice, hoping the little dog was still alive. "I'll hold Audrey here."

Alice quickly patted her dog and jammed a chicken hot dog treat in her mouth to keep her quiet. No need for Bianca to hide a little deeper, away from the scary, big hound.

"Call your dog," said Alice.

It took Crystal's positive mama voice to encourage Bianca from a hole under a dumpster. The wet, dirty, shivering dog crept out on her belly.

Picking up Bianca, Crystal cuddled her close not caring if winter dirt stained her gray jacket. She ran her hands over the Westie's body. "Thank you, Alice. Oh, her feet are so cold." Crystal's face moved close to Bianca's ear as she spoke to her canine friend in baby talk. The parade of residents swarmed Crystal and clapped. Audrey received her customary hug, followed by more chicken treats.

"Alice, how can I thank you?" Crystal's eyes filled with tears. "When I called you, I never really believed a dog could find another dog. Audrey's amazing."

With Crystal carrying her Westie and Audrey stretching to smell the little dog's butt, the four walked back to the trailer. Crystal insisted on a reward for Alice of cranberry tea and snickerdoodles. They sat next to each other on the couch, a serving tray as the only coffee table.

"I miss the companionship of working for Flossy," said Crystal, placing a paper napkin on Alice's knee. "She was kind to me."

"You said you were afraid Phil might have taken Bianca," said Alice. "Why is that?"

"Everyone says he's bad." Crystal lowered her tea, her eyes like Lena's wide with fear.

"Did you ever have a run-in with him?" asked Alice.

Crystal shook her head. "Wasn't allowed to talk to him. Flossy wouldn't have it. I'd have lost my job. Miss Flossy was very particular."

Alice sipped the cool tea and bit into a cookie. She noted how Crystal avoided eye contact and absently stirred her tea as if questioning whether she should continue with the story. *What is she not saying?* Mentally Alice added Crystal to Phil's possible conquest list.

"Every time I pass the Mansion, I remember you and Flossy, playing Dominoes on the front porch in the summer."

"She was one for Dominoes, and she loved being outside. Everyone stopped to talk to her, even kids. I don't think any school band member ever passed without saying thank you for the trips to Disney World. They brought back trinkets for her. Flossy was generous."

Audrey lay flat in the living room area, eying the Westie who found safety around Crystal's ankles.

"Do you remember anyone in Limekiln named Deirdre Hart?" asked Alice.

"Deirdre Hart," Crystal's eyes became playful and moist as she smiled. "I can name four Deirdre Harts, but Alice, you probably know more than I do."

Alice felt confused. "Crystal, I don't know any. Who is Deirdre Hart?"

The younger woman's face wrinkled with disbelief. "Flossy's accent?" said Crystal as if she just needed to jar Alice's memory. "She never saw a dentist about her loose upper plate." Crystal paused, waiting for Alice to react. "Alice, Flossy's Dear Heart girls? Didn't you ever hear her call some poor soul *dear heart?* They were the ones at the end of their rope. Flossy kept their secrets and helped when she could. I thought you knew."

Crystal then imitated Flossy's speech pattern and *dear heart* became *Deirdre Hart*. Stunned, Alice sat back in her chair.

"No. I never knew." Audrey rose from the floor and lumbered over to Alice, placing her wet mouth on her owner's knee. Alice stroked her dog's head and ears. "Who were they?"

"I won't mention names, but one needed help because of alcohol. Another was beaten by her husband and wanted to get away. A young girl with drug problems." Alice guessed names of two but never spoke them aloud. "And, of course, me," said Crystal, her voice shy.

"You?" The admission surprised Alice.

"You must remember I couldn't hold a job when I was young. Dropped out of high school. Couldn't control my temper. Moved away until my twenties and came back to Limekiln after being homeless. Flossy took me in. Only God knows why. 'Dear heart,' she said, 'you need a break.' So I moved into the Mansion and stayed over twenty-five years."

Alice related the story of the young woman who searched for her mother and asked Crystal for anything she recalled of a pregnant woman of thirty-five who needed help in 1990, but Crystal looked puzzled.

"For important conversations with Flossy, I was dismissed," said Crystal. "Many women came to visit Flossy, and I used that time to do household work. You must know Flossy was good at keeping secrets."

"The girl said she learned about her birth mother because Flossy's great-grandniece is posting a blog of her aunt's letters. Anyone can read them online."

"Anyone?" Crystal's eyes grew big, almost bemused. "All of them?"

"That's the intention. For history's sake."

"I packed boxes of those letters when Flossy moved to Oklahoma. Oh, my! Lots of people will be unhappy. I only read a handful, but Alice," she moved in closer, "those letters may cause embarrassment." Her face reddened and she winced. "I'm not saying anything more in case the letter isn't posted, but Lena . . . Oh, Alice, I'm so sorry."

Outside the house as Alice and Crystal said goodbyes, Gina Pickler waved her cell phone, running toward them, her heavy body churning with effort, her coat unbuttoned and flapping open.

"Miss Butterman. Mrs. Tricklebank. I have news," she called. Both the women and Audrey stood still. Flushed, Gina said, "Do you know Mr. Marcel Polk? He slices lunch meat at Beckerman's? He texted Mrs. Zug who texted me. Mr. Greer walked into the police station. Said he didn't kill Mr. Mills. Hasn't done all those terrible things. Oh, I'm out of breath."

Gina's hand went to her chest as she took a moment to pull two deep breaths.

"How does Marcel know that?" asked Alice.

"He delivered sandwiches to the firehouse and saw Mr. Greer enter the police station next door. He *had* to know what was going on, so he went into the station and asked if they also wanted sandwiches for dinner. That's when he heard Mr. Greer proclaim his innocence."

Audrey's head tilted, and she sat as if wanting to hear more.

"If Phil's not doing these things," asked Crystal, holding Bianca close to her body, "then who?"

"I don't know," said Gina, the excitement of mystery thrilled her eyes, "but he has to be innocent if he walked into the police station. Don't ya think?"

"Last night I was awake thinking about the fire," said Crystal, "listening for a break-in or the whoosh of flames. Does this news make us safer or is it more threatening because we don't know who is trying to hurt us?"

Alice took a moment to think. *An unknown threat?* Remembering Emily, Alice said, "I'm thinking at least some of the destruction belongs at Phil's door. Do you recall any of Phil's special friends, someone who would help him?"

Both women shook their heads.

"Only Richie," said Crystal. "Poor Richie."

"Phil was very taken with your neighbor," said Gina. "When her name was Mrs. Sweet. I remember she and Mr. Greer came to the peony farm near the interstate where I worked. He insisted she have our best smelling white peony. *Beauty for a beauty*, he said. Wouldn't let her leave until she picked one out."

"Who paid for the peony?" asked Alice, remembering Phil's con-man style.

"As I recall, she did," said Gina. "But he was so sincere, so loving."

"Was this before or after Charlie Sweet was killed in a car crash?" asked Crystal, her eyes narrowing.

Alice looked at Crystal, wondering at her suspicions. What might Flossy's housekeeper know?

"Oh, I'm not sure," said Gina, "maybe before."

Conversation drifted to the holidays before Gina said, "The darnedest thing happened today. Do either of you know how to pick up thumb tacks? The grass in front of my trailer seems to be filled with thumb tacks. I tried my old Hoover, but that doesn't work. The contraption sucks up more dirt than tacks. Such a goofy spillage to happen."

"Might Phil be responsible?" asked Alice.

"Oh, I can't believe it's Mr. Greer," said Gina, her cheeks coloring pink. "Years ago, he never spoke to me, maybe just a nod. Wait," she said raising her index finger, "the only time he ever spoke to me was to ask, 'which peony has the best scent?' and I told him a white one. The tacks are probably an accident. Drop a grocery bag. Too lazy to pick up. What a nuisance."

With her left hand on the wheel and her right scratching Audrey's neck, Alice drove, wondering about Bianca being lost and thumb tacks in the grass. Were she and the residents of Limekiln paranoid, placing every mishap at Phil's door? After all, Bianca could have wandered off. A trailer resident might have dropped a bag and out spilled tacks. And what of the women at rock bottom, the Dear Hearts. Was Lena afraid it'd come out that she too received advice from Flossy? At least she knew the origin of Zadie's birth name. Alice felt certain the mother once lived in Limekiln and, more to the point, maybe still did.

"Who is she?" Alice asked aloud, and Audrey turned her head away from the smeared side window. "What do you think is Phil's game?"

Audrey dropped to the pickup seat with a groan and inched closer to Alice's thigh. Alice's hand followed her dog's neck and kneaded the muscles.

Although it was a thought that crossed her mind many times before, Alice felt a little sick at Lena being courted by Phil before Charlie's car accident.

"Why do solutions come piecemeal?"

Late in the day, Bobby's face turned all-lieutenant as Alice and Audrey walked into the police station. He stood talking to Officer Jinn at the main desk. He offered no greeting. Instead, his open hand directed Alice to his office.

As he closed the door, Bobby said. "Long day."

"You got Phil?" asked Alice, unwinding her scarf and giving Audrey a pat on the side.

"More or less," said Bobby. "Phil's claiming he didn't murder Richie and didn't do any of the destruction."

"Do you have any evidence?"

Audrey took the measure of the serious conversation and decided to lie down near the door.

"Please sit," said Bobby to Alice. "The county's a little slow with the holidays coming. Don't expect reports for a few days, but in the meantime, I've got the men checking Phil's story."

"Audrey found Crystal Butterman's dog today," said Alice. "And Mrs. Pickler has thumb tacks in her grass. Crystal is worried Phil removed the dog from her fenced pen. Mrs. Pickler thinks someone stumbled and the tacks scattered into her small yard. Maybe Phil's shenanigans?"

Bobby's face tightened, his eyes closed. "Not necessarily Phil."

"I know," said Alice. "We're being paranoid. Ever consider the confusion might be for a reason? A drip of little annoyances to make us stop seeing something larger?"

Bobby's concentration made him look prickly. "What big thing?"

"Don't know," said Alice. "How long is Phil in jail?"

"In twenty-four hours, we release him. We've got until tomorrow afternoon to find something."

Audrey's face rose off the floor as if she expected their visit was over.

"Technically," said Alice, her mouth wrinkled, her brow furrowed, "Limekiln should be at peace for the next several hours . . . don't you think. Unless he has a partner."

"Seems true," said Bobby with caution. "Or at a standstill until the next crisis."

"Did Phil say where he was during the time Richie was killed?"

"That's the thing," said Bobby, anger rising in his face. "We don't have an exact time of death, yet. But we have a pretty good idea of when Lena's fire started and when your meatball was pitched into your yard. For that, Phil claims he played cards at the tavern on Cannon Street, followed by a late breakfast."

"A rough crowd on Cannon Street," said Alice.

"We've had a few run-ins with them. Pulled them in for disorderly conduct. I'll be unhappy if they choose to give Phil an alibi."

"I'm not one to defend him," said Alice, "but he has been the Boogie

Man in town for a long time. We all breathed easier when he went to prison for three years."

"Then why did he come back?" asked Bobby, his hand tapping a pencil on the desk.

"I may know of one person being blackmailed." Alice felt guilty at not sharing the information until now. She had trouble making eye contact with Bobby.

"You never said." A sternness entered Bobby's face, and Audrey shifted her position to watch the lieutenant, but still stretched out belly down.

"Here's the thing," said Alice. "No evidence." Alice sat back in her chair. *Time to spill all the beans.* She confessed to Bobby about Emily Parker's one-night fling leading to being blackmailed through texting. "She supplied Phil with lists of sad sack houses up for sale."

"That's why you suggested we search real estate." He pulled a piece of paper closer as if wanting to write a note.

"Emily gave him lockbox codes," said Alice. "So technically, I guess, he didn't have to break-in."

"I read about her affair in Flossy's blog, and let's face it, Emily's a helper-type." His words sounded more like an accusation than a clarification of detail.

"But Emily has the wedding to plan and a marriage to repair," said Alice, shocked with Bobby's train of thought. "She has no time to *help* Phil. I think the codes were all the help Phil can expect." Alice's head wobbled as she weighed possible conclusions. "Really, Emily doesn't *know* it was Phil who texted with demands. How hard is it for someone to fake a text?"

Bobby ignored her question. "Is she willing to come in and talk?"

"Probably not willing, but she might be cooperative."

Alice saw an expression of resolve cross his face and knew he'd knock at Emily's door.

"If Phil's alibi holds for Lena's fire," said Bobby, "I open the cell door. Phil walks."

"This is how Phil operates," pleaded Alice. "Years ago, he manipulated Richie into damaging a homeowner's property. They then contracted repairs that never were done. For his next scam, he distracted homeowners to come outside and talk about needed repairs while Richie broke into the back and stole wallets and purses. In court Phil's defense was based on him not doing the actual stealing, don't you see? The blame-someone-else defense."

"I read his file," said Bobby, not liking being schooled.

"I feel Phil is doing these things through someone else," said Alice. "I just can't figure out his con. What does he want? I can't believe destruction and humiliation are enough."

"My men will find something. You hear new gossip, call."

Hoping a comical gesture might lighten Bobby's mood, Alice snapped a salute and said, "With the first whiff of scuttlebutt."

Audrey, however, was the one to nose the police lieutenant into finally taking time to scratch her head before he shifted conversation to his sons and their desire for a big dog.

Every evening Alice inspected and cleaned Audrey's ears, wrinkles, and feet, removing dust, dried mud and bits of debris.

"Maybe I should invent wrinkle wipes," said Alice lifting her dog's ear and wiping inside. "I swear your fur is like a dirt magnet." Bath time ended with a foot massage which the hound stretched into as Alice sang, "one little piggy."

As Alice sat on the couch with Audrey's head on her thigh, the hound fell into instant sleep. *How do you do that so quickly?* wondered Alice, and she stroked her dog's clean ears. Her mind worked on a timeline, rearranging events into a probable order.

Phil's first attempt to upset the town had to be his audacious threat to Emily Parker. Alice guessed the text message was sent before Phil arrived in Limekiln. Not that Phil would actually stop the wedding to announce himself as Trisha's father. Such an act had an audience way too big for Phil to control. He relished the manipulation of fear, not the actual strike. No, his text to Emily won the lock-box codes.

Second, the flood of Bait and Books' basement. Neda thought it happened on Saturday. But the shop closed early on Friday night. Young people in town headed for pizza and beer. After dark, no one would be near the book shop to catch sight of Phil. So far, no one reported seeing Phil on the prowl for any of the shenanigans.

Alice guessed the third event was the killing of Richie, but she had no information how long he'd been dead. That information languished at the county morgue. Most nights, Richie worked at a warehouse and left in the early morning when it was still dark. Since they found him on Monday, Alice reasoned he died either Saturday night or Sunday morning. The kicker for Alice was Richie's apartment. Messy but tidied the way her son might have quickly cleaned if he heard Mom at the bedroom door. Magazines and papers were intentionally pushed aside in a heap but the real mess of the hot plate left alone. Did Phil surprise Richie with an early morning visit? Was Richie a little drunk from his rumored routine of having a few drinks with the boys before returning home? Perhaps Phil walked him to the Mansion or texted Richie to meet him there? Or did Phil's accomplice create a pretext to escort Richie to his death? The toothbrush still bothered Alice. Why was it not at the sink?

Alice knew she needed to see Richie's second-floor apartment one more time. If Phil had been there, maybe Audrey's nose could sniff a clue.

Lena's fire at the cafe came early Monday before morning light. Phil grasped the importance of the bakery to Lena. For years, it was called Sweet's Treats, named after her late husband Charlie Sweet. If Phil started the fire in the wee hours of morning, the whole structure could have easily burned down, but with Limekiln coming back to life by six in the morning, someone surely saw and called the fire department. Did Phil set the fire just before dawn for the maximum impact of terror? And who did he want to scare? Cheryl or Lena?

Then there was the poisonous meatball. She was at Bait and Books when Phil tossed it into her yard. Full daytime. A risky move since her next-door neighbor Gretchen usually was on neighborhood watch, and Alice's house was down the street from Lena's. Of course, he probably predicted Lena wouldn't be home because of the fire, but how did he know she, herself, wasn't in the backyard with Audrey? A shiver went up her spine. Phil knew. He was watching her.

A fertilizer dump onto the Stringini front yard, Crystal's dog Bianca going missing, tacks thrown onto the small patch of grass in front of Mrs. Pickler's trailer - none of it made sense other than Phil striking fear into the town. For what purpose? Where was his payoff?

And then as bold as you please, Phil saunters into the police station and proclaims his innocence. No one saw him do any of the destruction, and the one person who could give specific evidence, needed prodding. Emily's affair was posted so what more did she think she had to lose if she spoke out against Phil?

Alice shook her head. "Phil doesn't work alone," she whispered with dread in her voice. Audrey raised her sleepy head, and Alice's fingers continued to pat her side. "Sshh . . . don't have to wake up yet."

Alice didn't feel nimble enough to dance through all the facts to a conclusion. *What's going to happen*, she wondered, *with Phil in jail, his alibi iron-clad, protected from blame*. It bothered Alice that Phil was hardened to the wreckage he left behind, never a soft spot. Taylor's story of Phil's boyhood game made Alice shiver. "Made ya blink," she whispered.

What calamity's next . . . to crank things up?

Chapter 10

Alice expected her house guests from Bottom Ridge on Friday. Phil was in custody at the police station until the afternoon, and Lena concentrated on the wedding cakes needed in six days.

Wednesday morning Alice faced Audrey, "You need serious playtime. C'mon. We're going to visit the new hounds at Kennedy Farms. At least your friends aren't complicated." Alice packed extra dog treats and explained. "I need time to think."

When Alice turned south in the pickup, her dog knew something was up and stood for the rest of the drive, becoming more animated as the pickup pulled into Kennedy's farm. Gurgling, bouncing, knocking into Alice's shoulder, Audrey barked straight into her owner's ear, then pivoted to smear the window with nasty, wet slime.

"I know you're excited. Give me a minute to park."

Once in the enclosed yard, Alice released Audrey from her leash to the delight of the other seven bloodhounds who also barked, bounced, ran, and tumbled until each settled into concentrated playtime.

A turtle as large as a dinner plate walked ever so slowly across the enclosed yard. Each dog bravely gave the turtle's backside a sniff before jumping backward and barking a warning to the others. Alice, James Kennedy, and his wife Donna watched, encouraged each dog to be respectful, and pleaded with the dogs to leave the snapper alone.

"What's a turtle doing out at this time of the year?" asked Alice as

GEORGANN PROCHASKA

she looked at fluffy clouds against a blue sky. The bright sun warmed her face, and she considered removing her jacket.

Kennedy shrugged. "Weather's been unpredictable. Maybe Boudicca knows winter will be mild. You ever have the pleasure of meeting our warrior queen?"

Alice nodded in the turtle's direction. "Nice to meet you."

Jimmy was a small wiry man in his sixties with ruddy skin. For December days he layered two shirts for warmth along with jeans and walking boots. His wispy white hair curled around his collar.

"Boudicca usually hibernates in the creek behind the trees," said Donna.

Compared to Alice's height at six feet, Jimmy's wife was tiny, probably lighter than a one-hundred-pound bloodhound. Donna bundled up in a wool coat, her hair parted in the middle, pulled behind her ears.

"She likes to snuggle in the mud. Isn't she a cutie? But she has a temper. I named her Boudicca after the legendary warrior queen." Donna's big grin made her seem younger as the sun highlighted her freckles.

"Been here for some time," said Kennedy. "In the summer, we usually don't see her until evening. Her walk tells us the temperature's close to fifty."

The two new hounds, Biscuit and Clementine, were getting the gist of being a pack hound as A.J. brought out an old, patched inner tube to share. Wearing it around his neck, A.J. had difficulty walking straight as the thing kept slipping off his head. Finally, he shook it free, and all the dogs pounced as the tube wobbled away before falling. Audrey curled into the center of the tube as if it were a dog bed, but first her shoulder slipped out of the crib and then a hip. She was too big a girl to cradle in the inner tube. It was the uplifting, silly moment Alice craved.

"Oh, Audrey. You're no longer puppy-size," called Alice with a grin.

"Clementine will have her puppies soon," said Donna, smiling. "We didn't expect that when we agreed to take her in.

Alice looked at the tan hound who carried chubby weight. "Puppies! You have to be so pleased. I've never seen baby bloodhounds. Must be so adorable with long ears and wrinkly feet. Why don't you look happy?"

"Because we don't know the sire," said Kennedy, his face stern. "No one knows. That's why the owners got rid of her."

"What difference does that make?" asked Alice.

"Won't be bloodhounds," said Kennedy as if his answer explained everything.

"I don't understand." Alice felt irritation rising.

"Biscuit and Clementine weren't treated well because people thought a bloodhound was cleaner, quieter, and a guard dog," said Donna, her voice soft. "Imagine what happens if a dog looks like a bloodhound but has no inclination to follow a scent because the sire is a collie and the dog wants to herd. What if someone wants a cuddler for the family and the sire is a territorial? People find all kinds of reasons to be mean to dogs. For these puppies, Jim and I have to find the right kind of family."

"But," Alice couldn't believe her friends weren't excited at the idea of wrinkly puppies. "Still, puppies have to be adorable," said Alice, hoping to coax excitement into their faces. "Nurturing makes a good dog, not biology."

"True," conceded Kennedy. "But nurturing often depends on people's expectations. Look at Audrey. Not everyone is kind. I tend to agree with you about her treatment when she was young. Why was she crated too long and left alone? Bloodhounds are sensitive and social. Why didn't her owner help develop her confidence?"

"Don't know," said Alice as she turned to look at Audrey's dark face and droopy eyes, wishing her dog didn't panic at the thought of being left alone.

Kennedy grabbed the inner tube and sent it flying through the yard. All eight dogs took off at a gallop to follow. "Don't worry. We'll vet owners. Give puppies away to people who see them as dogs to love," said Kennedy. "We'll teach them about hound weaknesses. Can't keep every dog although Donna wants to."

Tilting her head in a flirty way, Donna added, "A few more hounds can't hurt. Jim, wrinkly feet, so cute."

A sadness hit Alice. Here was Jim and Donna worried about placing puppies into understanding homes, so not to create dogs with wounded spirits. *Wounded spirits*, Alice's thought went to Flossy's Deirdre Hart and Lena, all wounded and eager to please. *Easy marks for a predator like Phil.*

"Now you look sad," said Kennedy.

"Remembering. That's all," said Alice.

"Audrey accepting the crate yet?" asked Donna.

"She's allowing it in the bedroom. Thinks it's a storage unit for her toys. She places her face in it, but that's all. I occasionally put a bone in the back, hoping she'll climb in after it. Audrey whines and knocks the crate about until the bone slides forward."

"Smart girl," said Kennedy.

"But here's my dilemma," said Alice, "what do I do about my grandson's graduation in May? I can't ship Audrey to California in a plane. The stress of confinement and loneliness of being with baggage will make her crazy. In fact, she could die. And no airline will put up with her slobber if I try to have her in a cabin with me. Railroad? She'd still spend time in a crate. And my truck's too old to drive from the Midwest to California. Not every motel takes a bloodhound. Where would we stay overnight? I don't know what to do."

Donna put her hand on Alice's shoulder. "Always can let her visit here with our big family."

"Thank you, but to do that we need more practice with her

transferring loyalty to the pack," said Alice, remembering the last time her hound thought Alice was leaving without her. As Alice walked to the truck for an additional sweater, Audrey galloped and launched herself at Alice as if she were a puppy wanting to be held. Both owner and dog hit the ground with a thud. At least none of Alice's bones broke, but she still felt guilt for frightening her dog. "I don't want her scared."

"It's a puzzle," said Donna. "You'll work it out. Maybe a new truck's in your future?"

As they left for home, Audrey stretched out on the bench seat of the truck with her head on Alice's thigh. Alice hoped the small grunts and gurgles belonged to memories of play, of being brave while facing a turtle named after a warrior queen.

Alice was tired after their visit to the farm, but as she pulled into the driveway, her adrenaline surged, her heart beat faster. The lights were on in their house, and the curtains and blinds drawn

"Who's in our house?" asked Alice aloud.

Alice grabbed her cell phone ready for 911 and crept up the back steps to the door. Audrey's wiggle in her hips and enthusiastic barking showed she had a different impression of what was going on. *Must be Lena*, Alice thought as she slipped her phone back into her pocket. Inside the yellow light of the warm kitchen stood her best friend.

"Surprise! Look who arrive two days *early*," Lena said with more teasing than glee.

Behind Lena stood Sylvie Jakubowski, Virgil Deke, and Gladys Wax, the three guests from Bottom Ridge whom Alice met as she and Lena searched for a child accused of arson and murder. Lena had a wide grin and mischievous eyes.

"We hitched a ride with the groom," said Silvie, a woman in her eighties, painfully thin with thick blue veins on the back of her hands. Silvie was a member of the Bottom Ridge garden club, called the High-Hoes. In this winter weather, she wore a Cuddly-duds turtleneck undershirt with a brown crew-necked sweater on top. A yellow puffy vest layered over both. Jeans and boots finished off her dressing.

"Your next-door neighbor thought we were breaking in and called Lena," said Virgil. He also was in his eighties, a couple years older than Silvie. Alice remembered his rope-like muscles from years of being a grave digger. His hair was buzzed to pink scalp, and although he was in the house, he wore a baseball cap. His shirt was buttoned at the collar with a plaid wool shirt and a blue vest snapped around his body. Virgil stood heavily enveloped in warmth. His cheeks were pink.

"Please, take off your vests," said Alice. "It's warm in here."

"Nah, you keep your house cool," said Virgil. "I like to set my thermostat at 78. Comes with working outside all summer with no air-conditioning."

Alice remembered the older gentleman on his riding mower, cutting the grass at the Bottom Ridge cemeteries.

"We brought dinner," said Gladys who bent over the open oven door, "so you don't have to prepare anything for us. As soon as this oven gets going, the house will be toasty."

Gladys was the oldest High-Hoe, close in age to Virgil. She was shorter than Lena and round like an old-fashioned tea pot dressed in a knitted tea cozy. Her face glowed as she stood.

"Dog like celery?" asked Silvie. "Made a meat loaf. Also, a killer mac and cheese. You like cayenne pepper?"

"Oh," said Gladys, "hope you don't mind. We had to rearrange the refrigerator."

"Virgil got hungry for lunch," said Silvie. "He ate your little weenies."

Alice felt her face flush as she looked at Lena who sucked in her lips as she barely nodded and seemed to suppress a giggle.

"The hot dogs?" asked Alice.

Virgil took possession of a leather chair, newspapers strewn at his feet. "Chicken, I think. Cute little things. Who makes them? Really good. Like to have them back home."

"A local chicken farmer," said Alice not wanting to embarrass Virgil for eating Audrey's dog treats."

"In case you're worried," said Silvie, "I left my shotgun at home. Trisha told us how you got a curious dog. Now that I see her, can see she's a handful."

Audrey's forehead wrinkled more than usual as she made her rounds to sniff each new guest. When she neared Virgil, she slipped on the newspapers and knocked her shoulder into the elderly man's knee before smelling Virgil's face, particularly his mouth. Before Alice could stop her, the hound's wide, long tongue gave Virgil a slurpy lick across the mouth.

"Shoot," said Virgil, the back of his hand drying his mouth. "She probably thinks I deserved a good cleaning after traveling."

Finally, Alice rallied. "Very happy you're here. I have two guest bedrooms: a larger bed downstairs and twin beds upstairs." Seeing two suitcases, two boxes with bottles and jars, and an old-fashioned hat box sitting in the living room, Alice turned to the two women and asked, "Shall I carry these up for you."

"Gladys took hers up already. Those on the floor belong to me and Virg. We'll take them in. No reason to bother you."

Lena's fingers covered her mouth, her eyes were laughing.

"Virg and I don't like skinny twin beds even when they're pushed together. You keep your house cool. Already found your extra blankets. Virg, it'll be cuddling together for warmth like when we go camping.

"Don't worry about entertaining us," said Gladys. "Saw your movie theater."

"One thing nice about being old," said Silvie, "we can see four movies for the price of one. No one challenges when they believe you're dithering. You'll see."

"You need help with this Phil fellow?" asked Virgil. "Sounds like a mean one. The groom filled us in on the way here. Too bad about his new mother-in-law."

"She have a long affair or a quick dilly-dally?" asked Silvie.

"It's in the past," said Alice, looking to Lena for help.

"John and Emily will sort things out," said Lena.

"No one expects drama at the wedding," added Alice hoping her conclusion was true.

"You got a computer?" asked Silvie. "Want to read that gossip blog everyone's talking about. Sounds like it's better than having an old-fashioned party line."

Gladys sang, "Tomorrow's five days until the wedding!"

Lena's eyes rolled as she crisply walked to the back door. "Time to go. See you all tomorrow."

"Thank you for coming down to help supervise," said Alice lowering her volume.

"They're such a hoot," whispered Lena. "Good luck tonight keeping them contained. I suspect Gladys will rearrange your kitchen cabinets and drawers by morning. You'll be lucky to find plates."

"When we met them last spring," whispered Alice, giddy with pleasure, "did you suspect Sylvie and Virgil were an item?"

"I know!" sang Lena with mock shock. "Good for them, but still a surprise. Better warn them about Audrey's rules. Hope they don't mind leaving bathroom doors open to accommodate her curiosity."

Alice squeezed her friend's hand. "Don't think that will be a problem for these three."

"Good thing Silvie left her shotgun at home. I can see them reprising their roles of town militia."

"That's all we need," said Alice and together the two women giggled at the image.

"I can see the headlines," said Lena, shaking her head. "Please keep the gentleman away from my crispy dog treats for Audrey," teased Lena, with a big eye-roll. "I'll send Julian in the morning to give them a tour of town and to take them to the movies."

"See you tomorrow?" asked Alice.

"Maybe." Lena mimed holding a large mixing bowl with one arm and stirring batter with the other.

Chapter 11

Audrey lay on the floor with her nose pressed to the bottom of the bedroom door as Alice finished watching the late news program on television. The three house guests had been in bed an hour. When the doorbell rang at 10:30, followed by an insistent pounding knock, Audrey was on her feet, barking, toenails raking stripes into the closed door.

"Audrey! No. Shh!" Alice hustled to slip on shoes and pull a robe over her pajamas. By the time Audrey bounded and Alice hurried downstairs to answer the door, Virgil and Silvie dressed in flannel nightclothes were opening the door to Gary Tuchman.

"I'm looking for Alice Tricklebank. Is this the right house?"

What's the town historian doing at my house on a Wednesday night? wondered Alice. "Yes, Gary. Please come in."

"Pardon my hair-do," said Silvie who had her hair tucked into pin curls held with bobby pins and wrapped in a scarf. "Getting ready for the movies tomorrow."

Normally Gary was a fast talker, but the confusion at the door slowed him down. His blue eyes, much bluer than Alice's owl gray-blue, kept blinking. His clothing bagged on his thin body. He wore khaki-colored pants and an oversized big jacket. A hat with dangling earflaps sat on his head. In his mid-thirties, Gary was angular and awkward. Walking to a chair, he bumbled into a side table and grabbed the lamp about to teeter to the floor as he again mumbled about finding the wrong house.

"Didn't realize everyone'd be in bed."

Alice asked him to sit. By the time Gladys came down wrapped in a pink chenille robe, everyone had found a chair.

"I'll make tea," announced Gladys. "Give our hands a good warming up."

"Sorry I ate all the weenies," said Virgil. "Alice here got little chicken bites you can't stop eating." Turning to Alice, he asked, "That farm you talked about, do they make big hot dogs or just little ones? Big fellow like this guy needs a good-sized dog."

Silvie disappeared into the bedroom long enough to find the box of chocolate-covered cookies. "Ready for a midnight snack? Brought these from home."

Alice checked her watch again. Not even eleven o'clock. She waited for Gary to be charmed by three walking history books, but his eyes were serious, gestures more clumsy than usual.

"Gary," she said a little breathless, "What's happened? Is everyone all right?"

"Yes. Well, no. Looks like Phil broke into the Historical Society Museum this morning." Gary's face sank into that of a hurt child. "Lots of mess and some theft."

"This morning?" asked Alice. "Are you sure it was Phil?"

"Who else can it be?" answered Gary.

"What was stolen?"

"Stuff. Well, a Les Paul guitar that once belonged to Charlie Sweet." Gary's hands gripped each other as if lathering soap suds.

"Les Paul?" said Virgil, "Remember Silvie? We all used to watch Les Paul and Mary Ford on the TV back in the fifties." Turning to Gary, he asked, "You had Les Paul's guitar here?"

Gary shook his head. "Not his personal guitar. A brand-named one, but signed by some musicians. I heard Charlie's brother played it."

"All by itself, the guitar had to be worth money," said Virgil. "Who signed it?"

"Don't remember. Claude Grouper, the last historian enjoyed music memorabilia more than me. He once put together a display of music from the fifties and sixties. We got a lot of signed music sheets on loan from Charlie Sweet from when he played drums in a band. Only the ones on display are gone."

"Let's talk to this Claude fella." said Virgil. "Maybe he knows who signed it."

"Can't," said Gary. "He lives in Reno with his grandson.

"He got a phone?" persisted Virgil.

Alice saw Gary become more rattled as he stood up as if to escape then sat back down. Gladys walked in with a tray. "Who's ready for tea?"

"I saw a set of Slingerland drums in one of the museum rooms," said Alice. "Were those Charlie's?"

Gary nodded. "Here's the crazy part of the theft. Besides the guitar, Phil took the only signed drum but left the rest of the drum set. Then he tossed a bunch of files around the room. The only file missing, however, is the one with newspaper articles on Charlie's accident. Musta been in a hurry? One of the news articles got caught in the doorway. Sorta crumpled now. Why would Phil want Charlie's file?"

"Probably not Phil," said Alice. "This morning he was in jail. The lieutenant told me he wasn't releasing him until this afternoon."

Gary shook his head. "Gotta be him." Hanging his head, Gary took a sip of tea. "You know the drums and guitar are on loan to the museum. They really belong to the Sweet children." Then looking guilty, Gary added, "Before I call the police, I want to talk to Lena. I mean she married Phil after Charlie. I thought Phil might have *permission* . . . "

"You haven't called the police?" asked Alice, her heart beginning to thump.

"Not yet."

"You talked to Lena, right?"

"Couldn't find her. Her daughter either."

Alice's hand circled in the air, urging him to speak.

"Thought you'd know what I should do," said Gary. "Don't want to step on anyone's toes. Lena and Phil, you know, rumors."

Alice bit her lip, astonished at Gary's thinking. He didn't call the police even though someone broke into the museum. He hadn't tracked down Lena although he wanted to talk to her about the theft. *No, he came here.*

"You said it happened this morning?" asked Alice.

"Usually we close the museum on Wednesdays. I went in before four this afternoon to check mail and found the mess."

"You didn't clean up, did you?"

"No. Of course not, but I did pick up all the papers on the floor. Mostly I made a list of what's missing. Took time to check everything."

So you did tamper with evidence, thought Alice. "Gary, you should call the police. Here's the thing," said Alice speaking slowly. "Phil probably got out of jail *this afternoon.* Bobby kept him in custody until they checked his alibi for the cafe fire."

"After he got out," asked Silvie, "could he have lickedy-split to the museum and caused the damage before this fella got there?"

Both Alice and Gary shook their heads. "Probably too many people on the street to witness him at the museum," said Gary.

"We need to consider," said Alice, "who else robbed the museum. If the museum was truly robbed this morning, Phil may have an accomplice."

Gary sat back in the leather chair, worry on his face. "What's happening with this town?"

"Pretty clear you got yourself a sneaky somebody else," said Virgil, "using this Phil fella as cover."

A sneaky somebody else echoed in Alice's thoughts. *Maybe also a sneaky murderer.*

Gary gave a sideways glance at the two older women dunking cookies into their tea. His nose wrinkled, and he tilted his head before asking very quietly, "You don't think Lena could still be in love with Phil?"

In spite of Gary's caution, Alice's answer came stronger than she intended. "NO! Lena wouldn't set fire to her own cafe nor threaten Audrey's life with a poisoned meatball." What we need to figure out is why Charlie's file is important. Most of the newspaper files can be found online. Why is this accident file significant?"

"I can never find anything online," said Gladys. "You have to have the right words or else you get gobbledygook."

"Slingerland drums?" asked Silvie. "Les Paul? Mary Ford was a pretty woman. Good voice. When was Charlie's accident?"

"In 1986," answered Gary. "I looked it up."

"When did Lena marry this Phil character?" Silvie's eyes opened wider, giving her a hawk-like face.

Gary stared at Alice, waiting for an answer.

"In 1987," offered Alice.

"Well, that's all right then," said Gladys with a smile. "Unless she was skipping out on Charlie before she married Phil."

Alice rolled both her palms over Audrey's ears to help ignore Gladys' question.

"How'd he die?" asked Silvie.

"In a car crash," said Alice. "The police said it was obvious he was speeding and lost control. He hit a tree."

"Oh," said Silvie. "I never trust reports. You live long as us, you find people lie for all sorts of reasons, or get sloppy. I suspect policemen get tired with drivers being irresponsible or tired of typing every little thing."

"You remember who investigated the accident?" Gary asked Alice.

Alice turned to Audrey feeling a sense of shock. She barely remembered the accident at all.

Chapter 12

As promised, Julian picked up his three former neighbors from Bottom Ridge on Thursday morning to drive them into town for a tour of the shops and then to the edge of town with the movie theaters. Alice also drove there and parked across the street from the police station in the grocery store lot. She and Audrey joined a cluster of five people who stood on the sidewalk, chatting and watching as if a new thrill was about to happen. The day wasn't cold or windy but depressing just the same with heavy gray clouds.

"Alice, we heard Phil walked out of the station yesterday," said one woman, "as confidently as you please."

"The lieutenant should have kept him in jail," said another.

"About a half hour ago," added a third, "Stephen Zug walked into the station. You heard about the flood at Bait and Books? Phil's doing. You just know it." The woman's chin came down with authority as her hands went into her pockets.

"Like his antics years ago," continued another. "Get a repair job by promising an inspection but using that time to remove roof shingles or cracking seals around roof vents."

"I heard," said a woman who puffed, heightening the importance of her words, "he once removed bricks from a chimney. Can you believe that?"

"Older folk paid good money for repairs, and he up and left before finishing the job."

"Fraud, pure and simple."

"Arrogant same as now."

"Stephen's still there," said the first woman. "Must be filing a complaint. We all know what Phil did to Stephen years ago."

"Won't do no good. Statute of Limitations. Too much time has passed for the police to arrest Phil. Stephen's out of luck."

"Wedding will be better with Phil behind bars," said the youngest, close to Trisha Parker in age. "You saw the blog posting about Trisha's mom? I heard Phil thinks he's Trisha's father. Poor Emily."

"Poor John," said the only man in the group.

Alice looked at Audrey who followed the lead of the crowd by facing the police station.

"Trisha must be crazy with worry, wishing for snow," said the youngest woman.

Everyone nodded, making sounds of sympathy, eyes not leaving the police station door.

"At least we know Emily's one-nighter wasn't with Phil," said the man.

"Although plenty women did fall into his bed . . . from what I hear," said the third woman.

Alice's ears perked up to the gossip. *Who fell for Phil's charm.*

"Who . . . canoodled with Phil?" asked Alice.

The women looked at Alice as if they couldn't believe Alice's stupidity.

"Your neighbor, Gretchen Kluski," said one of the women with certainty. "I don't know if they actually . . . canoodled, but Gretchen told me after her husband died, Phil came on like gangbusters. She threw him out of her house, more than once . . . or so she *said*."

"The rumor I can't believe," said the man, "was Gina Pickler. You don't like to hear of your kid's cafeteria lady playing around with the likes of Phil Greer."

"Where'd you hear that one?" questioned one woman. "No! Phil poured tacks in her front yard."

Tipping his hands upward and raising eyebrows, he signaled the statement proved the rumor. "He's getting revenge for something."

One of the older women swatted his arm. "Howard, he poured those tacks because Gina once *publicly* scolded him for littering. Being a bad example for the children. Mika Watson told me so."

The group stopped to stare at the police station.

The youngest woman, a Limekiln High graduate, reminisced about the cafeteria's mac and cheese. "The gooeyness stuck to your lips and coated your teeth. Loved it. The football players called it mortar." Her voice deepened. "Need a glop of mortar for the game."

Another woman went on to describe the turkey and dressing, but Alice tuned them out. She was busy remembering how Gina defended Phil who wanted Lena to have a white peony. 'Beauty for a beauty,' he said, encouraging Lena to pay for it.

The cluster of women drifted away. The man, however, Howard Winklesea, bank employee, stayed behind. He was a heavy man, face flushed, dressed in a gray suit, white shirt, and bright Christmas tie, all clothing too short and tight for his expanding girth. Trapped by a collar, his skin rolled over the top of his shirt, reminding Alice of Audrey's layers of wrinkles.

"You don't think Lena has anything to do with all this nonsense, do you?" he asked not as a question but as a criticism.

"No, I don't," said Alice. Her tone left little room for discussion.

"Because she wasn't exclusive, even when she was married to Charlie. He was older than she was by a good twenty years. I'm just saying . . . are we sure she hasn't taken Phil back?"

Alice felt fire in her ears. Her fists went to her hips, and as if picking up a cue, Audrey barked at Howard. "How exactly do you know that?"

"You were probably the only one in town who was blind to what was going on," said Howard in a heavy-handed way with a smug look, "and maybe even now? I'm asking because the bank holds the mortgage on the cafe. I'm worried she's repeating old mistakes and her daughter's gonna take the hit. Don't want the bank to lose money. But, I'm not judging Lena."

The hell you're not judging! thought Alice. Her reply might have been sharper, but she remembered how Lena had pulled away, hidden something from their friendship. "Look," she said, hoping her voice carried the authority of a teacher, "Lena's done with Phil. If he's doing these terrible things, it has nothing to do with her."

"I heard she's not helping the police," said Howard.

"She can't give what she doesn't know." By the look on Howard's face, Alice saw what she said wasn't helpful. "Howard, Lena has been a resident here a long time. She's added to the community by serving dinners for families in crisis." Noticing holiday shoppers stopping to listen, Alice upped her volume and flicked her warm scarf for drama. "How many times has Limekiln held fundraisers and Lena donated the whole buffet. We all know her. I think everyone needs to quit speculating on whether she's in league with Phil. We *owe* her that much respect."

"Whatever you say," said Howard grinning as he walked away.

"This is a good town," Alice called after him even louder. "People should pay attention to the blog's good letters and let the few hard moments go."

Embarrassed shoulders turned away from her. Alice hoped they got the message in spite of her street-minister volume.

As she turned to leave, Alice saw Julian a half block behind walking toward her. Without a word he turned and walked away.

Audrey gave a shimmy, and when Alice followed the dog's gaze, Rooney Santoro walked toward them. Still wearing camouflage pants and a black jacket from Emily Parker's rehearsal of the rehearsal, Rooney's first move was to grab Audrey's face and tousle it back and forth, much to the delight of the hound whose tail whipped with pleasure.

"You seem to be drawing a crowd," remarked Rooney with a grin.

"I'm being the town *scold*," said Alice with disgust. "Lost my temper when Howard berated Lena. Too many rumors floating about. Too many horrible things making people afraid."

"Maybe part of the rumors will have some truth soon," said Rooney. "Did Stephen go into the station?"

"Yes," answered Alice. "When I talked to Neda on Monday, she didn't seem to have any notion that Phil may have caused the damage to Bait and Books."

"I heard about the damage," said Rooney. The young woman looked up and down the street and lowered her voice to a whisper. "Actually, I hope Stephen is telling the police about his vicious attack years ago. At least I'm planning to join him in telling the truth. It won't mean anything to the police after all these years, but they should know how dangerous he can be."

"What do you mean?"

"Stephen's arm. My fault, sorta."

"Rooney?" Stunned, Alice continued. "The whole town guessed Phil broke Stephen's arm. How can it be your fault?"

"Phil attacked Stephen because he tried to defend me from Phil," said Rooney as she stuffed her hands into her pockets. "When I was in fourth grade, I was walking behind Phil. I think he thought I was following him. Anyway, when he turned around and saw me, he charged and grabbed me around the middle so that my shoulders and head hung upside down. He pulled me close to his hip and started jogging. I remember being in pain because the hammer he keeps in that loop on his pants kept digging into my stomach. I screamed. That's when Stephen attacked. He was a kid too, but kicked and punched Phil until he dropped me. Then Phil yanked Stephen's arm really hard, pulling it backwards. With Stephen on the ground, Phil took out his hammer and hit him twice, breaking Stephen's arm."

"Rooney, why didn't you and Stephen say anything?"

"We should have, but we were scared kids. Stephen's mom already had too much going on in her life with a new Bait and Books business. And the divorce was really hard on her. Stephen didn't want to worry Neda. I knew if my dad found out Phil tried to carry me off, he'd do his best to kill him. But I knew Dad follows rules even in confrontation. In my kid-imagination, I saw Phil pull something sneaky and kill my dad." Rooney shrugged. "Kids."

Alice put her arms around Rooney. "I'm so sorry. That's too much weight for any child to endure. I'm glad you're going to tell."

"Do you think Phil held a grudge against my dad for something. Is that why he went after me?"

"Could be."

"Anyway, I'm hoping the truth being out there makes a difference to Stephen." Rooney turned to look at the police station, a small sparkle in her eyes.

"I don't understand," said Alice.

"We were once . . . close. But after we graduated from high school, we drifted apart. The attack made us friends as kids, but when we got older, the attack became an embarrassment Stephen didn't want to talk about."

Alice took a deep breath, wanting to hug the younger woman again and apologize for the town not pressing for more information in the past. The truth arriving late, however, wouldn't bring charges against Phil. Too much time had elapsed, and Alice didn't see any pertinent clue in Rooney's story.

"Maybe this is a new beginning," said Alice, "for you and for Stephen."

"Let's hope so," said Rooney.

Rooney kneeled again to pet Audrey and complimented her shoulder muscles. "I don't know how you control her," she said to Alice. "Audrey, girl, you should be in a muscle magazine."

Alice waited in the pickup outside Beckerman's grocery store for her order to be bagged and delivered to her pickup. Junior Beckerman brought out the food, put it on the truck bed of the pickup, and leaned into the passenger window.

"Mrs. T., you hear about the tacks thrown into the grass around Mrs. Pickler's yard. Crazy huh? And the hay wagon for the kids to have rides on Friday? Burned last night. Why would Phil do that? Now the little kids can't have a ride in the parade."

"Why would anyone go after hay?" asked Alice. On her mental white board, she recorded the new information. *Last night fire hay wagon. What does Phil get out of it?"*

Junior shook his head. "My dad and Mr. Santoro are standing guard tonight over the fireworks for the festival. Not taking any a chance with Phil in town. Dad wanted to take a baseball bat, but Mom told him to take his gun."

Alice felt a shiver of worry at Limekiln residents arming themselves. Both Beckerman and Santoro were hunters, but Phil was conniving. "Please tell your dad thank you and to take care. No one wants a fireworks explosion."

When she drove home with Audrey next to her, Alice shook her head, uneasy at the news of a second fire. Burning the hay could be Phil who was released from jail yesterday afternoon, and the fireworks did make the town vulnerable. But why continue the destruction and terror? Nothing made sense.

"What a mess."

Chapter 13

Standing in the kitchen with cans of food on the table, Audrey stretched her nose toward the meat packages Alice held. A quick game of keep-away followed with the dog making a gurgling sound in her throat while eying the plump raw chicken wrapped in plastic. Alice air lifted packages over Audrey's head and into the refrigerator. When a phone call came from Henry, her grandson, Alice's mood turned to delight. "Did you receive my Christmas present?"

"Thanks, Gram, it's great. Arrived yesterday. That's not why I'm calling."

"What's wrong? Is everyone okay? Band trip still on?" The silence at the other end of the connection hit her stomach with dread. "Henry?"

"Everyone's fine, Gram. Slider and Dad are still going to France as planned. Part of a school Christmas trip. and Mom *insists* on coming with me to Hawaii for the band trip. Gram, I need a place to stay."

"What do you mean? What's happened?" Alice felt her heart pounding.

"After I graduate, can I come live with you?"

At his pleading, Alice closed her eyes and put the heal of her hand on her forehead. This was a loaded question with no good response. She heard her mother's warning bounce around in her head. Henry's deep, rapid voice held rejection. Several questions lined up in her thoughts. How bad had the argument been with his parents? How angry will her daughter be when Henry tells her he's moving to the Midwest to Grandma's house? And, what happened to college?

Alice couldn't imagine Henry really wanting to live in the Midwest. California weather and beaches were more his style. But she reflected on past phone call conversations with both Jess and Henry complaining about college choices. He wanted out-of-state. She wanted him living at home.

Alice found it hard to speak. The last thing she wanted was to disappoint Henry at a time his voice wanted a hug.

"Now, what's going on that you want to stay with your old granny."

"You're not so very old," said Henry with calculated charm in his voice. "Just old enough."

"So, you want to leave California and live with me?" said Alice. "I'd say that's pretty life changing. You know I'd love to have you here, but Henry, why are you really asking?"

"Just listen and don't get mad, okay?"

Alice felt her body tense. *Don't get mad* was one of her least favorite conversation openings.

"Details, please."

"January first is the application deadline for the university Mom wants me to attend, but I don't want to go there next year because they don't have a welding program. I want a welding school or at least a college with a welding program." When he pronounced *welding* his voice held possibility.

"Henry . . ." She imagined Jess's anger in orbit at hearing *welding school*. Alice wanted to ask, *have you thought this through?* But this was Henry. Of course, he had planned and charted out his life in detail. Alice felt clever in asking, "Your mom's not good with welding?"

"No," said Henry, calmer than she expected. "She thinks I'll ruin my life. Wanna hear my plan?"

"Shoot."

"Grandpa went to welding school when he graduated high school and then college. He told me it was the best decision he made. Practical knowledge to actually get your hands dirty with guys who know what they're doing because that's their job every day. Whether I'm an engineer or architect, I need to work with materials like Grandpa did." Henry's voice ramped up, frustrated and pleading. "Grandpa said architects make mistakes because they don't know the application side of design." His voice full of determination, Henry continued, "Gramps called those architects *pattycakes*. Gram, everyone protects me here from getting dirty, you know? I don't want to waste time with a design if it has no actual chance of being made. I don't want to be a smart pattycake. Tell me you understand?"

"Your grandfather did learn about metals before he enrolled in college." Alice stopped herself before launching into a history lesson. Times were different for Baer, money an issue. "Henry, California must have a welding school."

"They do. It's good." Henry's voice held back praise. "But, forty miles from Limekiln is a respected college with welding in its curriculum. A guy told me how he took a class where you take a bridge apart, cut it down by three inches, and put it back together. It's cool. I want to go there. Maybe transfer back to California where they have underwater welding."

For a moment, Alice's ears rang with an imaginary rant from her daughter. *That's crazy Henry. Stay at home with us.*

"How will this help you become an architect?" asked Alice.

"I don't want to design houses," Henry said with contempt before launching into the details of global warming and the rising oceans. "I want to build the next generation of hydraulic systems to protect cities from flooding. I want to go to the Netherlands and study their gates protecting the cities."

The last time Alice saw her grandson, he had gained fifty pounds of muscle, his new height topping Baer's by an inch. She remembered the seriousness that entered his face, giving him his grandfather's forehead of determination. Now, he also wanted to build security gates, not ornamental like his grandfather did, but ones to protect lives from flooding. Alice welcomed silence, too choked up with pride.

Knowing Jess would place a blistering call if she didn't handle this right, Alice said, "How about working a compromise with your mother. Come here for the summer. Take a couple of classes, see if you like it. Return home if you're allowed to attend a college with welding." Now it was Henry's turn to be silent. "You're invited to stay with me as long as you want, you know that. Talk to your mother while in Hawaii. Pretty mellow place. You might work a deal."

"I'm not sure it'll do any good."

Alice couldn't tell if he was disappointed or drafting a new plan of attack.

Lena came in through the backdoor, saw Alice on the phone, and mouthed, *dog treats*. She sat across from Alice and waited for the phone conversation to end. She fed three bits to Audrey who cracked cookies on her molars and dropped crumbs into Lena's lap.

Alice put delight and expectation in her voice. "Remind your mother you've never eaten rhubarb pie and want to expand your horizons by experiencing a crappie fry."

"Crappy?"

"It's a fish, pronounced *crop-pee*. You'll like it. I have a friend who'll take you fishing." Alice knew she was rattling on, but in the details, was a message to Jess. All would be okay. "I remember your mother wasn't so thrilled with fishing, but call Uncle Peter . . . although he may have loved the cooking more than the catching."

"I don't think I'll have time for fishing if I take classes."

"Sure you will." Hoping her voice sounded dreamy, "I think rhubarb was one of your mother's favorites."

"Isn't that red sticks?" He sounded doubtful.

"Not how I'd describe it. Henry, I'll love to introduce you to the Midwest. Strawberry picking. Tractor pulls. Covered bridges. Draft horses! Swimming at the lake! We'll have fun. Ask your mother to compromise."

The conversation drifted to an end with Henry's rebellion tempered and a promise to discuss his future with his parents.

Once Alice hung up with a sigh, Lena asked, "Henry? How is he?"

"Full of dreams of how to save the world."

Lena sat back in her chair, putting her fists on her hips. "Gosh, I wonder who he takes after?"

"He wants to come in June to live with me," said Alice.

"Sounds like you went way over the top of encouragement with fishing for crappie. He's just lucky you didn't mention the button museum. What lad can refuse old buttons?"

"Jess hates rhubarb."

"Even mine?"

"Even yours," said Alice raising an eye brow. "Their lives are too busy to visit. Henry really doesn't know what to expect. I don't want him to be disappointed in his decisions when he has such big dreams."

"I feel I haven't seen him in an age," said Lena. "Still think of him as little. He's probably no longer eight."

"Most definitely not," said Alice, her eyes glistening. "Six-two. All muscle. And the last time I saw him, working on a beard." Alice patted her knee, and Audrey responded by placing her front paws on Alice's thighs for a hug. "I miss my children and grandchildren."

"Good to hear he wants to visit. Wish my grandkids would remember they have a breathing grandma and not a picture when we Skype."

After a tour of the town with Julian, Alice's three house guests returned. Gladys entered first.

"Came back for another sweater before we go to the movies," said Gladys. "And a tinkle. Julian said to call when we're ready. He went home."

"Stopped at the grocery store for popcorn," said Silvie. "Don't like the yellow grease theaters use."

"That's when we heard someone tore through an apartment," said Gladys with eyes wide, "where someone had died. Lots of mess."

"Everyone talking about it," said Silvie.

Virgil took a seat in the big leather chair, and Audrey put her face on his lap. Alice heard Virgil whisper to Audrey. The hound licked her chops, then the strong smell of liverwurst caught Alice's attention too late to stop Virgil's sharing with her dog.

"Keeps their coat shiny," he said.

"Was the break-in at a house or an apartment?" asked Alice, turning her attention back to the two women.

"Apartment," answered Silvie.

"Did you hear the name Richie Mills?" asked Alice.

"Can't really say," said Silvie.

"Don't think anyone actually said," added Gladys.

If it were Richie's apartment, what was the intruder after? wondered Alice. *He has nothing worth stealing.*

"You want to stay for coffee?" asked Alice as Lena stood to leave.

"Nope." Lena's mood changed. "Don't you have a call to make to Jess? Sounds like you nosed into her business."

"I do need to call her, and I did invade, but I'm a grandmother. That gives me leverage."

Alice walked Lena to the door. Her friend whispered "This is me leaving because I know you want to talk about Phil and I don't."

As Alice turned, she thought she caught sight of Virgil sneaking an open package of liverwurst into the refrigerator.

Before Alice could comment, Silvie said, "Don't let us stop you from your snooping business. You call whoever you need to. We'll sit in the living room, in silence, right after we have some tea."

Gladys filled the kettle with water, and Silvie popped open a package of Windmill cookies.

"Hey," said Virgil, "We got a couple hours before that movie *Gravity* starts, why don't you call that Claude fella? I'd like to hear more about Les Paul."

"Maybe later," said Alice. "Time difference with Nevada."

"If he's an old fella like you say, he's been up for hours," offered Virgil.

Calls to Jess and Claude were on Alice's agenda, but she wished Lena were willing to talk about the events regarding Phil. She missed throwing out options of how details might line up with Lena taking each to some absurd direction. Their system worked to tease out the truth. But for Lena, discussing Phil was off limits.

Alice's first call went to Jess who didn't pick up. In desperation to talk to someone, Alice's second call went to her next-door neighbor Gretchen, who according to gossip, maybe knew Phil far too well.

"Come on over," said the owner of Audrey's cat friend. "I've got hot chocolate and stories."

Chapter 14

"Gretchen, I've had house guests for a night and a day and I'm worn out," said Alice after she pulled a reluctant Audrey through the back door. "My whole routine has been thrown off. They're lovely people, but I catch them watching me after they've slipped people food to Audrey. A few moments ago, Virgil fed liverwurst to my girl here. No idea how the fat will hit her intestines." Alice took a deep breath and allowed her shoulders to relax. "I'm on guard all the time. And Phil in town? They're entertained by what's happening."

"Do they move things around?" asked Gretchen. "My mother-in-law used to rearrange my cooking utensils. Throw out anything she didn't like. Don't get me started on the linen closet."

By architectural design, Gretchen's house appeared very much like Alice's. The difference came in decorating. Alice's Spartan home accommodated a clumsy bloodhound. Gretchen wasn't a collector like Lena, but she dearly loved her grandchildren. Framed photographs covered end tables as did crayon artwork. Boxes of toys filled plastic milk crates. What distressed Audrey was the scattering of catnip mice and feathers dangling from sticks for Sheila, the menacing cat. The hound's paw tested the feathers that moved with her breath.

Gretchen also loved holiday sweaters bought at craft shows. The one she wore had the back of a cat in front of a Christmas tree and fireplace with a collection of presents and a rocking horse. Her short hair, freshly cut and colored for the holidays, was reddish-brown and straight.

Audrey moved to lean against Alice's leg, but her neck was bent low with her attention on the couch across from her. Plopping down flat and making a squeaky whine, Audrey attempted to see under the skirt of the couch. Sheila's soft, white cat paws slipped out from under and pulled back, causing more whining from Audrey followed by one deep bark.

"My refrigerator," said Alice, leaning forward to pat Audrey to divert her attention, "has little containers of leftover food they brought from home. I hardly know what's in all of them."

"Guests will do that to you," said Gretchen with a snicker. "I'm glad I'll be flying out the day after Christmas to visit my boys. The last time my youngest grandson visited, he tormented Sheila with attention. She's old like us. Took a month before she stopped hiding under the bed."

Alice and Gretchen talked about family Christmas traditions, gifts they wished they could buy rather than giving impersonal money, and Alice's care of the cat while Gretchen was out of town.

"She probably won't go outside if the weather turns nasty," said Gretchen. "Just visit with her for a half hour. Bring Audrey. Sheila needs to know someone's here. When do you see your grandchildren?"

"Not until spring. This Christmas my grandchildren are busy with school activities. My son Peter is hosting a family holiday reunion at his Bed and Breakfast."

For a moment, Alice felt lonesome. Skyping wasn't a good substitute for hugs. Quickly, she reminded herself children need to build their own life experiences.

"Did you read Flossy's blog today?" asked Gretchen.

"No."

"Remember the Orchard Lady?"

Alice nodded. Picking apples as a family was a fall tradition.

"A hoarder. According to Flossy's blog, the barn was filled with junk. Same with the press room for apple cider." Gretchen's eyes grew big. "Flossy wrote warnings to the daughter of possible law suits if someone got sick. Who knows if the cider had contaminants?"

"Well," said Alice, "I guess it doesn't matter now. We lived through those years. I don't remember getting sick. The daughter made a bundle selling the land for warehouses and storage buildings."

"Funny," said Gretchen. "Hoarding to organized hoarding." Alice's neighbor grinned at her own snide remark. "How's the hunt for Phil going?" Gretchen lowered her chin and looked over the top of her glasses. "I've been fending off calls."

"You haven't heard?" said Alice. "He walked into the police station and proclaimed innocence."

"Lieutenant Unzicker doesn't believe him, does he?" Gretchen sat taller and her voice rose with shock. "They didn't let Phil go?"

"Had to. No evidence."

Gretchen sputtered. "This is absurd. What about the meatball?"

"Still no report from the county," said Alice, squirming at her frustration. "If it is poison, no actual evidence Phil was the one who threw it."

"The burning of the hay wagon before the children's parade?" Gretchen's body moved to the edge of her chair. "Do you believe it? You tell me who would be so inconsiderate other than Phil."

"The police will investigate," concluded Alice. "We know Phil's sneaky. Most of his dirty dealings have been at night. So far no one saw anything."

"You don't think Lena's interested in Phil again, do you?" Gretchen's face flushed. "Because when he lived down the street with her, married or not, I felt *threatened* every day."

Alice found herself defending her friend yet again, knowing Lena'd never help Phil. If for no other reason than Julian's temper was ready to explode. Lena's grumpy partner had one thing in common with

Baer, problems may best be solved behind a barn with one good pop in the chops.

With a naughty grin Lena might break thy-neighbor's-husband commandment, but she'd always supported the community. She'd never collude to burn a wagon or destroy hay rides for children.

"Gretchen, you've lived in Limekiln almost as long as I have. Do you remember anything about Deirdre Hart?"

"No. Can't say I do. Why?"

Alice related Zadie's search but left out the significance of her mother's name.

"Sometimes it's hard to tell if a woman is pregnant," said Gretchen. "Take Neda Zug for example. She's about the right age for the girl's mother and used to have a round body type when she lived on the farm. Difficult marriage. Divorce. She was never the quilting and canning type, you know what I mean? I always expected her to move away to the big town like Memphis or Cincinnati."

Alice knew as Neda aged, her intensity had softened. She joked with fishermen and shared book passages with readers. Of course, Stephen's arm probably tempered her aloof spirit, made her softer, more careful about the feelings of others. Still, many in town called her standoffish. Didn't like that she closed the doors to Bait and Books promptly at five.

A dark place in Alice mind wondered if the violence to Stephen had been revenge on Neda. Could Neda be Zadie's mother? Phil, the father? Alice struggled with bits of detail like Phil's threat to claim paternity at Trisha's wedding. Did Phil get the idea of claiming paternity from Flossy's blog, or did he know of a baby daughter given up for adoption and used the storyline as a weapon against Emily Parker?

"Of course," interrupted Gretchen, "could be any woman in town. Phil wasn't picky. He even targeted me after Terry died. I gave him the heave-ho real quick. Can't imagine what he was thinking."

"His voice can be buttery," said Alice, remembering Lena's despair, "filled with tones of remorse."

"All of us can be foolish with men," posed Gretchen with a scowl. "I think it's easier for us plain women to grow old. Not so much to lose. Lena was a pretty girl, and she knew it. Don't think pretty girls are prepared for the layers of insults that come as we all age. Maybe a buttery *sorry* from a guy is easier for them to swallow. To me it sounds like grease."

"Got another morsel on that nonsense for ya," called Silvie as Alice and Audrey returned home from Gretchen's. "Woman called. Said a school painting got slashed. Some guy got conked on the noggin."

"Do you remember who called?" asked Alice.

"Nope."

Alice checked caller I. D. *Mrs. Pickler.*

Nonsense was a good word for the more recent destruction. The theft of Charlie's guitar and drum from the historical museum could have been for money or maybe aimed to hurt Lena and her children. The burning of the hay wagon was a slap at Limekiln itself, but only an inconvenience for a town surrounded by farms that grew grains. Alice knew another farmer would easily supply a substitute wagon. The slashing of the picture at the high school? Downright meanness. Who was the target of Phil's anger this time? With school security tight during the holidays, did Phil break into the school? Or did the custodian allow him in? Alice hoped a *conk on the noggin'* produced a witness.

Mrs. Pickler's phone went to voice mail.

Alice wanted to yell stop. Stop with the destructive dirty tricks. Stop violence. Stop with the blog gossip. Stop the search for a mother. Stop Lena from hiding out whipping up rum custard and frosting. Alice felt so far she had done little to understand the mysteries in town and needed to refocus Lena as a friend interested in snooping, willing to talk about the past. To do that, Alice needed to work up her own courage to tell one truth about Baer and their marriage.

Virgil sat in the leather chair with another handful of Lena's dog biscuits, tempting Audrey.

"Don't you worry about Audrey," said Virgil. "I'll keep her busy. You call that Claude fella. Find out what he knows."

Chapter 15

At Virgil's insistence, Alice called Claude Grouper who lived in Reno with his grandson. She remembered him as a broad-shouldered heavy man who shortened over the years. When she and Baer moved to Limekiln, Claude had been in his forties but appeared older. Even then, Claude enjoyed his role of Santa.

"Claude, this is Alice Tricklebank in Limekiln. How are you?"

Virgil scooted his big chair closer to Alice, laced his fingers over his chest, and winked approval of her call.

"Alice, good to hear from back home." Claude's voice was thin, but his tone cheerful. "I'm getting along. Some days immobile, some days a kicker. How's home?"

"We're getting ready for Christmas, and did you know Trisha Parker's getting married?"

"She sent me an invite," said Claude. "Said I could wear the red suit one more time. Can't come though. Her mama having heavy doings?"

"Emily's plans are over the top. John's, too. Trisha wants snow for Christmas Eve."

"Then she'll get it, knowing John," said Claude. Alice heard his delight.

They both laughed in appreciation of parents who break their backs to do the impossible for their children. Conversation drifted into his family and how much he missed his wife Teresa.

"What a wonderful person," said Alice. "So surprised to hear she had passed."

"Baer, too. Shocker to hear." Both took a moment of silence. Claude said, "I appreciate the call, but what's up."

"Phil Greer's back in town," said Alice.

"Thought he was in jail?"

Alice explained the hardships and snafus happening in Limekiln, including the theft of the guitar and one drum from the historical museum.

"I remember him as a nasty dude," Claude's voice sounded younger. "But he's none too smart if he took only one drum. To sell it for real money, he needs the whole set. Did he take the paperwork too."

"Gary said he went into the file cabinet and got it. One newspaper article about Charlie's death got trapped in the front door."

"That was the file I put together on Charlie. For the good stuff, he should have gone after the old steamer trunk in the immigration display. Gary mention the trunk?"

"No. It sounded like Phil pulled the folder from the file cabinet. What's in the trunk?"

"Charlie and his brother once played in bands, mostly together, sometimes apart. The trunk has signed photographs of all the music celebrities they worked with when called to open a concert or fill a spot in a band. One picture shows Rick Nelson signing the guitar. Of course, Charlie got Les Paul's and Glen Campbell's signatures on it. One picture has the Monkees lined up to sign it, too. The big names on the Slingerland drum are Gene Krupa and Lionel Hampton. Boy, does that bring back memories of the old, old days. Probably can't say it today, but back in my day, we all wanted to hear Krupa's jungle beat."

"I never knew Charlie collected pictures and autographs," said Alice.

Audrey climbed onto Virgil's lap, almost hiding him. At first Alice thought the elderly man waved at her to pull the dog off, but Virgil said in a loud whisper, "Ask him what the guitar is worth. How many thousands?"

Alice turned away, concentrating on Claude's information.

"Got signed music sheets too. I always wanted to do a display, but over time my fingers wouldn't let me. Damn arthritis. So, Phil didn't get the mother-load?"

"I guess not. Claude, did you keep a file on everybody in Limekiln or just Charlie?"

"Like I said, I kept the monied items in the trunk, but I got about twenty files on Limekiln residents in the file cabinet," said Claude. "Sounds like Phil knew about the newspaper clippings I kept on Charlie's accident."

Alice filled him in on Flossy's blog of letters throwing the townspeople into a tizzy. Although Alice hadn't kept up with all the posted letters, she guessed Phil had read them all, mining them for embarrassing moments of the past to force cooperation from residents now.

"I'll have to look up that blog. See what ol' Flossy thinks of Charlie's death," said Claude. "I didn't like the way he died. Charlie wasn't a speeder. If anything, people yelled at him for driving too slow. He once told me his head got filled with music, and he slowed down to appreciate it. When he had an accident caused by speeding . . . just wasn't Charlie."

"I wondered about that myself. I thought he might be rushing home to Lena."

Claude's hum sounded like doubt. "Did you know a few months before he died, Charlie loaned the historical museum all of his music, photos, guitar, and drum set. We even got some stage costuming. He asked that I keep it safe. Got a retired lawyer over in Plum Valley to draw up papers giving his children ownership but loaning it to the museum for twenty-five years."

"Really? Why?"

Claude's voice deepened. "I think he saw Phil moving in on Lena.

I don't blame her. Charlie was over twenty years older. Lena was a firecracker. Charlie may have seen her flattered, maybe tempted. After all, she had a reputation." Claude cleared his throat.

"Yes, I know," said Alice, "but I have a hard time seeing Lena cheating on Charlie with Phil. She loved Charlie."

"Maybe she didn't cheat. But an older man with an aggressive younger guy paying attention to his wife? Maybe Charlie wasn't so confident. All I know, he wanted to protect his kids by putting something aside for their future. Why do that unless he felt threatened? I'm pretty sure Phil had a lot to do with Charlie's death."

"But, Claude, the investigation concluded it was an accident. His car hit a tree." Alice felt shaken.

"Lot of empty fields surrounding that road. Corn and soy . . . not many trees. Funny how the one lonely stand of trees and Charlie's car veers into it."

"The police didn't find any evidence of another car," said Alice, not liking her own growing suspicions.

"Who was looking?"

"Don't know."

"Buddy Wink," answered Claude.

"Oh." Alice remembered the smiling, cartoon-like police officer, known to have a little nip on the job.

Also, known to be accommodating, to look the other way, cut corners to keep the town peaceful. After Charlie's death, Buddy resigned and moved away. Not wanting to ask too many questions if his moving-on was his own idea, the town breathed a sigh of relief.

"You know the first rumor was suicide, don't you?" said Claude.

Alice was shocked. "No. I had no idea." She swallowed hard. Who would say that? Who would think that?" Alice felt her heart race. Why did she not know this? Alice's mind went into a whirl. "Did Lena know about the suspicion?"

Claude cleared his throat with a cough.

1986 was the year Alice's brother Billy was in the thick of his troubles. Both she and Baer tried to talk sense into him, but as an investigative reporter, Billy's passion to expose fraud blinded him to dangers. Then Billy's wife learned she had cancer, and with Billy off tilting at windmills, Alice tried to help his wife. When Charlie died, she and Baer were out of state.

"There is no way Charlie would kill himself," insisted Alice.

"That's what John Parker and Scott Stringini told Buddy Wink."

Hearing *Stringini* knocked against the story of the fertilizer dumped on his lawn. *Parker* triggered details of Emily Parker being blackmailed, her marriage to John threatened.

"Why did they speak up for Charlie?" asked Alice.

"Scott's dad was Charlie's long-time friend, and John took music lessons from Charlie. Had great respect for him."

"So, to cover the rumor of suicide, Officer Wink probably concluded Charlie's death was an accident," said Alice. Claude kept silent. "But there had to be an insurance investigation, right?"

"Don't know all the details," said Claude. "Far as I know not much insurance involved if the police filed a report of an accident and no other party named. Don't think Charlie had life insurance."

"Poor Lena." Alice's stomach flipped with the realization. "She knows the rumor of suicide, doesn't she?"

"She's aware," said Claude. "I told only a handful of people. My wife knew, of course Parker and Stringini. I took pictures of Charlie's car after the police were done with it."

"And?"

"To me it looked like Charlie was sideswiped," said Claude. "All dented up in the back too. Hard to believe a car hit a tree all by itself when both the side and the back have damage."

"Any paint residue left on the side of Charlie's car? Maybe red?" asked Alice leaping to conclusions as she remembered Phil's red truck.

"How'd ya guess?" Alice heard Claude's snide smile.

A question nagged at Alice. Were the dents and scrapes made at the time of the accident or days before? Bobby would want evidence.

"Where are the pictures?" asked Alice.

"One set was with the stolen file. But before I left, I gave that young lawyer in town a duplicate envelope of pictures. Bet Phil didn't steal that one. Not from Gilly Chapel."

Promising to keep Claude informed, Alice thanked him and said good-bye.

She always thought of Gilly as the strongest woman in town, able to make powerful men in court cower. Luckily for Alice, Gilly was her lawyer too.

Her brow furrowed as if worried, Audrey jumped from Virgil's lap to sit in front of Alice.

"So, did that fella tell you how much the Les Paul is worth?" asked Virgil. "Tens of thousands or hundreds of thousands?"

"He didn't say," said Alice, her mind churning because of Claude's bombshell information - *Phil killed Charlie*. What if Phil started the suicide rumor to stop the investigation? Now Phil's orchestration of a con fell into place with a practical revenge in mind. Get money. Hurt Lena through her children. Other mishaps in town were drama to keep the police occupied. Of course, the theft occurred when Phil was in jail, obviously done by an accomplice. If the thief were caught, it wouldn't be Phil who went to jail. With the accomplice blamed, Phil could skip with items to fence.

But so far, his antics went after reputations and property. Were these just the warm-up act announcing Phil was back in town? Compared to the destruction of Stephen's arm, the burning of Lena's cafe and tossing a meatball into Alice's yard were small aggravations. Charlie's death was the infinite loss for Lena. Richie's murder as punishment for testifying against him? Bizarre, even for Phil.

If Lena's correct and Phil wants to leave infinite pain as his revenge, stealing a guitar isn't big enough, thought Alice.

"What's the bigger picture I'm missing?" Alice whispered to Audrey. "Can't help but feel something earthshaking is coming."

Chapter 16

After Julian picked up Alice's houseguests for an afternoon at the movies, Alice and Audrey walked into Gilly Chapel's office off the square between Dilly's Hive Fresh Honey and Courtney's Cards and Candy. The juxtaposition of Dilly and Gilly always made Alice smile as if they were characters in one of Maud Hart Lovelace's Betsy-Tacy books. She pictured Dilly and Gilly, as two little girls planning a picnic, high on a hillside overlooking Limekiln.

Gilly's office had five pink and white poinsettia plants in front of the secretary's desk. On the wall hung red ribbons with Christmas cards from friends and clients.

Jade, the young secretary, sat behind her desk with a small electric heater glowing nearby to take the chill off her work space. The floor felt cool, the heat apparently rising to warm the ceiling. Alice's six-foot height felt the blanket of heat hovering around her head and shoulders. She pulled Audrey close. No reason for a dog's curiosity about a heater to burn a nose.

At hearing Alice's voice, Gilly left her office and came to stand next to Jade's desk. Julian called Gilly *Spitfire*, often referring to her build as being a fire hydrant. Gilly's height was maybe five feet tall when she wore heels. Her career wardrobe dressed her in a blue or black suit. When not in court, Gilly wore jeans, a sweatshirt, and running shoes. She spent little time on her appearance. Her hair, brown and short, fell like the character used in the Buster Brown ads when Alice was a girl. Yet, this former student, now Alice's lawyer, rescued her from legal tangles like the one that happened in Bottom Ridge. Alice trusted Gilly with her life.

Alice and Audrey went into the coolness of her office. Alice found relief from the cloud of heat by sitting in the client chair. Gilly told her secretary to hold all calls.

"Moments ago," said Gilly, "Claude Grouper sent me a message to give you the file I've been keeping for him. I've never read it. What's this about?"

Alice explained the death of Charlie Sweet and Claude's concern that it wasn't an accident. He believed, as Alice suspected, Phil murdered Charlie. Alice wanted the truth to come out.

"I can see Mr. Grouper building a file," said Gilly. "Nice man. I felt sorry for him when he moved to Reno. So bent over. He couldn't even stand straight. His fingers twisted with arthritis. You should see his signature."

"Do you remember when he played Santa?" asked Alice.

"Of course. Didn't need padding, and he had a real white beard. Always carried candy in his pockets, and when we kids saw him around town, he'd put his finger to his lips, tell us he was on vacation. 'Don't blow my cover,' he said and gave us candy."

Alice's hand stroked the top of Audrey's head as she remembered Claude and missed having him in town. "A super nice guy."

Alice's musings were cut short as Gilly turned to business of gathering facts.

"With all the turmoil that's going on with Flossy's blog - don't get me started on *that* - and Phil's destruction in town . . . if Phil caused Charlie's death . . . you think this file has proof? It's been how many years since Charlie died?

"Over twenty."

"Did anyone other than Mr. Grouper find Charlie's death

suspicious?" asked Gilly. She pulled a legal pad and pen from a pile on the desk.

"John Parker and Scott Stingini," said Alice. "They spoke to the police and insisted it wasn't a suicide. Of course, you heard the Stringini family had their front yard destroyed with fertilizer."

Gilly's head bobbled as if weighing the crazy circumstances.

"I can see," continued Alice, "Phil warning Scott he can hurt him anytime he wants."

"Open the envelope," said Gilly, "let's see what Claude put together."

With that Alice slit the paper to expose a picture collection of the wreck. Nine 8 x 10's were in the envelope, showing severe damage to the front of the car, a side that looked like it had been sideswiped, and possible ramming damage to the dented back."

"And they called this an accident?" asked Gilly, shaking her head with judgment and a frown on her lips. "Who was the cop who handled *this*?"

"Buddy Wink. No longer with the force. Sort of an Officer-Friendly type or a boozy uncle."

"Before my time," said Gilly. "So, a rumor about Charlie's suicide may have influenced the investigation to bury evidence and call the crash an accident because it was kinder to the family."

"Seems so," said Alice.

"No one who saw these photos today could think this was a suicide or accident," said Gilly. "Wink put his foot in it."

"Can we prove Phil forced Charlie off the road and into the trees?" asked Alice. "Look at the red striping on the car. Phil had a red truck." Even as she said it, Alice doubted the photos held any proof, but she hoped there was something she wasn't seeing. "Evidence of murder?"

"Nope. Not unless someone kept a door from Charlie's car *and* after twenty-some years we can get our hands on Phil's truck with the original paint scraped off *and* we can prove that Phil was actually behind the wheel of said truck the night of Charlie's accident and the damage didn't happen days before."

Alice's shoulders slumped. "Too much to prove."

"That would be my guess. Anything else in the envelope?"

"Looks like handwritten pages of Claude's notes." Alice peeked inside to make sure it was empty. "Nothing to test DNA. We got nothing."

"No witnesses came forward?" Gilly asked.

Alice shook her head. "Not that I heard."

"Any *rumored* witness?" Alice heard in Gilly's voice that they were dead in the water. "Anyone gossip about overhearing Phil threatening Charlie?"

"The only person who would know about Charlie is Richie, and he's dead," said Alice all the while wondering if Phil broke the police tape and searched Richie's apartment for some revealing evidence that the accomplice didn't find at the historical museum. Once they knew of a break-in, Bobby's men would have searched a second time.

Wonder what they found? thought Alice.

"Alice, these pictures are useless without corroboration. Lena can't give us anything?"

"She's in a muddle with Phil coming back." Alice sat back in her chair, her mind cataloging residents who might have known Phil's antics more than just in rumor.

"If people thought Charlie's accident was a suicide," said Gilly, "some friendly protector may know of the incident and have kept quiet all these years about a fact or two. Always a chance. What does your small-town nose tell you?"

"I got nothing," said Alice.

"Lot of you old-timers around," teased Gilly. "Looks like Lena may hold the key. Time for her to speak up."

Indeed, thought Alice. *Not as easy as you think.*

Chapter 17

Late in the afternoon Alice and Audrey waited in Bobby's office while an officer searched the storage facility for the old file on Charlie's death. She and her hound played what-hand-is-it-in? Hardly a challenge for a bloodhound whose nose instantly went to the hidden treat but Alice enjoyed the look on her dog's face as she brought both hands out from behind her back. With a wrinkled brow, Audrey looked dismayed before nosing Alice's hand.

"You're not going to find it this time. I got you fooled." Alice tipped her fists first with fingers down, then up, then down again. Audrey gave her the look of *Seriously?* and trapped Alice in the chair with her front paws while stretching under Alice's arm to retrieve the treat hidden on the seat behind her owner. Alice was laughing as Lt. Unzicker walked in carrying a folder.

"I reviewed the medical examiner's report," said Bobby. "We have a problem."

Alice pushed her hound away from her lap and stroked her dog's ears to signal playtime was over.

"What did you find?"

"The reports aren't very consistent." Bobby looked annoyed. "Tell me again what you remember about the accident."

"In 1986 Lena was thirty-six years old and Charlie was fifty-eight. My memories are scattered because at the same time of Charlie's accident, my brother's wife was diagnosed with cancer, and Baer and I went to help. When we came back, Charlie had died and Lena was devastated. Many days Baer and I took care of Lena's children." Alice's head dropped to focus on Audrey rather than make eye contact with Bobby. "Lena took it hard. She wouldn't get out of bed. I begged her to eat."

"How long after his death did Lena remarry?" asked Bobby.

Alice looked up, feeling alarmed. Where were his questions leading? "Nine months."

"Did you suspect foul play in Charlie's death?"

"It seemed odd that Charlie was speeding, but . . . at the time, no I didn't suspect anything." Guilt crept into her thinking. "Everyone talked of the accident. Charlie's children were crushed after their father's death. Baer and I ran off to help my brother and ran back to help Lena. Guess I never noticed anything else."

"I gather," said Bobby, "given the dynamics of their marriage, wouldn't do for Charlie to be late for dinner. Pleasing Lena had top priority."

Alice didn't like the sarcasm in the way Bobby framed Lena's marriage.

"I wouldn't have said it like that. I agree it's unlikely Charlie was speeding, but then they had children who needed a dinner routine."

"Mr. Grouper, the previous historical museum director, told you someone suspected suicide. That right?" Bobby's tone wasn't accusatory but asked for clarification.

Alice repeated the story of the musical instruments being loaned to the museum for twenty-five years, and Claude's suspicions that his friend Charlie was murdered by Phil. Officer Buddy Wink had a reputation for looking the other way. Rumors of suicide were squelched by John Parker and Scott Stringini."

"I remember Wink from when I was a kid," said Bobby. He knew how to engage a classroom of little kids. When I think back, he was like Big Bird in a uniform. Great guy, but I wouldn't like to work alongside of him now. Where did he move?"

Alice shook her head. "Not sure. I heard west," said Alice. "Supposed to have a horse farm where he gives lessons to disable children."

"I can see that. Much more his style."

Bobby picked up a pencil and tapped on his desk. Audrey stood to attention as if a treat were about to appear.

"The guitar and drums and all the signed music sheets and photographs," listed Bobby, concentration lining his face. "Could have been given back to the Sweet children two years ago."

Alice blinked. She hadn't bothered with the math.

"So, that you know," said Bobby, "with Lena's permission, we've secured the trunk with the photos and sheet music. My sons and I watch all those shows on television from the Road Show to Las Vegas Pawn. To my untrained eye, the trunk alone could contain a bit of money."

"Baer and I knew Charlie played drums, but we had no idea he had connections to stars. One of my houseguests suggested it could be in the hundreds of thousands of dollars."

"Nah, not that much, but a decent amount." Bobby threw the file on the desk. "Police reports don't give us any answers, only more questions. The medical examiner stated the cause of death was inconclusive. He wrote one wound isn't consistent with a head-on accident with a tree. Either Charlie struck his head on a rounded item within the car or a hard object hit his face on the left side near his nose."

Alice felt a chill. "When Phil walked in to the station to declare his innocence in Richie's death, did he have his hammer hanging from a loop on his jeans?"

"Sure did," said Bobby.

"What did Wink write in his report?" Alice's mouth was dry.

"Descriptions of the car, the tree, and Charlie." Bobby shook his head. "Totally inadequate descriptions of the scene." Bobby shuffled a few papers. "I noticed, however, he *didn't* mention the scrapes of red paint on the driver's side of the car or any follow up to the medical examiner's report. Even our official pictures show Wink was negligent in his recording of detail."

"Does the report name who found Charlie?" asked Alice.

"Named Roger Zug as the farmer out in his field working late. Zug said he heard the sound of the crash and called for help."

"Roger Zug," said Alice, swallowing hard. "Stephen's father." Alice held out her palms as if weighing the information, and Audrey's paws again trapped her in the chair. Fishing into her pocket, Alice brought out a treat.

"What are you thinking?" asked Bobby.

"Too much of a coincidence, don't you think?" asked Alice. "Roger hears Charlie's accident and a couple years later his son's arm is brutally broken by Phil."

"But between those two events are years," said Bobby. "Besides, the report records Zug heard the crash, not actually saw it."

"Yes, I know." Alice bent forward to focus her thinking. *Phil attacked Stephen, wrenching his arm and breaking it with a hammer.* The timeline was wrong or the police report incomplete.

Audrey pushed her nose under Alice's arm as her owner gave the down command. The hound gave a small whine before she hit the floor.

"Rooney Santoro thought Stephen came to her rescue," said Alice, "but what if there were an older grievance, causing Phil to stage a situation in front of Stephen? What if the attack turned out to be a warning to Roger or payback for a threat Stephen's father made. Maybe Phil figured Charlie told Roger the cause of the accident."

"Then why didn't all of that appear in Wink's notes?" asked Bobby. "Wink only writes Roger called in the accident."

"You need to track down Roger," said Alice. At least he's still around. Sold the farm after the divorce from Neda. I think he works at the herb farm."

"We'll find him. See what he remembers," said Bobby scratching out a note. "Tell me. Go through the sequence of events starting with Lena's marriage to Phil nine months later.

"Not much to tell other than their marriage was stormy. Married three years, but separated during that time at least twice. Actual living together time, less than a year. The official divorce came in 1990." Alice bit her lip. "Baer didn't like Phil, and Phil didn't care for me. During those years, Lena and I met after school for dessert at the cafe."

"Phil stayed in town after the divorce," stated Bobby. "How'd he take it when Lena married again?"

"Rocky. But I think by that time he and Richie were in the roofing business - not that he tried that particular scam in Limekiln. We were his haven of sorts. He duped people in the surrounding towns, gave them shoddy work, if he worked at all, or skipped with the money before the job was started."

"Promising a new roof and not delivering," stated Bobby and he started to tap the pencil again until Audrey lifted her bright interested face. Bobby stopped tapping.

Alice nodded. "People can't resist saving money. Phil promised a deal-deal."

"When did Neda and Roger divorce?" asked Bobby.

"After Lena did. Probably in '93 or '94. Why?"

"Curious. Stephen's attack happened a year or so later," said Bobby.

Alice sighed. Why had Phil attacked Stephen years after Charlie's death? Maybe the two events were totally unrelated, and Phil just a mean guy with a temper.

"I guess we wait for you to find Roger Zug," said Alice, planning her next conversation with Lena.

As she rose to leave, Audrey pulled at the leash, leaning in to give Bobby one last sniff, but Alice held tight. "Did the photographs of the shoe prints found at the Mansion give any clues?"

"Not yet. Richie's feet were much bigger. Phil's the right size, but the day he came in, he was wearing loafers. Not a shoe match. At least we got the pictures on file for comparison when needed."

"Never pictured Phil with a wardrobe of shoes," concluded Alice with a big grin. "Can't be staying in empty real estate."

"Briar is already on it," said Bobby. "Alibi and address doesn't hold up. Guy out near the interstate claimed Phil is only a drinking buddy. Was doing him a favor when we called for a *reference*."

"I hope he surfaces again soon," said Alice.

"Me too. But I want more than a vagrancy charge. We plan to let things play out a bit more. I really want to nail this guy. Smug and arrogant. Likes to control a situation and that makes him overconfident. Let me remind you, though, he is dangerous. So, you be careful. He may not be done with you or Lena."

"Do you mind if I see Richie's apartment again?" asked Alice. "I heard about the break-in."

"Jinn checked it out when Mrs. Kennan called. He thinks kids got curious. Nothing was different. He asked Mrs. Kennan to lock the door and keep a key. We'll call her and let her know it's okay for you to enter."

"And Audrey?" asked Alice nodding her head in the dog's direction.

"Audrey too," said Bobby, giving a sigh that sounded like an indulgence. "Where would we be without a bloodhound?"

"Meant to ask, did Richie have anything unusual in his pockets?" asked Alice.

"Not really," answered Bobby. "Cigarettes, wallet, work I.D."

"Keys?" asked Alice.

"No keys, but pain meds. Oh, I guess the toothbrush is a little odd. Why do you ask?"

Alice tilted her head back and forth. "Just curious."

"Right," said Bobby with clear doubt in his voice.

On the walk back to her pickup, Alice put determination in her step, but Audrey stopped to shimmy a welcome. Alice twisted to look at the people on the street. All were shoppers with their own holiday agendas, Christmas just days away. As far as Alice could tell, no one stood out as a friend to merit the dog's shimmy. What did the dog detect? Who was watching?

Chapter 18

Friday morning Alice felt lucky to find Lena at home. She and her dog stood at Lena's locked door, tiny bits of icy rain falling in a shower from a brightening sky that hinted it would be over soon. But the umbrella didn't fully protect Audrey's back.

"May we come in?" asked Alice.

Lena apologized for the delayed welcome, and Alice escorted Audrey into the kitchen but kept her near. From the duffle she carried, Alice pulled a large blue towel to dry Audrey who never complained about receiving a vigorous rub. Out of the corner of Alice's eye, she caught an orange foam Halloween pumpkin wearing a purple and black Mardi Gras mask.

"You packing away Christmas and moving on to Mardi Gras?"

Lena looked at the pumpkin sitting on the kitchen counter. "No, but that isn't such a bad idea. I'm not liking this Christmas season." Lena washed her hands. "I'm ready for lunch. You want a tomato stack? Sliced tomatoes, melted white cheddar, mayo, and black pepper."

"For breakfast?"

"I was up at four this morning working on wedding cakes. Beckerman's allowing me to use their ovens and freezers." Lena popped a tray of open-faced sandwiches into her oven. "The tomato stacks are my first lunch."

Motioning for Alice to move into the living room, Lena folded a kitchen towel. The living room was a scary experience for Alice who steered her bloodhound around a large Christmas tree and table surfaces decorated with more dancing Santas. One persistently chanted "Ho, ho, ho" with any movement in the room. Audrey went into suspicious barking, warning Alice of something strange in the room. Alice pulled her dog close, fearing Audrey's tail might whip the Christmas tree clean of ornaments. Lena switched off the Santas.

"You here because of the mental telepathy I sent you about my research on Zadie?"

"What did you find?" asked Alice wobbling Audrey's cheeks to keep her dog quiet.

"You said Zadie was born in early November, 1990. I figured not many people hide a pregnancy in the eighth or ninth month. You and I should remember someone in town who was big with child. So, I went to our local paper for July and August to see who is listed as travelers in *Society's Focus*."

"Lena, that's really smart."

"Girl born in Iowa, only stands to reason someone left Limekiln to go nest." Picking up a collection of pink Post-it notes and pushing a pile of printouts aside, Lena said, "I miss the old days of having the *Society's Focus* in our local paper. The column identified who was in town visiting, births, deaths, hospital stays, whose horse died, which kid got elected class president, who attended birthday parties. You know real news that meant something to people."

"Privacy issues kicked most personal news off pages. People get touchy about a whole town knowing they were in the hospital," said Alice.

"Oh, like Facebook is concerned about privacy," argued Lena, securing Post-its to the coffee table. "Not that I'm not on it every day posting and reading messages. Hit *Like* whether I do or not, but it's a whole lot harder to find who attended a birthday party or if I should send a get-well card to the hospital or home."

Alice smiled. "It was good of you to search the newspaper for information. I'm sure Zadie will be grateful even if we don't find specific details."

"Not hard to research," beamed Lena. "The newspaper came out on Thursdays. I only had to read eight pages." Lena pulled the leash from Alice's hand. "Let the poor dog breathe. She's not going to hurt anything."

Facing the kitchen with Audrey's nose in the air, the two women scrambled back to the oven. Putting on oven mittens, Lena pulled toasted sandwiches, slid them to a plate, and marched back to the living room with Audrey close to her hip. Alice held napkins and forks.

Sitting on the edge of chairs, hovering over the coffee table to protect their sandwiches and note-taking from Audrey's nose, Alice asked, "What did you learn?"

"Not much," answered Lena, tapping each note before her. "I ruled out all the girls off to college. A farm family moved but not anyone to consider because they had a daughter in her twenties. Flossy Grueber, way too old. She went to visit her family in Oklahoma for a couple months. A group of girls and their parents went to Boston for a concert. Again, too young. Neda Zug went to her niece's wedding in Cleveland, gone a month. Didn't take her son. He stayed with his father." Lena glanced up from her list. "That's all I got. The only potential woman is Neda. But, I'll keep looking and try May and June newspapers next."

"Sounds good."

The women ate in silence as Audrey talked her disappointment in grunts of not receiving melted cheese from Lena's tomato stack. Lena shushed the dog, and like a kid, Audrey went to her owner, begging. Alice searched pockets, coming up with a chip of a leathery dog snack. The hound accepted the treat, but her face registered disgust.

"Did the newspaper record if Flossy's housekeeper went with her to Oklahoma?" asked Alice.

Lena took a big forkful of gooey cheese that slipped from the bread, and with her cheek stretched with sandwich, she said, "The paper didn't say if Crystal went with her or not. She may have stayed at the house."

Audrey's tail hit a silver bell hanging on the tree. The hound eyed the sparkling sound and barked her authority at it.

Lena stretched to steady the bell and said, "Another angel got his wings."

Alice nodded, but kept her comment to herself: *Happens a lot with Audrey.*

"You know," said Lena, "I hardly ever saw Crystal away from the Mansion. I don't think she belonged to a church. Probably the old lady kept her as a prisoner. That's what I think."

Not wanting to hear a repeat of Lena's distrust of Flossy, Alice asked, "Where's Julian? He doesn't know what he's missing. These sandwiches are really good."

"Out for gas. I swear every time the car uses a pint of gas the man thinks he needs to *top off* the tank."

Anticipating the real conversation she wanted, Alice's knee jumped. She hoped the revelation of what she knew would only pour out a demitasse of secrets and not give Lena a body blow.

"Lena, I came to talk about something different. We need to put order back in *our* lives, and you're going to help me." Alice took a deep breath, drawing strength from the smell of toasted cheese lingering in the air. "I haven't seen you this walled off since Phil split. Your divorce from your first husband Zack and the one from number four, Fritz, were easier. Why are you so unhappy that you can't talk to me?"

"I don't know what you mean." Lena leaned back in her chair, creating distance.

Alice put her hand on her dog's back, feeling the heat deep in Audrey's fur, and took strength. Her dear friend had a fragile ego for all her flamboyance. She needed the truth.

"Here's the thing," said Alice, "Remember how Baer once broke a guy's nose with one punch. It wasn't right, but it felt good. I was proud to have him in my corner, defending me. Of course, I was afraid charges would be brought against him, but he said men who knew each other had an understanding about punching each other in the face. I never understood it myself, but the guy never brought charges."

"What are you saying?" said Lena looking puzzled.

"Are you reading Flossy's blog every day?"

"Aren't you?" asked Lena. "Julian reads it every morning before me. Did you know when your chicken dog-treat guy, Mr. Tran, went for citizenship papers, Hazel Graybill wrote a letter praising his good character. With her last name on the Graybill Hospital, nobody would dare question Mr. Tran's citizenship."

"I think that's commendable," said Alice worrying the discussion had slipped away from her.

"It *is* commendable. However, she never told him she was born in Canada and was smuggled into this country as a baby in a picnic basket."

"I can't believe that's true," laughed Alice. "Border agents monitor food, even picnic baskets?"

"According to *Flossy*, these didn't. See, you can't trust everything Flossy believes. A lot of her information can be dangerous. What if the government takes away Mr. Tran's citizenship because of what Flossy wrote?"

Lena stacked plates, turning away from Alice.

"Our neighbors are loving the underbelly of the town way too much," said Alice. "But Lena, ninety percent of Flossy's letters are filled with congratulations. We can't let one *misstep* destroy us. That's what I was trying to get at with Baer's story."

Lena gave Alice her *a-lot-you-know* face, stepped over Audrey, and removed dishes to the kitchen.

"I know why you're checking the blog," called Alice. Truth came easier with Lena in the next room, but she knew her next words would be a shocker. "You're afraid I'll see criticism of you for trying to seduce Baer."

Silence followed. Nothing moved.

Lena returned to the living room, her face drained of color.

"Alice . . . I never . . . Was the letter posted?"

"No. Years ago Baer told me." Alice kept her voice soft, sorry she hadn't confessed this knowledge before this.

"Years ago . . . he told you?" Alice nodded. "I never meant . . . don't know what I was thinking. Alice, nothing happened. Baer was a gentleman."

"I know," said Alice. "Phil left. I'm guessing you needed . . . reassurance."

"I am so sorry. What must you think?" She pulled a kitchen towel tucked into her waist band and covered her face. "I've been so worried about when the letter will be posted." She lowered the towel and asked, "Can you ever forgive me?" Her fortified wall of emotions broke and she wept.

Alice reached for her friend's hand.

"Hey," said Alice, "we're friends. We forgive the big, ignore the little, and allow the comic."

Lena squeezed Alice's hand, inhaling back tears.

"I know you like Flossy," said Lena, once again in control, "but I thought of her as judgmental. She poked her nose into business that wasn't hers. How could she have possibly known about my *mistake*? Unless Baer told her."

"Or Cheryl?" asked Alice remembering how Lena's daughter despised Phil and told Alice's daughter Jess of the log she kept of every mean thing he said or her mother did. "Daughters hear things, and didn't Cheryl play Dominos with Flossy?"

"Cheryl! Of course." Becoming serious again, Lena said, "You're right. It all happened after Phil and I had a nasty fight. He listed women he slept with. I threw him out, but the names were shocking. What a skuzz."

"As we said two eons ago when we started teaching," said Alice, thankful they were talking. With a silliness in her voice, she said, "A *pluperfect skuzz*. Remember the man who rode a bicycle and sharpened knives? Want a ride young lady?" asked Alice imitating his raspy voice.

"I had forgotten that. He gave me the shivers." Lena laughed. "Never knew what it meant but *pluperfect* had such drama to it."

"As Julian would say, are we square?" asked Alice.

Lena smiled with tears returning to her eyes. "We *are* best friends."

"Of course. And someday you'll tell me about the dance of the seven veils you promised Baer."

"He told you *that* too! Your husband was a blabbermouth. I saw it in an old movie. Thought it sounded exotic. Baer being a world traveler, gallivanting around, installing ornamental gates. I wanted him to see me as worldly." Covering her face again with a kitchen towel, Lena said, "How am I going to explain this to Julian?"

In that moment, the two women switched their attention to Audrey whose curious nose clicked on a swaying Santa. Alice reached to turn off "Here comes Santa Claus."

"Lena, Bobby needs your help. We know Phil has an accomplice. It's not a coincidence the theft from the museum happened with Phil in jail. Although it's painful, will you name women who may be helping Phil?"

With her determined eyes ready for revenge, Lena said, "Gladly. I bet most of the names he gave me were lies, but I'll list them."

"And by any chance did you save a pair of Phil's shoes? The work shoes he used to wear?"

"Are you kidding me? That was over twenty years ago. That would be plain creepy. Ick."

Julian flagged down Alice as she and Audrey walked home from
Lena's. He pulled to the curb and got out of the car. He wore a heavy
jacket and jeans, his head covered with his orange bandana, but no
gloves on his hands. Julian's eyes sagged, making him look tired and
worried.

"Car gassed up?" asked Alice.

"Yeah, yeah. You talked to Magpie about that damn blog?" asked
Julian. "Discover the millstone she's been carrying?"

Julian's endearment of calling Lena *Magpie* still grated on Alice, but
it was preferable to his previous nickname of *Fatty*.

"We talked," said Alice softening her voice. "She might be better.
At least she and I are friends again, but she's worried. What's up with
disappearing for gas?"

Julian shuffled his feet, his face scowling more than usual. "Stopped
in to see your lieutenant about his releasing that asshole ex. No evidence
to hold him, he says. Wants to catch him in a major slip up. Magpie's
in danger. That's all I know." Julian jammed his hands into his pockets.

"We're all on guard, Julian," said Alice. "Bobby's good at his job. His
men will find Phil."

"Not if I find him first."

Alice's stomach tightened. Julian had a stocky build with good
muscle development, but Alice questioned whether he could take Phil
on. Phil calculated every move and carried a hammer. "You can't go
hunting for Phil."

"Why not? Lieutenant said he's sure Phil has more in mind for
Magpie. Worries me. I dropped her off at Beckerman's about four this
morning." Julian's eyes turned to slits, his jaw tight. "You know men
from the warehouses lied about Phil's alibi for the time of the cafe fire."

"I guessed Phil has connections," said Alice.

"Early this morning after a few beers at the tavern, men talk."

Alice felt afraid for him. "Julian, you can't just go around looking
for Phil."

"Want to let him know I'm watching. Lieutenant's sure Phil has an accomplice." He looked over his shoulder up and down their street, paying attention to a car that passed them.

"But, you have to be careful."

"I plan to stay close to Magpie." Julian's chest puffed out. If he were a dog, Alice would say his hackles rose, making him more threatening.

"I know you'll take good care of her," said Alice, and she touched his shoulder.

"Lieutenant said *you* need to be careful too," said Julian, poking his index finger in Alice's direction. "You got someone watching your back? 'Cause I dropped a hint to Virgil to watch you like a hawk."

"Virgil? You shouldn't have done that." Alice took a deep breath, a new worry forming.

Virgil was muscle strong, but for a man in his eighties, perhaps bone fragile. Although she had seen him drop an assailant with a good chop to the neck, Alice feared a fall could shatter him like fine glass.

Back home, Silvie was the tough one who toted a shotgun on her dog walks. Now Alice worried Virgil might be emboldened to prove he was a tough old bird like Silvie.

"Tell Virgil not to worry about me," said Alice. "Phil or his accomplice went after me already. They won't try that again. Besides, I have Audrey."

"Not much of a guard dog. 'Course Phil don't know that."

Alice noticed Julian's ears turning red with the cold.

"Any idea who's his accomplice?" asked Julian. "Might need to talk, you know."

"No suspects yet," answered Alice, not wanting to share any more guesses with him. "Lena's putting together a list of suspects."

"Good. You hear on television of some lonely woman trying to help reform a prisoner. Could be someone in Limekiln likes bad guys."

"Thanks, Julian," said Alice. "I'll ask Bobby if he has checked with prison correspondence. Maybe find a pen pal."

Julian nodded and turned to leave. Before he closed his car door he said, "The little one, Gladys, invited me and Magpie to dinner tomorrow night. She's back at your house making a food list for Irish Stew." He scratched his head. "Think she's planning to send Virgil out in your pickup for kraut and caraway. How does that make it Irish stew?"

Alice shook her head.

Ready to volunteer for shopping, Alice hurried home, worried Virgil would drive her temperamental pickup into town. And worried about Julian stalking Phil. Very worried Virgil might want to be a hero.

Chapter 19

Alice picked up Gladys' food list and drove into town. With a few free minutes, she decided she needed to search Richie's apartment again. The police checked it out after an intruder broke the crime scene tape, but Alice had questions and wanted to see Richie's space again. As she parked in front of the bungalow, Rooney parked behind her pickup. The young woman hopped from her car before Alice could calm her bouncing dog. Alice struggled with unhooking Audrey from her safety tether, grabbing the dog's leash, and hoisting the duffle bag onto her shoulder.

"This is a surprise to see you," said Alice as Rooney stood by the passenger door.

"Saw you in the truck. I'm curious about your dog. You on a hunt?" Rooney pointed to the duffle.

"No. I take the duffle everywhere. It has Audrey's things - cleaning supplies, treats." Alice didn't add the medical supplies.

Rooney came around and kneeled, to give Audrey a deep scratch. The dog's muscles melted with delight as she flipped onto her back, right there in the street.

"You do that and she will be your friend for life," said Alice.

"Nothing like a good belly rub. Mind if I join you?" With one eye squinting against the brightness of unexpected sun, Rooney tilted her head to gaze up at Alice.

"I don't expect to find anything interesting, but if you want to come along, all good," said Alice.

Rooney stood and together they walked the narrow driveway into the bungalow's backyard. As the clouds rolled over the sun, the day returned to being gray. Alice pulled her scarf a little closer around her neck, and Rooney zipped her jacket.

"What are you looking for today?" asked Rooney as she, Alice, and Audrey faced Richie's attic apartment.

"Audrey and I were here before," said Alice. "The police have been all over his apartment for a second time after the break-in, but I want to look again." Alice scanned the yard. "No common thief would think Richie owned anything worth stealing."

"This okay with the lieutenant?" asked Rooney.

"He mentioned the broken police tape," said Alice. "Sounded like an invitation to me." Alice grinned at Rooney who looked uneasy. Placing her hand on Rooney's forearm, Alice said, "He told me Mrs. Kennan has the key."

"You know everyone says Audrey's the best show in town," said Rooney. "Even little kids I talked to lit up with excitement. This'll give me a chance to see what it's like to work with a dog. You mentioned a dog breeder?"

"I did. He's got his hands full. One dog is about to have puppies."

Rooney hummed and walked toward Richie's stairs. Alice stopped. The younger woman looked back at Alice whose eye reconsidered the dirty black pickup parked next to the garage with its nose forward.

"Quite a rust bucket," said Rooney.

"It is. This is Richie's pickup." Alice walked from the passenger side to the back. She crouched down. Audrey's nose playfully swiped at her owner's ear. From the back of the pickup, Alice squeezed between the truck and the garage to check out the driver's side.

"Old dents," she called. "Some of these may be new." She pulled on latex gloves and ran her hand over the driver's door. Bending low Alice studied the rear of the truck. Audrey's nose was right with her. "Look at this dent in the back, Audrey. Would you say this is new?"

Audrey made a noise, a cross between a gargle and a woof. Rooney joined Alice in the back, tramping on plants.

"I have no idea," said the younger woman. "Could be a recent accident."

"I wonder if the police checked out the pickup," said Alice, taking pictures with her phone.

"Why would they?" asked Rooney. "Wasn't Richie killed at the Mansion? He walked there, right?"

Questions swirled in Alice's head. The back of the pickup had been hit from behind. The shallow dents and scrapes of silver on the driver's side resembled sideswiping. Or maybe she imagined rear-ending and sideswiping because it was what happened to Charlie's car.

"This is all wrong," declared Alice.

"What's wrong?"

Alice shared her guess that Phil killed Charlie by forcing him off the road, first by ramming the car from behind and then sideswiping it into a stand of trees.

"Phil probably stopped long enough to make sure Charlie was dead," said Alice.

"Of course, he did," assured Rooney. Her hands went to her pockets, hunching her shoulders.

"If Phil wanted revenge," posed Alice. "Maybe he waited for Richie to leave work in the early morning . . . played tag with this pickup and forced Richie off the road, just like Charlie."

"But he doesn't kill him that way," said Rooney her voice full of doubt. "Maybe he just wanted to scare him."

"Scare him for a couple hours or days," continued Alice, "then kill him? Don't get the impression that's Phil's style. Frightening him should have been the beginning of revenge."

"That doesn't make sense either," said Rooney. "Some guy rams my car, he's not luring me to the Mansion later."

"Exactly," said Alice. "If Phil went after Richie, to scare him, maybe announcing he's back, why would Richie agree to meet him . . . or *any-one* . . . at the Mansion. Unless he trusted the caller."

Alice spun looking at the yard. Audrey also came to attention a low grumble in her chest.

"If the plan was to kill Richie, why not shoot him here?" asked Alice.

"Too many witnesses?" offered Rooney. "Right?"

Both turned to view yards next door. Sightlines were blocked by high wooden fences on both sides. Mature evergreen trees blocked the view from upstairs' windows.

"Only Mrs. Kennan and her children can see anything," said Alice.

"Not much of a yard for kids to play," said Rooney. "The separate garage and Richie's truck take up a lot of room."

"Look at the kid's toys," said Alice. A plastic playhouse stood near the fence along with a boy's small bicycle lying on its side.

"What of it?" asked Rooney, following Alice's inspection.

"Toys were in the yard," said Alice deep in thought, "when Audrey and I were here to pick up a trail. I saw them, but because it's so ordinary, I didn't *see* them."

"Alice?"

"Ever notice how a picture - let's say of a pumpkin display - becomes more interesting when you notice the little chicken in the background. Then you realize it's not a grocery store display. More like a farmyard."

Rooney frowned with confusion in her eyebrows. "I have no idea what you are talking about."

"A little detail tells a story, gives a notion."

Rooney gasped. "Ah, like when you taught us about symbols in literature." After a quick intake of air, she said, "You think the murderer is Richie's neighbor?"

"Oh no. No! But the toys tell a clear story. Do you think it would matter to Phil to shoot Richie even with Mrs. Kennan's children play-ing in the yard?"

"Not in the least. Phil liked to terrify kids. Never cared about the wreckage he left behind." Rooney's face hardened.

"Someone else called Richie to the Mansion," said Alice. "Someone who cared about children. Think about it. To convince Richie to leave, it had to be a person who was non-threatening to lure him away."

"Could be anyone in town."

"Let's get the key and look inside."

Mrs. Kennan, a young mother in her late twenties, gladly turned over the key, shoving rambunctious twin daughters from the door and the allure of the bloodhound. The young woman's blonde hair was pulled back from her face yet some strands worked free. She wore a long-sleeved T-shirt and jeans. When his mother asked, a small boy retrieved the key and snuck a quick pat of Audrey's face before hand-ing the key to Alice.

Rooney and Alice walked up the outdoor stairs, easier this time for Audrey since the ice melted. The winter gloom allowed little light inside the apartment, and a chill filled the room.

"I didn't expect this," said Rooney. "Was it this messy when you saw it the first time?"

"Pretty much."

Alice released the leash, and Audrey jumped on the bed, tuck-ing her long legs and feet under her. Both women stopped to look. The dog's head went down and her eyes closed. She apparently had no interest in sight details, and even with Alice's coaxing, Audrey still snuggled deeper into the rumpled bedding.

"Okay, fine," said Alice to her dog. "I'll apologize to Bobby, but hav-ing you on the bed probably doesn't mess up the crime scene."

"Shouldn't she be doing something?" asked Rooney.

"She's reserving her strength," said Alice with a hint of sarcasm. "But most likely she's not detecting any new smells."

Alice turned on a lamp by a chair and the florescent light over the hot plate. The search by the police or the intruder dislodged items from drawers. Black dust from collecting finger prints coated the top of the sink. Behind the chair, the pile of newspapers, girly magazines, and racing forms once pushed into a heap now had more order than Alice remembered. A shirt, previously draped on the back of a chair, hung from a hanger on the clothes pole, acting as a closet. Alice touched the shirt. Did the police choose to hang Richie's shirt smoothed and buttoned?

"How can people live like this? It's dirty." Rooney made a face.

"The dirt wasn't here before. Regular dust yes. Black dust is fingerprinting."

"On television cop shows," said Rooney, "the police take pictures of prints with their phones."

"We're still a rural community. I suspect we're old-school."

"Sad little apartment. Sad little life," said Rooney, looking around.

Alice felt protective of Richie and of Rooney. The young woman's tone sounded more like a criticism of her struggle with decisions. Would she leave the military and return to *sad little* Limekiln or stay in and continue working in housekeeping, whatever she meant by that?

Taking a deep breath, Alice made a visual sweep of the apartment, everything mostly the same, even the pile of dirty laundry. She peeked into the bathroom.

"You're making your I-don't-trust-you face," said Rooney. "Every kid in class knew when you weren't buying a lie."

"I'm not trusting the scene," said Alice ignoring Rooney's reference to memories of high school students. "Something's off."

Alice rapidly opened all the cabinet doors and dresser drawers. After that, she opened unsealed cardboard boxes. When Audrey's head lifted off the bed, Alice stood back.

"You're right to lie there," said Alice. "Audrey, we're done. But don't you get any ideas about that brown sock monkey I found in the bottom drawer. Not yours." Alice slipped a treat to Audrey who climbed off the bed.

"Anything significant?"

"To the murder?" Alice shook her head. Her thoughts went to the apartment door and the intruder. The yellow police tape had been broken, but the door showed no signs of being forced open. "I've seen what I came for. How about we go to the Mansion?"

"In my whole life growing up," said Rooney with a grin, "I was never invited into the Mansion. It scared me as a kid. I figured you had to be proper if you lived there."

"Proper is a good word for Flossy's style. She lived in by-gone times. Tried to keep her father's world alive." Alice smiled, "Want to snoop?"

"Of course, I want to snoop."

Returning the key to Mrs. Kennan, Alice asked, "Was the door locked when the police left the first time?"

The young mother launched into a story of what she knew, being home with her children, remembering Richie's steps upstairs and then down, guarding the key for the police, being afraid to let the children play in the yard. Her hand pushed loose strands of hair out of her face as the three young children stood behind her staring at Audrey, one protecting a bowl of Spaghettios.

"The door was locked."

"Do you remember the exact day Richie left the apartment?" asked Alice.

"Officer Jinn asked me the same question. I've the children, you see. I never paid attention." Her eyes narrowed almost saying, *It's not my fault.* "We were away when the intruder came. Later, I saw the yellow tape flapping and called the police. Officer Jinn told me the door was still locked and asked for the key."

Concluding with the small talk of goodbyes and thanks, Rooney, Alice and the hound retraced the path to the Mansion, the same route Richie took to meet his death. Sure enough, the backdoor to the Mansion was unlocked, and as they ducked under the police tape and into the mud room, Alice saw the pale, dirty footprint was gone. Though the door into the kitchen, both women commented on the stale air and oily smell.

"It's like industrial furniture polish," said Rooney. "This place smells like a museum."

The house was a timepiece. Very few pieces of furniture remained, but those that did were of dark-stained, carved oak. The ceilings high. Kitchen huge and white. The front door meant to dazzle with the view of the grand staircase. Parlor, dining room, sun room, office, all carried the power of sophistication.

"Wow," said Rooney. "Now I understand why kids weren't invited inside for tea."

The second floor held six small bedrooms, all small except for one which sat next to the only bathroom. A back staircase to the third floor hid behind a narrow door. On the attic level, three tiny bedrooms tucked under the eaves of the house with a closet that held a toilet and tiny sink. No corner of the house had cobwebs or dust. Alice found herself wondering who kept the house clean? Crystal?

"Why are the attic rooms so small?" asked Rooney.

"Way back when, the Grueber family had a staff of servants," said Alice. "This is where they slept. At one time my son thought he wanted to renovate the Mansion for a bed-and-breakfast. But with only one full-size bathroom . . ."

"Yuk! No one would sleep up here. It's cold now and probably hot and stuffy in the summer."

"One of these was Crystal Butterman's room," said Alice. "Do you remember her? Flossy's housekeeper?"

"I do. Never saw her anywhere but here. Always in the shadows. Kinda creepy."

Both women turned as Audrey's body shook with three sneezes.

"Flossy lived downstairs and Crystal upstairs? Downstairs is beautiful, but I can't even imagine living up here." Rooney's tone was full of judgment. "It makes me angry. Crystal was a servant?"

"That's how it worked for the wealthy of Flossy's generation," said Alice. She pictured Crystal's defeat in being homeless. Of course, a job of cleaning and caring rescued her, made her feel safe. "Flossy was probably more generous than most."

"But still, Alice. I thought Crystal *lived* here. That Flossy was a *nice* person. Only scary because you had to be perfect and not spill anything."

"Again, for her generation, she was pretty nice."

"How did Crystal stand it?"

Alice let the question go. For Rooney, she had no way to explain the bond that formed between a Dear Heart and the employer who offered room and board. Long ago, Crystal once expressed her feelings about the house. "I feel I owned the Mansion," she said with a grin. "This Cinderella bought it with dusting and scrubbing."

Back downstairs in the living room, Alice checked the hardwood floor, noting the stains from Richie's murder.

Alice wished she could bounce ideas off Lena, but Rooney always seemed to be at her elbow. And why was that? Maybe Limekiln was as boring as her daughter Jess thought. Or maybe Rooney saw Audrey as the best entertainment around. But leaning against Alice's pickup while her dog sloshed down water from a portable bowl, Alice wove details into imaginings as she might with Lena.

Wouldn't it have been storybook detail if Richie's black pickup was once transformed from Phil's red truck? But even with rust, Richie's truck was a much newer model than Phil's from all those years ago. Richie's pickup was bashed and scraped in a similar manner, but with a car. If Phil did it, whose car did he use? Why had no one piped up about a car being stolen? And why hadn't Richie told about Phil's attempt on his life?

"Alice, what are you thinking?" asked Rooney.

"Richie backed into a parking spot, perhaps to hide the damage next to the garage wall. Why?" asked Alice while nervously tugging on her own ear. "If Phil wanted Richie dead, why not surprise him at the apartment and blow him away? Why bother to bang up the old truck?"

"Where'd Phil score a gun?" asked Rooney with new authority in her voice, her posture tall.

Alice smiled at Rooney copying her and slipping into the role of crime solver.

To Alice's knowledge, Phil had never used a gun, preferring to inflict pain with a hammer-bashing.

"Don't know where Phil got a gun," answered Alice.

"Should we take paint scrapings off the truck and give them to the police?" asked Rooney with serious enthusiasm.

"No. I'll text Bobby. Better if they take the evidence and match it to a car manufacturer. When they run it through a database, names of owners with silver cars will pop up."

"Why do you think it's a car and not a truck?"

"Phil knows how to swipe a car off the road," said Alice. "A pick-up would match the tonnage of Richie's truck, but a car probably doesn't have the heft." Alice stopped, picturing the truck. "Besides, the scrapings on the pickup are low."

"Still, it's been a valuable day of snooping, yes?" said Rooney, her face brightening as if she looked with admiration at Alice. "Anything I missed in the apartment?"

"The tidying," said Alice, "my son Peter did the same kind. Last minute layering of clothes and papers as if piling became the same as cleaning." Alice grinned. So did Rooney.

"Stephen's room was like that in high school," said Rooney giving Alice a sideways glance. "He helped me study."

"Here's the thing," said Alice, not wanting to explore Rooney and Stephen's relationship just yet, "Phil would know how much force he needed to push a truck off the road. Why try it with a car?"

"What are you saying?"

"The swipe was a scare tactic," said Alice.

"To make Richie run?"

"That's where the theory falls apart. Phil ran Richie off the road to scare and torment him. Saying *I'm back* and *I'm coming after you.* But there's much we don't know. What caused Richie to go to the Mansion or Phil to shoot him?"

"The accomplice?"

"Likely a female," continued Alice. "She may have contacted Richie and convinced him to walk with her to the Mansion. He agrees, maybe to hide for a few days. Not knowing Phil waits for him."

"I can see that," said Rooney. "Makes sense."

Alice gave a big sigh because the theory had niggling holes. It made sense for Richie to escape but not for Phil to shoot him. She needed Lena to sit with her and spin possible scenarios. Out of their wild plotting came nuggets of truth. With three and a half days left before Trisha's wedding, Lena was up to her elbows in frosting, busy baking individual wedding cakes for the tables when she wasn't calming Julian, or helping to entertain the three guests from Bottom Ridge. Lena had no time to sit with Alice and spitball the possible.

Audrey finished her big drink of water and tipped her bowl. Alice warned Rooney to back away. At that moment, Audrey gave a power shake, slinging ribbons of water caught in her wrinkly jowls. Rooney's arms shielded her face in defense. Still, both women laughed.

Later while Alice and her dog sat in the parking lot, waiting for Gladys' grocery items to be delivered to her pickup, Alice's thinking went into a loop. She struggled to fit pieces of the puzzle together into solid fact. If Phil wanted Richie to twist in fear, why didn't he wait longer before shooting him? Or could Lena's first reaction be correct, and Richie's death had nothing to do with Phil? Did Richie have another enemy angry enough to shoot him?

Audrey tilted her head, and Alice gave her one of Lena's crunchy treats.

"After we make our delivery to Gladys, you and I are going to visit Lena, again. Maybe we can shake a few knots loose about Richie's past."

Audrey collapsed to the seat with a groan, her head, as usual, on Alice's thigh.

Scratching the top of her hound's head, Alice grappled with the riddle.

It's the toys in the backyard for Mrs. Kennan's children, she thought, *and the vintage sock monkey with tags in Richie's bottom drawer. And the toothbrush and the tidying.* Alice felt she had new insight into Richie. Girly magazines disguised under newspapers. Alice came to a conclusion in the form of a question: *Was the respected woman in Richie's life the one who invited him to the Mansion?*

Chapter 20

Steam clouded the windows of Alice's kitchen as Gladys cooked and wafts of pork and sauerkraut filled the air.

"Flavors have to marry," sang Gladys, "as my grandmother used to say."

With tomorrow's dinner preparations in full swing, Gladys banished the homeowner and dog from the kitchen. Alice suited up Audrey and walked to Lena's house.

Alice sat in Lena's kitchen, Audrey at her side, well away from Lena's living room and the coffee table, newly decorated with Lena's delicate porcelain manger scene. Alice's intent was to plan the logistics of entertaining the Bottom Ridge guests at the evening's parade and festival, but mostly to pump Lena for information on Richie.

Lena volunteered to drive the elderly guests into town, freeing up Alice to snoop at the town square holiday festival. Before Alice introduced the topic of Richie, a forceful knock hit the door. Phil barged in, demanding to speak with Lena. The house became hot and stuffy as if no fresh air existed.

At first Lena blocked his path to the couch, but Phil easily pushed her back with his forearm nearly causing her to stumble. Like a warrior, Julian rose from his seat and beelined for the intruder. Then Lena pushed Julian backward as if this were her fight alone. Alice sat fidgeting with her cell phone, watching and listening to the dynamics in the living room, ready to call 911. Was this the moment Bobby wanted? Was Phil about to overstep, and Bobby could arrest him for disorderly conduct or domestic abuse?

Audrey reflected the tension, sitting then standing, pulling toward the living room, all the while whining. More slobber than usual formed on her wrinkled lips. Alice wiped it away while listening for trouble, something more than just stinging insults.

"You plan to tie the knot?" asked Phil sprawled out on the couch, looking possessive and defiant, his chin raised.

"Not your business," said Julian whose body stood taller on guard, a badger ready to attack.

"Tell you what," said Phil "You give me twenty-five thousand, and I'll sign annulment papers. Make your marriage all legit., and I'll go away."

"Not going to happen," said Julian who sat with care across from Phil, ready to spring.

Lena went to Julian's side and edged herself onto the arm of the chair. "What are you talking about? I have *three* living ex-husbands. One before you and one after you. Why would I pay you for an annulment?"

Phil's smile turned smug. "Do you indeed? Not many women with three living exes."

Alice felt sorry for Lena who had walked into Phil's trap of reminding Julian he would be the fifth in a string of husbands, and although not mentioned, a string of lovers as well.

"Why aren't you in jail?" asked Lena, frustration in her voice.

"Who's seen me do anything wrong?" countered Phil.

With that, Alice concluded, *This visit isn't about money or an annulment. Phil is setting up for something. Maybe an alibi. Proof he is innocent when some harm happens during his visit. Who was the victim this time?*

"She'll leave you same as me," said Phil.

"Maybe I'm not the same kind of bastard as you." Julian leaned forward, breaking contact with Lena's protective hand, his keister barely touching the chair seat. Even from a sitting position, Julian could to look down on Phil.

"You love her," Phil said as an accusation and chortled like it was damn funny.

"I do."

Lena's hand reached to caress Julian's back. Phil snickered.

"Your funeral, man," said Phil with a grin.

"Time for you to go," ordered Julian as he stood ever so slowly, his eyes on Phil. "Leave. Get out of here!"

Lena flinched. Julian's hands were at his sides, knuckles whitening in fists.

Phil raised his palm and smiled at Lena. "Think about the money. If you believe the stories in town, I'm a bad guy." Phil stood with a winning grin on his face. "Might not want to take too long to decide my retreat from your life."

"Look," snarled Julian turning to face Phil full on, putting his hand on his rival's chest. The muscles in Julian's face were taut. Ready for battle. Alice stood as Audrey pulled forward.

"She's not paying you a dime," said Julian. "You try to hurt her or her family, I'll stop you."

Alice felt her heart hammering. Breaking up high school fights were tricky once one testosterone male put his hands on the other.

But Phil reacted with a snort, underscoring Alice's conclusion: Phil's visit had a different motive.

"Lena, got yourself a tough guy, a regular Bugs Bunny. Will he shoot an unarmed man? Ooo! Maybe blow me up?" Phil mimed a cartoon explosion. Julian's face reddened.

Alice found Phil's arrogance maddening, and if Audrey had been a different breed of dog, she'd be tempted to order, "Sic 'em."

"You threaten this family," snarled Julian, "I'll take you out."

"Good luck with that. Good to see you, Alice. Woman's got a mind like a steel trap. Makes for a good witness of me being threatened."

Phil saluted and walked out, the hammer swinging against his thigh. "See you in court."

The replay of Phil's visit and Julian's threats to "kick his ass," only succeeded to upset Lena. The more Julian claimed territory as Lena's guardian, the more Lena pleaded for him to ignore Phil and be careful. Neither listened to Alice's theory of why Phil chose this day to visit.

Get under Julian's skin. Wind him up. Make him rash. For the next time.

Alice shivered at the thought: *Next time.*

Chapter 21

The noisiness and glitz of the Town Square Holiday Celebration on Friday night pulled even the farm families into Limekiln. Excited children squealed. Adults filled the air with shouts and high pitched laughter all aimed at cheering rings to drop over old-fashioned milk bottles or hula hoops to trap a stuffed animal. Family dogs whipped tails in joy as if the festivities happened for them. Alice admired the courage of everyone willing to celebrate, leaving their homes unguarded with Phil now in town.

Everyone gossiped about the three vandalized homes with families away for the holidays. In one, a window was broken. Another had strips of siding pried away from the house. In a third a neighbor found frozen meats pulled from the freezer and left on the living room couch. All the destruction was senseless, but proved the vandalism wasn't a kid spoiling for naughty fun.

Alice spotted her house guests in front of church carolers as they sang near the WWII tank. Alice always wondered why the Catholic choir had twice the number of men, the Methodists, mostly women. Joined together, they possessed a powerful voice. Close to the tank stood a booth for hot cider and cookies. Steam filled with sugar and cinnamon lured skipping children. At the other end of the square near the clock tower stood the soup and bread competition as amateur chefs offered ladles of homemade soup and freshly baked bread.

Stomachs literally growled at the fragrance of thick oxtail broth with vegetables or the buttery smell of chicken noodle soup. To vote for the winner, each vote cost a dollar. Every year the money went toward a town project. Between the two stations of food, fairy-lit Christmas trees brightened the square.

Tonight, the mayor would announce the winner of the best house decorations and the Top Elf, a recognition of the best community helper.

Over the years, various firemen and policemen had won for their rescues. Alec Stringini won for his work with Boy Scouts. Even shopkeeper Dilly won for rescuing the September Corn Feast from a wandering hive of bees. More than once Lena won Top Elf for her generosity.

As in the past when too much drizzle claimed the needed snow, the children's snow sculpting competition was canceled. Instead, residents were encouraged to dress up their pooches for the title of best reindog. Audrey took pride in her working dog vest, but drew the line at fluffy antlers tied under her chin. The bloodhound apparently had dignity standards, pulling at the ribbon with her paw and chewing it into a mess while Alice tried to pry it from her dog's mouth.

"Okay, I get it. No reindog title for you."

The dogs led off the town parade followed by the hay wagon with children, pulled by Eli Moneyheifer's Belgian draft horses. Eli's thickset body dressed in a dark blue shirt, stiff new overalls, and a tweed sport coat. A jaunty brown fedora, meant for Sunday church, submerged Alice into memories of her father's hat, one he treasured from the 1950s. Grateful hands clapped appreciation as Eli passed, and he soberly tipped his hat. The German band, scouts, various displays from organizations like the Button Museum and Timber Haven filled the Square until Santa appeared on a bright red tractor, shimmering in the Christmas lighting. Cheers from the crowd stopped all gossip.

Alice never tired of the free and easy tradition. Silvie, Virgil, and

Gladys joined the festivities and wandered about the square, participating in the eating of homemade foods and watching games of chance. Neighbors greeted each other as usual. The gathering was ordinary, common, run-of-the-mill fun, almost.

The enjoyment, however, struck Alice as wary pleasure. Smiles and laughter yes, but also sideway glances, looks over shoulders, eyes scanning the crowd, hands gripping children a bit tighter. Whispers shared impressions from Flossy's blog or fears of what Phil would do next.

The entire police force milled about in full uniform. Everyone was on duty, ready and watching. Waiting.

When Alice spotted Old Adam, custodian at the high school, she went to his side. Old Adam wasn't as old as Alice, probably in his forties, but his hairiness at the age of fourteen allowed him to purchase beer easily for his friends. If you wanted booze, Old Adam was your go-to man.

"Adam," called Alice. Audrey, always ready for new smells, backed away, giving him a wide berth. "Heard you had damage at the high school. Phil's doings?"

"Be my guess," said Adam, "You know I was the one hit over the head." His hand went to his head and rubbed the spot of the strike. "I was on my rounds of the school, making sure all was locked up for the holidays, when someone hit me from behind. Not out long. When I woke up, called the police."

Alice hummed empathy, and Audrey opened her mouth in a big yawn that sounded like a sympathetic whine.

"Where were you in the school?" asked Alice.

"In the back. Near the dock." Adam looked away, his cheeks reddening. "Figure I messed up when I came in that day and didn't lock the door behind me. Probably got what I deserved for a security lapse, but then that kid's painting got slashed. That big gray and beige one of the woman that hangs outside the principal's office. Feel bad about that. Guess Phil don't like modern art."

Alice shook her head. She remembered the painting. Why would Phil go after an acrylic painting of a young woman, her face filled with yearning and loss?

"You were struck near the dock, but the painting's on the other side of the school?"

"Yes ma'am."

"Any other damage? Anything of value taken?" asked Alice.

Old Adam scratched his head. "Not that I know of. No other damage that I saw."

"Before you got hit, did you hear anything? Smell anything?" asked Alice.

"Not really. With all the disinfecting at the school, to me everything smells of soap. Coulda used a bloodhound." Adam shook his head and reached down to tousle Audrey's head, making her ears flap. The dog responded with a big sneeze, so hard her front paws left the ground. Alice remembered the strong soap used for cleaning the school. Adam continued, "I just can't believe I was that stupid to forget to lock the door."

They finished their conversation with Adam deciding he needed to vote for soup before walking to the beer wagon.

When Alice saw Crystal Butterman standing in front of carolers, she said to Audrey, "Let's go see Crystal."

Small talk about the evening gave way to Alice describing her visit to the Mansion. "I'm so impressed. The Mansion's been empty for almost five years, yet there isn't a cobweb or dust bunny in sight."

"The family asked me to look after the house until they find a buyer," said Crystal. "Funny, it looks smaller to me now that the furniture is gone. I like to go back and remember old times. Sit on the stairs. Don't get me wrong, I love having a place of my own, but I miss the people who visited Flossy. It was like they chose to visit me too."

Alice took her hand. "You did good work caring for Flossy."

Crystal looked embarrassed and broke eye contact.

"I'm not liking Flossy's letters being posted," said Alice.

"Seeing names in print takes away how funny Flossy could be." Crystal grinned. "Once she shared a funny letter with me and asked if she was being a *pip*. She had an odd sense of humor for all of her rules."

"Did she mind when people teased her about *dear heart* sounding like *Deirdre Hart?*"

"Not a bit. She even used the name when she wrote letters to them." Crystal's smile quickly faded.

"Did you ever travel with her when she went to Oklahoma?" asked Alice.

"No, I never did," said Crystal. "Why do you ask?"

"My daughter couldn't wait to leave Limekiln. I believe she said there wasn't enough action here. Not enough to do."

Crystal rolled her eyes. "Flossy gave me plenty to do. She always had guests at her house. I met her family when they visited. Lovely people. She visited them every two or three years. Stayed a couple months. When she went on vacation, I had a respite."

"What did you do with your time, while she was away?" asked Alice, hoping her voice reflected wonder and not nosiness.

"Major cleaning," said Crystal, rolling her eyes. "Air out the house. Wash down walls. Clean the pantry. Make things sparkle for when Flossy came home." A big grin followed. Crystal's eyes brightened. "And lots of pretending that I was the lady of the house."

"Not even a chance to get away for lunch with friends?" asked Alice.

"I didn't have many friends," said Crystal, her eyes following a child with cotton candy. "My life was quiet."

"I always thought Richie's life was quiet. Maybe that's why Phil got his hooks into him."

"He was a nice man . . . most of the time," said Crystal. "Sometimes I saw him walk to the tavern for an early dinner."

With a bounce of enthusiasm, Alice shifted topics. "My grandson wants to visit this summer from California. Can't imagine how that will work out . . . him away from the ocean? I hope his visit lasts more than a week." Alice shook her head and watched the crowd tighten, waiting for the announcement of Top Elf. "You never wanted to see anywhere else?"

"No," said Crystal. "We all get used to a place, not exactly stuck in the mud, but comfortable. I moved around a lot as a kid. As an adult ended up homeless - as you know - but I did make one friend. Rita and I worked for a summer on a Mississippi River gambling boat as singers and dancers. Rita played the banjo. One year when Flossy was away, I went to visit Rita's family in Iowa."

A cheer went up from the crowd. Crystal looked frightened, but Alice launched into a another story of when she worked as a roller-skating car hop for a hot dog stand. Before she described spilled trays and bruises, a fifteen-minute warning blasted the fireworks were about to begin.

Alice put her hand on Crystal's shoulder, "If I bring a lovely woman to see you tomorrow morning, will you help her understand Flossy's Dear Hearts?"

Crystal bit her upper lip and nodded.

Alice tugged Audrey toward Roger Zug.

"Heard about your hound," said Roger with his usual dull affected way of expressing himself. "I like dogs, but not as good at sniffing as a pig is. A pig's not as willing to show off as a dog, so I don't expect we'll see the FBI or airport security using pigs anytime soon."

Both Roger and Stephen were almost as tall as Alice, but Stephen took his good looks from his mother's side. Roger's face held deep furrows as if nothing in life was fun. He wore an old jacket, jeans, and work boots. Earmuffs arched over his head and cuffed his ears.

"Pigs, huh?" said Alice. "Definitely not FBI ready. You handling Phil being back in town?"

"Me?" asked Roger. "Don't like the man. Stephen told me only a couple years back that Phil wrecked his arm. Neda and I always suspected it because of the rumors we heard, but mostly because Phil told us about teaching him respect." Two boys ran between then in the direction of the fireworks. "No secret I wanted to kill him." His eyes narrowed, face darkened.

In spite of Stephen's attack being the most emotional moment in his life, Roger's tone held no menace, his voice too highly factual.

"A terrible thing," said Alice.

"Oh, you don't want to hear about our old troubles," said Roger glancing into the crowd.

Alice quickly said, "Claude told me you made the call about Charlie Sweet's accident. You saw the pickup speeding away."

"I did."

Roger didn't seem surprised by Alice's information. "Thought someone raced off to find a phone to call for help. I hurried to the car, but saw Charlie a goner. When no ambulance came, I called 911. Couple years later when I moved into town, I learned Phil owned a red pickup. Wondered if Phil was the driver that night. Never knew him before Neda and I divorced. When Claude showed me the pictures, I spoke up. You know that first cop never asked me any questions?"

"So, after Claude showed you the pictures, you told the police?"

"Nah." Roger shook his head. "Just to Claude first. Told him what I saw. Then, I faced Phil, man to man. Told Phil my suspicions. Asked him if he murdered Charlie." Roger's eyes again became slits and Alice bit her lip, fighting tears. "Told him about the photographs, too. Never figured he go after my kid. Stephen was hurt the day after I accused Phil. Now I'm more inclined to keep my mouth shut."

"Phil knew about the photographs of Charlie's car?" asked Alice.

Roger nodded.

"Did he know who took them?"

"I lied. Told him I saw police photos." Roger pulled closer, his voice with an eerie lack of emotion. "I figure Phil learned about them from Flossy's blog. There's her letter to John Parker, asking if the rumors about Charlie were true. Asked if anyone could view the pictures at the museum. Most people wouldn't understand the significance of photos, but if Phil came upon the letter in the blog, he'd know."

"Wow. Flossy's blog." Alice wanted to kick herself for not plowing through the hundreds of letters posted on line.

"This is what I learned," said Roger. "Phil's like a poisonous snake. No negotiating with him." He pointed at Alice. "You tangle with him, you better kill him because if you don't, you're in for great hurt. I figure to test that theory the next time I see him. Kneecap him for what he done to Neda's shop. Up to him after that. Don't mind killing a snake. Now, if you don't mind, I'll go for a cup of hot cider before the fireworks begin."

Alice felt a chill in Roger's words. She felt Phil had outmaneuvered the town. *What's next?*

The first blast of fireworks shattered the sky to a chorus of "Ooo!" Alice scoured the crowd for someone else who held secrets, but the crowd moved toward the field for the sparkly spectacle. Alice and Audrey walked back to her pickup to head for home. Her bloodhound didn't let loud noises bother her unless it was a surprise. Gunfire during the day didn't startle her, but booms and bangs at night made Audrey jumpy. Time to go home.

Labeling her fears as ridiculous, Alice placed a late evening call to Zadie Vanek.

"I know this is really short notice, but can you come down to Limekiln. I want you to meet a special woman tomorrow morning who knows about Deirdre Hart."

"I'll be there by morning. Thank you. I have news for you too."

In the quiet of the house with soft explosions echoing from fireworks in town, Alice chose to talk her ideas through with Audrey. The bloodhound sat attentive to her every word.

"Just hear me out, okay?" said Alice. "Richie left his apartment with someone who he didn't see as a threat. He took his toothbrush.

I'm guessing he planned to be gone for a few days. Would he have done that for Phil? No." Audrey's tongue lolled out of her mouth, her eyes in total ha-ha-ha agreement with Alice. "Don't you listen to anyone who suggests it was Crystal who met with Richie at the apartment." Audrey pawed at Alice's knee. "I know, I know. I figure she hung up his shirt and buttoned it after she broke the police tape on his apartment door. She didn't do that out of guilt. I think she was saying goodbye."

Seeing her dog eye Virgil's slippers, Alice quickly picked them up, away from Audrey who lunged, only to snort in defeat. After throwing the slippers into Virgil's room and closing the door, Alice retrieved the bucket and rag to wipe saliva and snot from the wall and lamp.

"Anyway," continued Alice, "what could Phil have possibly said to Crystal to convince her to work with him? Besides, you and I have been in Crystal's trailer. No trace of Phil. No, Crystal isn't the lure. Can't be." Alice curled onto the couch and patted the seat. "Snuggles!" Her hound leaped up and, never aware of her size, snuggled like a lap dog. Alice's arms circled her dog's body as she threw her head back and closed her eyes.

"You'll see. Crystal's not the accomplice. Because if she is, Zadie's in for a whirlwind mess, a storm too horrible for words." Alice felt her dog's warmth bring sleep.

Chapter 22

On Saturday Audrey's barking woke Alice before dawn. Lying in bed, Alice heard Gladys' footsteps padding in the hallway toward the bathroom. Downstairs the guest room's squeaky door opened, followed by more footsteps and whispers. By the time Alice dressed, Audrey wiggled at the closed bedroom door. When Alice opened it, Audrey angled past her and raced down the stairs, woofing the whole way.

The lights in the living room were on, and Silvie and Virgil peeked through the curtains.

"You got a somebody in your driveway. Car woke us."

Virgil stood in his pajamas, his quilted vest over the pj's top. Silvie also in printed pajamas and matching robe, pulled the curtains open.

"No point in pretending we're not here," said Silvie. "She's coming to the door."

Zadie entered the house without knocking, and everything became noise, led off with Audrey barking. Silvie's greeting went into questions for the young woman and a reminder of a morning still dark.

Wrapped in her bathrobe, Gladys pulled pans from the kitchen cabinets. "Coffee? Bacon? French toast just like my mother used to make?"

Virgil continued to invite the young woman into the room, pressuring her to sit in the chair he claimed as his own. In the din, Alice tried to explain Zadie's visit, but her words were lost in the circus of questions.

Only Audrey's baying stopped the chatter. Once all attention went to the hound, Audrey pushed and angled her way to Zadie and gave her crotch a good deep sniff.

The young woman instantly sat in Virgil's offered chair and removed her coat.

"This is Zadie Vanek," said Alice. "She's just had a long night of driving. Please let her catch her breath. I called her yesterday because I know a woman who can help her find her birth mother." Enthusiastic questions were about to return, when Alice said, "Hold your thoughts. Audrey needs to go out for her morning walk. I'll be back in ten minutes."

Alice attached a leash, grabbed a big flashlight, and donned an old gardening jacket. Audrey bolted for the door. Luckily the timer on the Stringini deer had turned off all lights and movement. Alice and Audrey walked their regular route down the street, the big flashlight lighting the path.

Well, she's here, thought Alice. *I hope I'm doing the right thing.*

As Audrey squatted, Alice planned. *We'll take this slow. No need to shock Zadie or Crystal with the news. Maybe in a few days. Let them get acquainted first.*

The surprise for Alice came when she and her dog returned.

"We're pregnant," exclaimed a breathless Silvie with delight. "Our girl here is pregnant. The father sounds like a dog. Wants to get on with his career. Suggested she put the baby up for adoption."

Zadie looked embarrassed and struggled to keep eye contact.

"If you can't find her birth mother," said Gladys, "maybe she can move to Bottom Ridge, and we can take care of her. I love babies."

"No jobs in Bottom Ridge," said Virgil. "Better if we visit her. That way we can take turns helping with the baby. Got five great-grands. Diapered every one of them."

"You see, Alice," said Gladys, "she has a nice young man who wanted to wait to get married, but the baby won't wait. And she needs to work. This is where a mother would step in, but her adoptive parents, lovely people but sickly, can't care for a child. Zadie wants to talk adoption with her birth mother, but *we* think maybe her birth mother can help. Is it possible to find her?"

"We volunteered our help just before you walked in," said Virgil.

Zadie sat looking as overwhelmed as Alice felt. Taking the leash off Audrey, Alice asked, "Can we all sit down?"

They all did except Gladys who announced she didn't want to burn the bacon and rushed back to the kitchen.

"I was only gone ten minutes," said Alice.

"More like twenty," said Silvie. "Knew she was pregnant as soon as she asked to pee. And your dog there put her nose right into the girl's belly. Sure sign."

Alice didn't refute Silvie's claim about Audrey's ability, but she knew Audrey's target was a crotch sniff.

"You're pregnant?" asked Alice, and Zadie nodded.

In a quiet voice bordering on tears, Zadie told of her adopted parents, one with Parkinson's and the other with a bad heart. A baby added complications the young woman had no idea how to handle.

"Logically, I should give the baby up," said Zadie, her eyes only watching the attentive hound. "I wanted to find my birth mother to ask her how she found the courage.

A chorus of sympathetic hums followed as the three elderly house guests looked to Alice.

Well, Baer, thought Alice, *this information puts a whole urgent spin on Zadie's introduction to Crystal Butterman, housekeeper, caregiver, lonely woman.*

Chapter 23

Gladys Wax set the dinner table for her invited guests as a thank you to Alice for being their host. The menu was her *Irish* stew with spaetzle. Lena hovered over Gladys' shoulder, questioning each ingredient until she pulled Alice aside.

"That is *not* Irish stew," whispered Lena. "It doesn't have a bit of lamb in it. She's using pork, onions, potatoes, caraway, garlic and sauerkraut. It looks like soup. Whoever heard of Irish stew with spaetzle?"

"It will be good whatever she calls it, and don't you think there could be a story behind the recipe?"

"The meal is German," said Lena with conviction. "Not Irish."

"This is my grandmother's recipe," said Gladys, sounding defensive and giving Lena a little push toward the living room. "During World War II my grandmother wasn't about to call her special dish *German*, not in a town with a military base. Our family got used to calling it Irish stew. Wafts of garlic and kraut steam rose to the ceiling, a little black pepper caught in Alice's throat.

Coughing, Alice pushed on Audrey's behind to encourage her to leave the kitchen to Gladys who was humming to herself as she stirred the pot. Alice didn't want her dog to beg for pieces of pork soaked in sauerkraut.

"Think about tomorrow's morning walk," Alice whispered to her dog. "I shudder, absolutely shudder, to think what effect kraut might have on a hound's digestion. Liverwurst was bad enough." The hound tilted her head as if considering the consequences.

"Time to spill it," said Silvie as they entered the living room. "What happened today with Crystal and Zadie?" Virgil, Julian, and Lena stood around the table and stopped talking. Gladys leaned against the doorway, holding her wooden stirring spoon.

"I assumed the two women needed time to become accustomed to the idea of being mother/daughter, but I was wrong," said Alice, holding back a memory of happy tears. "When we walked into Crystal's trailer, they *knew* each other. I think it's the eyes. And a narrowness in their body structure. I didn't notice it when we spoke separately, but families are stamped with hundreds of visual similarities."

"They look that much alike?" asked Gladys.

"When they're together, you can see it," said Alice. "Uncanny."

"I inherited my pear shape from my grandmother," said Lena, smoothing wrinkles in her shirt. "And if you saw my uncle Ed, you'd see my ears."

"That's without earrings. Right?" said Julian laughing at his own joke. When Lena fired up her prune face, he patted her on the butt.

"Back to the story of Zadie, please," said Silvie with obvious impatience.

Alice told of Crystal's homeless past shaping her decision to choose stability for her daughter and herself.

"Zadie's struggling with that same decision of how to give her child a good home. Learning she's about to become a grandmother, Crystal called it her second chance. By the time I left, Crystal and Zadie were planning to haul Crystal's trailer up to Wisconsin where the young woman's parents own acres of land. Crystal's more than willing to help with the baby and Zadie's adoptive parents."

"There you go," said Virgil. "A happy ending."

Alice hoped he was correct.

As Gladys carried a soup tureen from the kitchen, they gathered in Alice's dining room filled with wonderful smells of home life. Everyone laughed and joked, admired and complimented.

"Doesn't this feel like a Christmas card?" said Gladys.

Alice looked at her friends decked out in winter sweaters, and her mind took a snapshot.

After dinner of a delightful German-Irish stew-soup, Lena shoo'd everyone out of the kitchen.

"The least Alice and I can do is wash dishes," insisted Lena. "Gladys put all this work into a creative dinner and deserves to watch *White Christmas* or *The Bishop's Wife* on television."

"Loretta Young. Mighty good looking woman," said Virgil winking at Silvie.

"Then it's settled." Lena held up her hand to stop Julian from rising. "We got this."

After scraping bowls, Lena pulled Alice aside. "Okay, who's the *father* of Zadie?"

"Crystal didn't tell me or her daughter."

"But you know. I *know* you know," said Lena raising her eyebrow. "In 1990 Crystal was thirty-five, and Phil and I separated. Please tell me it wasn't Phil."

"That was my worry at first, but no, it is not Phil."

"How do you know?"

Sadness overcame Alice. "Richie's her father."

"Oh," said Lena, "OH! Are you sure?" asked Lena in a soft voice.

"Very sure. As we said at dinner, no matter how we try to disguise it, we look like our parents. Crystal's hand went to her mouth the moment she saw Zadie. Then when she insisted her daughter sit, I recognized what I found familiar about how Zadie moves, Richie's same crooked stance like a kink at the back of their necks. Very noticeable as they stood or sat. You know how Richie had that permanent tilt with his head forward. He always complained of headaches. The first time I met Zadie, she twisted her head and popped her neck, you know, like athletes do."

"I hate that sound," said Lena. "I told my boys to stop it. Why do boys crack joints at the dinner table?" Lena sighed and looked away. "So sad. Zadie finds her mother and must learn about her father being murdered."

"When I searched his apartment, I found a brown sock monkey in the bottom drawer of an old dresser. Never been played with. Still had tags. No way of knowing if he kept it as a memory of his daughter, but . . . "

"You're intent on making me cry, aren't you?" said Lena with one hand on her hip. "Richie must have missed his daughter."

"On that second visit, I saw someone had been there and hung up his shirt." Alice went through the description of the apartment. With a certain amount of organization taking place, Alice ruled out Phil as the first guest into Richie's apartment or the uninvited visitor after the murder.

Lena agreed. "Phil wasn't one to be impressed with cleanliness."

"That second time a person entered the apartment," said Alice, "it was someone who cared. The police didn't find any evidence of a break-in other than broken police tape. The woman who lives downstairs keeps the key. She told the police she hasn't given it to anyone - well - other than me."

"The intruder had a key of her own," said Lena with sudden insight. "Were Crystal and Richie having a thing all these years?"

I'm guessing more off than on, but yes they maintained contact. Probably Crystal wanted to take one last look and say goodbye."

Lena removed her hands from sudsy water. "In her situation, I'd have married Richie." Lena scrubbed a pot and sloshed it back into the water. "Marriage would have saved both from awful lives because you'll never convince me Crystal enjoyed taking care of Flossy. That woman wasn't as good as you think."

"I agree Flossy had her faults," said Alice. "I also don't believe Crystal was happy, but she was secure. And as *you* know, marriage is tricky."

"True. Silvie told me she thinks I use marriage as a crutch," said Lena, "asked me why Julian and I are getting married. Can you believe that?"

"What'd you say?"

"Love," tossed off Lena. "Silvie doesn't think that's a good enough reason." Lena rolled her eyes, but looked put-out.

Alice squeezed Lena's shoulder. With Julian in the next room, she felt uncomfortable whispering with Lena about her future. Instead she continued with information about Crystal and Zadie.

"Crystal told us of being frightened at the thought of being homeless again, only this time with a baby. Lena, the truth is Flossy didn't want a noisy baby in the house. If Crystal kept the baby, she'd be out of a job. And let's face it, Richie, nice man, but too malleable. Phil easily twisted and manipulated him into committing crimes. Could Crystal with a baby and no job have pulled Richie into a picket-fenced life?"

"I see your point," said Lena. "Even so, Phil probably killed him or had him killed for spite."

"Maybe."

"Maybe? Now you're in doubt?" Lena spilled water and rapidly wiped it up, her face becoming rosier. "Who else would want to kill Richie?"

Alice sat for a moment, her brow wrinkled like Audrey's. "The police found Richie's toothbrush and pain killers in his pocket."

"Toothbrush? Seriously? How is that a clue?"

"People leave their home with pills all the time," said Alice, "but why take a toothbrush unless he was planning to hide out? Someone safe came to Richie and warned him about Phil."

In a loud stage whisper Lena said, "I told you Phil had an accomplice. I told you."

Alice's mind swirled with possibilities which she cast aside as soon as a picture formed. Lowering her voice and once again checking that they weren't overheard, Alice said, "I want you and Julian to be careful.

I don't like that Phil came to your house. He didn't come for money. If he wanted cash, he'd have approached you in a different way. I think it was some kind of set-up or cover."

"Alice, Phil is *always* after money. You know that." Lena went back to spooning leftover spaetzle into a plastic container. "That's why he became a thief." Waving the wooden spoon in the air, Lena asked, "What do you mean by cover? Cover for what?"

"Something big that he's planning. I don't know what." Lena stopped working and looked confused. Alice rose, took her elbow and steered her friend closer to the door. "We have two things to worry about."

Lena butted in. "Only two?"

Alice ignored the intrusion into her thinking.

"Someone other than Phil killed Richie, and when the police held Phil in jail overnight, his accomplice robbed the historical museum."

"The accomplice," said Lena with a knowing nod and a pointed finger. "Wait until I tell Julian I was right." Lena's eyes grew big. "Tell me you're not thinking the accomplice is Crystal. Is that why you're so upset?"

"No," said Alice, "definitely not Crystal. Lena, the robbery at the historical museum was messy. The killing of Richie, planned."

"Two accomplices?" Lena's fingertips covered her mouth before saying, "We have two stupid women helping Phil?"

Alice shook her head. "I worry about why Phil came to your house. Why was he so testy with Julian? Why did he point out I'd make a good witness? Lena, he has to know you've been working on wedding cakes at Beckerman's in the early mornings, so why didn't he offer you, and only you, the deal of an annulment when you left the grocery store kitchen?"

"Because Julian always waits for me," said Lena. For a moment, she had a look of peace and contentment. "He drives me to the store at four in the morning and waits until I'm done. No way Phil can catch me alone."

"Julian doesn't always stay."

"Where does he go?" asked Lena.

"Hunting for Phil."

Alice expected Lena to explode, but her friend embraced silence, and they both turned to kitchen work. Alice frowned as she stacked plates a little too harshly, causing them to cackle. As if in a coordinated dance, the two women finished wiping and stacking until the kitchen was clean. Both folded kitchen towels and removed their aprons. Lena joined Julian in the living room by wrapping her arms around the rough, retired truck driver and giving him a kiss.

"We need to talk. At home. Right now."

Although Audrey 's nose was interested in the kiss, she left Virgil and leaned into Alice's leg.

"Don't get up. We're leaving." That said, Lena and Julian walked out.

"Whoo-boy," said Virgil, "Glad I'm not him. Sounds like a blister-his-hide moment."

The women kept silent. Audrey curled up at the bottom of the stairs. All the others went back to watching the movie.

For Alice, something still wasn't right. Two patterns of behavior collided in her thinking, but she couldn't identify both as conspiracies. One involved an accomplice - almost playful - tossing a meatball, robbing the museum, and hitting Old Adam over the head, followed by slashing a student's painting of an unhappy woman. The other pattern was a cold darkness all by itself.

Chapter 24

Before dawn, Alice heard Gladys move around the house. Audrey heard it too. The dog stood at Alice's bedroom door, ready to be released, but Alice wanted a moment more of quiet before the day raced into church activities or stories about the blog or worry about Phil or wishes for a snowy wedding. Staying in bed, Alice put her hand over her eyes to block the sense of craziness. *Two days until the wedding.*

When a sweet song played on her phone, her son Peter's ring, Alice sat up in bed. Her dog recognized it was time to lie down with her nose pressed to the sliver-sized opening beneath the bedroom door.

"Hi Mom. I'm catching you before church to say Merry Christmas," said Peter. "Won't have time Christmas Eve or Christmas. We have a family reunion of twenty-eight people. Full house for us. Glad to have the work."

They talked of his bed-and-breakfast and her last visit. He told stories of New England and the beauty of being in mountains with snow. She related Trisha's desire for snow at her wedding, but rain and gray days persisted. He asked about her house guests.

"Jess said you encouraged Henry to stay with you this summer."

"I didn't encourage him, exactly." Alice's hand went to her forehead, her eyes closed. "But I did say *yes* when he asked if he could stay. Is Jess livid? She hasn't called back."

Alice's usual Sunday filled with Skyping grandchildren. After her previous talk with her grandson, Alice feared her daughter might be peeved. Since childhood, Jess's hurt feelings moved her into a huffy silent world.

"No. She thought you made a slick move with hyping rhubarb pie and fishing for crappies. I mean, I love preparing crappies, a very versatile fish, but outside the Midwest? Compared to ocean fish? I don't know if a West Coast kid will enjoy fried foods. Anyway, Jess and Henry have compromised. Henry will spend the summer with you going to welding school and return to California in the fall for welding classes there. Who knows? Maybe Henry'll pick up Dad's business making ornamental iron gates."

"He wants to make the kind of gates that protect cities from rising oceans."

"Ambitious," laughed Peter. "Wonder if he has any idea of the amount of schooling he'll need? Well, Jess and Henry are off to Hawaii where the band is playing in a parade, and Juliana is off to France with her father, a daddy/daughter thing. Jess said to tell you not to expect a phone call until after Christmas, but they'll all post pictures on Facebook.

They thanked each other for gifts.

"I know Meg and I only sent a gift card, not very personal, but it's meant for you to fly to California for Henry's graduation."

"I'll try," said Alice not wanting to discuss the impossibility of Audrey on a plane.

"You can't miss Henry's graduation from high school."

"I'll be there," insisted Alice.

"What you going to do with Audrey?" asked Peter. "You said she's a big dog. What is she, over a hundred pounds?"

"Give or take." The direction of the conversation bothered Alice.

"Meg and I worry she's too big for you to handle. I don't want you hurt. It's not like Jess or I are next door to help you if you fall. I have friends whose mothers. . . "

"Oh Peter, so good of you to call. Look at the time," said Alice not wanting to hear the old-lady-breaking-a-hip speech again . . . not from her youngest child. She was only in her sixties for goodness sake. "I have house guests waving at me with questions. Tell Meg merry Christmas. Your gift, so generous. Love you. Bye," Alice hung up.

Audrey looked at Alice and sneezed sending dog snot smack against the bedroom door. Alice had to smile. It was as if her dog said, "That's telling him."

By the time Alice and Audrey returned from the morning walk, Gladys had breakfast prepared: hot coffee, a big pot of oatmeal, and sliced bananas. No amount of suggesting kept Gladys from taking charge of the kitchen. Despite being a guest, she needed to work for her keep. Silvie shrugged when Alice turned to her for help with Gladys.

"You can't stop her. For some women housekeeping is a drug. Cooking gives her a useful feeling."

Wearing an apron but no coat, Gladys collected a bucket of water after breakfast.

"It's not that cold this morning," said Gladys, "maybe at freezing, and your back stairs have paw prints and winter slop." She gave Audrey a scolding look. "I'm not going to church until I see this house spic and span. Christmas is days away."

Alice sighed, tired of battling. She and Audrey went to the back-yard for playtime, Audrey's nose and eyes searched for the cat. When Gladys put the bucket down, however, the hound ran to the bucket and plunged her whole face into the pail, splashing water. As she pulled her head back, water slid down her face, curling into wrinkles. Gladys pushed closer to the pail, but there was no time for Alice to warn her to back away. When Audrey did a muscular shake, skin flapped, sling-ing streams of water in the older woman's direction.

Too late, Alice ran forward with apologies. As water ran down her face and seeped into her clothing, Gladys stood motionless. Taking off her own sturdy brown jacket, Alice wrapped it around the little woman, all the while biting the inside of her mouth to keep from laughing.

"I'll go in to shower," said Gladys, giving Audrey a dirty look.

"Nice and hot. You don't want to catch a cold." Alice apologized again and helped Gladys into the house. "Don't worry. I'll clean up here."

Alice wiped Audrey's face and paws before wiping the stairs. Back in the house, she found Gladys had thrown her damp jacket on the back of a kitchen chair to dry.

"Very naughty of you," said Alice to her hound as she hung up the damp coat over the dryer.

She pictured the comic dousing of Gladys. Laughable, really, but once she had put her hands on the jacket, she felt a chill of foreboding. Out of the blue, sometimes puzzle pieces fall together into a pattern.

Is the universe sending a warning?

Chapter 25

While Gladys sang in the shower, Audrey crooned in a low gargle punctuated with powerful woofs and one long howl. The dog growled, unhappy over a closed bathroom door.

A call came from Lena. "Alice," she screamed into the phone, "Julian's gone."

"What do you mean, gone?"

"Gone. Not here. Missing. Can't find him."

"Where are you?"

"In town. Remember, Alice, I told you Julian drives me to Beckerman's? Well, when I finished this morning, no Julian. He's not napping in the car. The gas station hasn't seen him. His phone is off. I even checked the brew pub. The man would eat beer ice cream if it existed. Alice, he's nowhere. No one has seen him. I have no idea where he might be. I told him not to stalk Phil."

Alice asked Lena to take a breath and back up in her explanation. "Any idea how long he's been gone?" Alice heard church bells in the background.

"No, but I've been looking for almost two hours. His phone goes straight to voice mail. I've left at least ten messages. Alice, he promised me to stop hunting for Phil."

"Lena, maybe he lost track of time," offered Alice, knowing Julian would never be so lax with his commitment to keep Lena safe. With

Phil in town, there was no way he'd indulge in a tavern stop for two hours of beer drinking. "Cell phone needed recharging? Lena, maybe he ran into someone he knew. After all the wedding is the day after tomorrow. People from Bottom Ridge might be arriving in town today."

Silvie and Virgil listened and signaled to Alice in the kitchen asking questions. "Did something happen to Julian?" Alice hit s p e a k e r on her phone so they could hear Lena.

"We drove into town early this morning," said Lena, her voice building a controlled panic. "Julian's car is parked in the grocery store lot." Her voice cracked with a sob, her tone a high-pitched squeal of breathy fear. "Alice, I'm worried Phil got him."

"Have you called the police?"

"No." Lena hesitated. "I didn't want Julian to get mad at me for being a worrier. You know he doesn't like fuss."

Alice felt her body sag. *Why is everyone leery to call the police?* "Blame me if he complains. When we hang up, you *call* the police. Let them know something suspicious has happened. This isn't like Julian. They'll understand."

A whimper came from Lena. "I was going to make him vanilla French toast with hot cinnamon apples when we got home."

"*Lena*, we have all kinds of maybes here. I'll get Audrey ready, and we'll be there in five minutes."

Two elderly guests circled her with questions about Julian, and Audrey bounced with excitement, barking and hopping as Alice strapped the hound into her bright green padded vest. Alice's mind churned through the possibilities. Maybe Julian saw Phil in town and decided to follow him. *Very likely*. Or maybe Julian got dizzy or sick, and someone called for help. *Not likely*. Walking to a store on the square to sit down? *Again, not likely*. Nothing open other than places Lena already checked. At least they knew Julian was on foot. Audrey could find him.

Alice layered on her cold weather clothing of a turtleneck, long scarf, and Baer's trusty wool shirt that had seen her through many practice searches with Audrey.

Alice's hands shook as she opened the backdoor, the chorus of comments and questions still ramping up behind her. "What should we do?" "Give Julian our best." "Went for a beer, I bet." "How far to the hospital?" "Known him since a boy." "Never thought I'd outlive him."

"Have good thoughts," squeaked Gladys, wrapped in a robe and shiny from a warm shower, her hair still damp. "He's only missing. Right?"

Alice rushed into town with Audrey, parked her pickup in the grocery store lot, two spaces from Julian's car. Lena and June Beckerman stood outside near a high stack of logs packaged for winter fireplaces. Audrey's nose went to the wood pile before sniffing June's crotch.

Lena's face puffed with crying. June's arm gripped Lena's shoulders. True to her reputation for glitz, Lena was dressed for winter in pink tennis shoes sparkly with sequined snowflakes, light weight pants and swaddled in a dyed, rosy-pink rabbit jacket. Alice's stomach clutched. Lena held three of Julian's bandanas against her chest. Would Audrey's nose confuse Julian's sweat with Lena's heavy perfume or the rabbit fur?

"I didn't want to leave her alone," said June, "but I have to get back to work."

Both Alice and Lena thanked the younger woman, and after June went into the store, Lena said, "I went through Julian's car and found his bandanas for Audrey to sniff."

Alice pulled out separate plastic bags for each scarf, hoping Lena's perfume hadn't contaminated Julian's odor.

"Have you called the police?"

"Well, if Audrey can find him . . . I didn't want to bother them if Julian's not in trouble."

Alice knew not to argue and planned to call the police as soon as she and Audrey were away from the store and Lena.

"Promise me you'll at least stay in Julian's car while we're gone. Call me if he comes back."

"I want to go with you," said Lena, whining like a child. "Look. I wore my old Keds."

Alice didn't want to hurt Lena's feeling.

"Lena, if this is a long search," said Alice as carefully as she could, "you aren't dressed for mud, in spite of wearing sneakers. The temperature's hovering around freezing. Audrey may cut corners and not stick to a sidewalk or road. You don't want to ruin your clothes, Besides, what if Julian comes back, looking for you. No one else will think to call me and let me know."

Lena took a deep breath. "Okay."

Opening the first bag and asking Audrey to sniff produced the response Alice expected. Audrey sat down, and her tongue lolled out of her mouth, apparently detecting Lena's perfume as no challenge to finding Lena. Alice removed stray pink fur from Audrey's nose and wiped her face with a damp cloth, hoping the spice bomb scent Lena wore didn't remain.

The second bag drew Audrey's closer attention. Following a quick sniff, her nose swept the ground near Julian's car, left and right, up and back, until she gave a pull. As Alice and Audrey turned the corner of the grocery store, Alice called Bobby's phone number at the police station. A woman answered.

"Suzie, volunteer on phones today. Is this an emergency?"

"Yes and no," said Alice and proceeded to give details of Julian being missing, maybe in trouble.

"Where are you?" asked Suzie.

"In the parking lot behind Beckerman's Grocery Store. Moving toward the field."

"Mrs. T., are you on a search with your dog?"

"Yes."

"Well then, everything will be all right. Our officers are out on a call. I'll let them know you're on a case and get back to you as soon as I can. Keep Lieutenant Unzicker informed when you find Julian. Merry Christmas and a happy New Year."

Alice expected an all-out team of police to join her search for Julian. She felt let down. *My own fault,* thought Alice. *Going my own way for too many years. Well, Audrey, we're on our own for a while. I'm bigger than Phil. Not so sure I'm as crafty.*

Audrey sniffed around the base of a dumpster as Rooney Santoro jogged up, dressed in fatigues with a light runner's jacket. She stopped.

"Audrey looking for a spot?" Rooney asked with a big grin.

"Actually, she's following a scent. We're trailing." Audrey took off with a jolt. Alice hung onto the leash and followed.

"Mind if I join you?" called the younger woman, picking up a jogger's pace.

"Fine with me." Alice felt a wash of relief to have company.

The hound caught where Julian left the dumpster and followed a scent path through a field to the road fifty feet behind the grocery store. The asphalt road quickly changed to packed dirt, rutted with ice-glazed water in the hollows, but muddy thickness where the sun hit.

"It's been a long time since I was on this road," said Rooney. "I don't even know the real name. Dad calls it Duck Blind Road."

"When I first moved to Limekiln," said Alice with a weak smile, "Everyone called it Washboard Road. Probably not the real name. No idea what it's really called."

Audrey continued sniffing with thorough concentration, sweeping back and forth, careful not to miss the scent, then bounding forward, nose to ground. Alice and Rooney jumped ruts, twisting to a new direction as Audrey pivoted. Her pace slowed but thrust onward like a projectile.

"If I owned a hound, is this what I could expect?" asked Rooney.

"Pretty much," answered Alice.

Up ahead across another field, Alice saw the trailer village where Crystal and Gina lived. Audrey charged into the weeds, her tail moving like a windshield wiper, beating the tall, dry grasses. She pulled Alice across a paved road directly to a trailer in back with a green stripe. Alice looked for a wiggle to come into Audrey's shoulders. She hoped her dog's breathing might quickened with a find, but no such luck. Audrey kept them on the same twisting crazy path as she swept back and forth verifying the trail. The hound's nose didn't rise to the air, nor did she bark to announce her search was over. Instead, she thrashed about a parking spot, riddling out what had happened to the scent trail.

"Can you knock on Mrs. Pickler's door," said Alice. Church bells rang off in the distance, and Alice hoped the cafeteria lady was at home.

"This is where Mrs. Pickler lives?" asked Rooney, her voice sounding like a kid's. "I always think of her as living behind a cafeteria line."

Alice grinned at the memory of her own students' shock at finding her in stores buying birthday cards or bleach like a real person. Audrey approached the door but pulled a paw back.

"Thumb tacks," said Alice. "Mrs. Pickler never picked up the tacks." Alice checked her dog's paws and held the dog back. Audrey looked at her confused.

"Rooney, please knock," asked Alice. "I don't want Audrey hurt. Ask Mrs. Pickler if she knows where Julian went after he stopped here."

"How do you know he's not inside now?"

"Audrey's body's telling me he's not." Seeing Rooney wasn't going to knock without an explanation, Alice said, "Hard to explain. Audrey's not breathing like he's here. Her body doesn't have the right wiggle. Her nose isn't in the air. She's not barking. But, Julian was here."

Audrey leaned toward the door for another sniff. Turning, she backtracked to the driveway along the village, her nose once again sweeping, searching for a new path to follow.

Rooney knocked on the door. Gina Pickler answered, dressed in a well-worn beige terrycloth robe and a towel wrapped around her head like a turban. Alice noticed her shoes were covered in dried dirt, a dried leaf stuck to the sole. Before Gina spoke, Audrey cut and ran toward the door, ignoring a prick of a tack, dragging Alice behind her. Her nose touched Gina's shins before going to the air as she sniffed the heat inside the trailer. Almost with a disgusted snort, the hound turned away.

"Oh my," sputtered Gina, and Rooney rapidly explained their search for Julian.

"I've been in the shower," said Gina. "I don't think Mr. Mueller was here, but if he knocked, I never heard it."

Both Alice and Rooney thanked the plump cafeteria lady who stood in the doorway waving goodbye with girlish wiggling fingers.

"Now what?" asked Rooney.

"We try again."

The three went back to Duck Blind Road. Alice pulled out the third bag with Julian's bandana, and held it open for her hound to inhale. It took seconds for the dog to wrench away and race back to Mrs. Pickler's trailer, only to cross the street and sweep the ground where a car should be parked.

Her nose worked with steady determination, frantic sniffing, but the trail had gone cold. Alice worked to calm her dog by giving her chicken treats. At first the hound rejected the interference of a treat, nose going back to the ground. Alice knelt in front of Audrey, holding her face in both hands and ruffled the top of her head, but the dog thrashed away from her in a frenzy to follow Julian's odor.

"It's okay," soothed Alice. "You're a good girl." She continued her whisper, maneuvering Audrey's attention away from the impossible task of following a car.

A car had gouged fresh deep ruts into the mud of the road. Soft mud also oozed around three sets of footprints, a small set of treaded prints similar in size to those left behind the day Richie died. Alice snapped a picture with her phone.

"We're done, girl."

"What just happened?" asked Rooney.

"Trail's cold," said Alice feeling sad for Audrey who liked nothing better than a hunt. "But we have three sets of foot prints. Looks like Julian and two others got into a car parked near the trailer."

"You think the car belonged to Mrs. Pickler?" asked Rooney. "She didn't seem to notice her car was missing. Should we go back and ask?"

Alice scanned the trailer village and ignored Rooney's question. "No, not yet." She continued to weigh the possible choices. "Phil'd never drive Julian back toward town. More likely in the opposite direction. The question is why."

"This road doesn't go anywhere," said Rooney. "Guys usually don't come here unless they're planning to shoot duck. And this close to Christmas, nobody's hunting." She turned to face Alice, "There's nothing we can do?" Rooney looked disappointed.

Almost every one of Audrey's searches had been controlled with a short leash. In only one search was her dog loose with two other bloodhounds. Other than that, Audrey had few practices on a long twenty-foot lead, free ranging for human odors. Sending her dog far out ahead wasn't Alice's favorite method. Sometimes Audrey disappeared in tall grass, sending shivers up Alice's spine. With Audrey's nose intent on a scent, maybe she wouldn't see a broken bottle tossed into a field or the danger of a speeding car racing toward her.

"Rooney, up for an experiment?" Alice took a breath.

"Sure," answered the younger woman.

"Hold Audrey for me. Careful, she may give a jolt if she becomes interested in a smell."

Rooney wound the leash around her hand and gripped it until her knuckles whitened. Alice lifted her bag off her shoulder, secured

Julian's bandanas, and searched for the thirty-foot strap. Clipping the longer tether to Audrey's harness, Alice removed the shorter leash.

Quickly she explained how bloodhounds are expected to search sometimes without a scent. "What if a person is lost, and we don't have a specific scent to give the hound to sniff? A trained dog can still find a human scent. We humans have a distinctive odor to a dog."

"Crotch odor," smiled Rooney. "I love this dog. May have to own a hound."

Alice's smile was coy. "Puppies are about to be born at Kennedy's farm, but you need a high tolerance for slobber?"

"Nobody's perfect," said Rooney with a glint in her eyes, "but until I figure out my life, I probably shouldn't adopt a puppy."

Alice squeezed the younger woman's shoulder. "Warning, this will be our first real ranging search."

Free of being limited by a shorter leash, Audrey moved forward, muscular shoulders sending her in bounds like a powerful ballet dancer. Much too fast for Alice's comfort. Twenty feet ahead Audrey stopped and turned to look back, and Alice knew her dog still needed the assurance that her owner followed.

"In all the years I've lived in Limekiln," said Alice, feeling a soft cool wind hit her face. "I don't think I've ever been out here. How far is the duck blind?"

"A ways," said Rooney, "a mile or so. You good?"

"We train several times a week and take long walks every day. I'm good."

"Dad used to take me hunting. We'd walk here carrying our gear."

The two women talked softly about their fathers until Audrey woofed. Both picked up the pace, shortening the dog's lead.

"You'll see the duck blind on the right," said Rooney rapidly. "It looks like somebody's weather-beaten old shed," Her eyes traced the horizon, intense and wary. "It's long. If we go inside, we'll need to open the wooden awning for light. Inside the door, is a pole to push the awning open. The pole slips into braces on the window frame to hold the window covering open. Can't believe anyone's hunting. Not now." Turning solemn, Rooney said, "You said Audrey's not a guard dog?"

"No, she's not. Why?" Alice felt her heart beating faster, watching Audrey's determination.

Rooney's face changed as if her own alert training took charge. Her eyes narrowed, and the muscles around her mouth tightened.

"Up ahead I'll leave you," said Rooney, her voice serious, business-like. "I'll take a separate path to the waterside. You and Audrey continue. Don't make a turn until you see the picnic table. The blind's down the hill."

Alice felt the cold as the density of intrusive silver maples increased, and the wooded area darkened. In previous sunny patches, ruts were filled with water. Here the density of trees allowed ice to skim over pools in tire ruts. To Alice it seemed a car had recently driven down the road.

Taking a deep breath, she watched Audrey's body language change. The dog's nose twitched in the air before barking and giving a happy wiggle.

"She's detected something," whispered Rooney, alert and moving silently. "I'm off through the underbrush. Don't call for me. Let Audrey do what she does. Okay?"

Alice nodded. That was when she noticed a lump near Rooney's ankle beneath the fabric of her pants, and her thoughts went to her husband.

Baer, she's got a gun!

Chapter 26

Walking turned difficult in one sunny patch as Alice and Audrey picked up gooey mud that stayed on shoes and paws. In all likelihood behind them in town, the temperature had risen to comfortable moments when the sun peeked from behind clouds, but in the forested trees of evergreens and stubborn silver maples holding curling leaves, the gray canopy of clouds kept the temperature around them hovering at freezing. Alice felt a chill hit her cheeks. Audrey's nose was in the air, tether taut. *Dogged,* thought Alice.

Rooney was gone. Alice felt as if she were on patrol alone, the only sounds were the soft rustle of her own padding feet. She spotted Rooney on a parallel course between trees. The younger woman moved with military precision, put her finger to her lips before silently placing two fingers below her eyes, and pointed to a narrow path through weeds. Alice took the gesture as an order. *Quiet. Watch out.*

Audrey turned again to check on Alice before her head swept through the air. The dog picked up the pace, outdistancing both women.

"She's caught a scent," whispered Alice to herself.

As the ground sloped downward, the road narrowed to a single lane. *Almost there*, thought Alice. Audrey's movements sent a message. Her muscular roll in her shoulders and her breathing a touch heavier triggered Alice's hope. *Julian*, thought Alice, not wanting to consider

THE CASE OF THE EX WHO PLOTTED REVENGE

why the love of Lena's life was in a duck blind. The hound strained against the long lead, pulling her owner straight ahead.

Out of her peripheral vision, Alice caught sight of Rooney just as determined moving through the underbrush, gun raised.

She clearly thinks trouble lies ahead, thought Alice.

Alice's mouth went dry, and she reeled Audrey closer to her by half. Here she was with a dog who at best could be a scary barker and very able to knock someone down, but she didn't bare teeth or snap. Audrey's main defense was the yuk factor of drool. When Alice hesitated with a tinge of fear, she felt a tug from Audrey whose wrinkly face turned as if to say, *Will you keep up?*

No sound came from Rooney. She was no longer in sight.

What if they were moving toward Phil holding a gun on Rooney?

Next to the road sat a weathered picnic table. Alice pulled her eager dog close to her hip and patted her side. No car was in sight, yet tire tracks and small foot prints flattened the ground with use, not design. Alice saw the steep path to the duck blind was slippery. Ice broke and grass crunched as she and Audrey began their descent. Wetness soaked into her dog's fur, darkening her legs and belly. Audrey began to bark in a series of big, excited, baritone woofs and lost her footing. Her chest hit the ground, her nose came up covered with icy snow. One good shake and the icy snow flew through the air.

The duck blind seemed eerily quiet and just as Rooney had described. It appeared to be a modified twelve by twenty foot, red cedar, storage shed. From the road, Alice couldn't see the awning opening Rooney described, but she concluded the window was waterside. Alice reviewed Rooney's instructions. Over the window was a hinged wooden flap that Alice needed to prop up with a pole. She moved closer to the duck blind and tried to peer through the slight spacing between boards. Something was on the floor but the room was too dark. There was one closed door. No padlock. Alice knew she didn't dare call Rooney's name. Goosebumps covered her arms.

Grabbing Audrey's collar, Alice walked her dog to the door and slowly pulled it open. As Rooney instructed, Alice found the long stick by the door and struggled to push open the heavy wooden awning and snap the supporting stick into place. Through the window overlooking the slough, the frosty world of a skim of ice and tall trees was worthy of a photograph. Light entered the duck blind.

Julian lay on the floor, hands zip-tied in front of him, ankles bound with a shirt, mouth taped, body naked.

In the cold damp of the room, Julian's skin took on a silvery green glow despite his black tattooed arms. Plastered against his scalp, his hair looked thinner. Eyes glazed. Someone had spilled slough water over his body and left him to die of hypothermia. Judging by Julian's non-response, Alice thought he had been there for a couple hours.

Alice dropped the leash and took off Baer's big woolly shirt she'd been wearing and covered Julian with it. She pulled the tape from his mouth, but Julian had no reaction. His lips fell open, eyes dull. The plastic zip tie was too tight for Alice to undo as were the remnants of a shirt tying his ankles. Her throat constricted as she tucked the blue shirt closer around Julian's body. As Audrey's nose twitched, Alice frowned at the earthy smell of stagnant water and beer. Several crushed cans lay strewn on the floor, the liquid contents puddling on the floor around Julian.

"Let me," said Rooney from behind her. The younger woman held a knife with a blade big enough and sharp enough to skin a bear. In seconds Julian's hands and feet were free. Still, he didn't move.

"Why isn't he shivering?" asked Rooney.

"Not good," said Alice. "His breathing is too shallow. We need paramedics, fast." She crouched and put her ear to Julian's chest. "Call 911."

Rooney tried her phone but had no service in this rural area meant for hunting. "I have to find a spot with reception. You need the gun?"

Alice shook her head. "Whoever left him to die in the cold won't be back." Alice touched his cold face. "Before you leave," said Alice as she wrestled with Julian's shoulders. "Help me pull him up."

Alice sat on the floor behind Julian, straddling his body as if on a toboggan. Together the two women maneuvered his rag doll body into Baer's shirt and then positioned him with his back to Alice's chest. Alice draped one hand over the wool shirt, holding it tightly across his chest. Julian's head fell to one side, his mouth open, without a sound.

"He'll need more heat than this shirt can give," said Rooney. "You know skin to skin contact is best for warming up someone?"

"Not going to happen," said Alice. "We got this." Alice gave a weak smile. "Audrey. Come on girl. Snuggles." She let the blue shirt fall open exposing Julian's chest.

Audrey responded by placing her head upon Julian's belly, eyes raised upward for approval.

"You can do more than that," said Alice with hyped enthusiasm. "Julian's cold. Snuggle time."

With damp belly fur, the hound crawled onto Julian, chest to chest, and lay with her head placed on his shoulder, her nose against Alice's neck.

"We'll be fine until the paramedics get here," said Alice. "Nothing better than dog heat."

"Man, she's long and flat," said Rooney. "She's got his thighs covered too."

Rooney tried her phone again. "The duck blind just doesn't have service. I'll have to backtrack to get bars before I call. You going to be okay? Sure you don't want the gun?"

"No gun. We'll be fine for now. Hurry. His heart isn't beating right."

Once Rooney left, Alice assessed Julian's condition. Besides being really cold, he had been beaten and had a number of facial cuts, his hands purple bruising. Alice guessed both hands had been hit with a hammer, breaking bones, Phil's chosen method of assault when Julian was defenseless. No cuts were on Julian's knuckles. No opportunity to fight back. His wounds would heal over time, but his irregular heartbeat frightened her. Alice fought tears and panic.

"Julian, how you doing?" asked Alice. He didn't move or respond. "Rooney will call the paramedics, and we'll have you warm and in a hospital in no time."

Cradling Julian, Alice felt tears slipping from her eyes. Hugging Baer's shirt and remembering the night he died, Alice said, "You're not dying on my watch, Julian. Absolutely not."

Audrey's warm doggy dampness reached Alice's nose as her dog's heat turned the wetness of her fur to warming therapy. *Nothing like dog heat*, thought Alice, alone in the silence.

Coldness penetrated her body through her back pressed against the cracked wooden wall and the cold moisture that wicked from the floor through her jeans. She shivered and hugged Julian closer, imagining Audrey's dog heat seeping through Julian to warm her too.

"Did Lena ever tell you about the time she gave me a candy-making lesson?"

Audrey's head rose from Julian's shoulder as if she wanted to hear this interesting story. Alice's fingers went to Julian's pulse. His heart seemed stronger, still skipping beats, but less frenzied to catch up. She launched into the ingredients of candy making, praising Lena's superior skill.

"All went well in the kitchen until Lena took a phone call. I mixed ingredients of sugar, butter, marshmallows, peanut butter, and Rice Krispies." Alice took her time listing the ingredients as she shivered and stuttered her words in the cold. Why was time passing so slowly?

"I rolled out small balls - more difficult to do than I thought. You wouldn't believe how chocolate gets under fingernails. With Lena still on the phone, I reasoned how-hard-can-it-be to roll peanut butter into warmed chocolate. But as my fingers dipped and rolled the balls, the warmed chocolate melted the peanut butter and marshmallows into slippery goo. The first one fell apart as did the second and the third. No amount of scooping kept the concoction together."

The hound raised her head from Julian's shoulder with a look of concern.

"I'm okay, Sweetie," said Alice, remembering Lena's rescue of the fourth treat. Her friend loudly reminded her that she had forgotten to refrigerate the balls before dipping. Alice tearfully grinned at the memory of Lena laughing at her melted chocolate stripes on Alice's hands, arms, and face. *I forgot the cold*, thought Alice, wishing she could do the same now.

Julian's shoulder quivered - a good sign - and Audrey caught him off guard and licked his face twice, wiping away some of the blood.

Alice was grateful when the EMTs arrived. Her teeth chattered with the cold, but Julian's eyes were much less glazed, movements small and awkward. He seemed confused even as they carried him to the ambulance and loaded him in the back. As they worked on him, Alice heard Julian say, "Sucker punched."

A police car accompanied the ambulance, and Officer Briar offered the back seat for Rooney and Alice to keep warm. When Audrey bounded in first with muddy feet, he might have protested, but Alice quickly joined the dog.

"Shotgun," called Rooney as she took the passenger seat.

Briar jammed up the heat and agreed to drive them to the hospital in Graybill Bend, twenty miles from Limekiln. As the road shifted from dirt to pavement, Alice saw her phone had bars of service. She called Bobby and told him about finding Julian, assured him she was okay, and asked him to go personally on a wellness check of Mrs. Pickler.

"Audrey took us to Mrs. Pickler's trailer. She answered the door but said she hadn't heard Julian knock. Said she'd been in the shower. It's possible I guess, but the timing's wrong. Her car isn't near her trailer, and she was wearing dirty loafers with a maple leaf stuck to the bottom and no socks. Be sure you go inside. Insist. Make sure she's okay."

"Not my first rodeo," said Bobby to Alice's orders.

Alice apologized for being bossy.

"I understand," said Bobby in a more subdued tone. "You've had a tough morning. I'll check on her because I trust your instincts, and if it is Phil's rat hole, I'll have someone check with the Greer family in Whittle. Better let them know Phil's on the run. See what they know. Tomorrow, come around the office and explain the maple leaf to the bottom of Mrs. Pickler's shoe."

When they ended the call, Rooney asked, "You think Phil forced his way into Mrs. Pickler's?"

"Possibly," said Alice, "but no. I believe Mrs. Pickler is playing Bonnie to Phil's Clyde."

Chapter 27

Lena paced the waiting room of the Graybill Bend Hospital. Alice nodded to a hospital office worker dressed in a blue suit and holding a clipboard, walking behind Lena.

"I can only stay a minute," said Alice assuring the hospital worker she and her dog, both rough looking and stinky, wouldn't be contaminating the area for long. "How's Julian?"

"They have him in the emergency room," said Lena. "They asked me to wait here. I need a hug." Lena viewed her best friend with shock. "Your jeans are dirty. Is your turtleneck still damp? Alice, you look half frozen!"

"You still want a hug?" asked Alice stretching out her arms, inviting.

"Yes," answered Lena, and with a step away from her best friend, Lena threw her rosy rabbit fur covered arms around the neck of the surprised hospital woman with the clipboard. As she pulled herself away, the hospital worker blew feathery rabbit fur from her lips.

"Not me?" asked Alice who stood amused.

"Not yet. You and Audrey both need a shower."

"May I suggest," said the woman, "that I take all of you to a room near the loading dock? Our maintenance crew uses it as a coffee room, but they won't mind if a dog hangs out. I'll come for you when the ER is ready for family. Not the dog, of course," said the woman to Alice. "just Mrs. . . . . what is your name?"

"Mueller," said Lena. "I'm Mrs. Mueller. Julian's wife." Lena gave Alice a warning glance to keep her mouth shut.

Alice knew Lena and Julian had worked this scheme before.

Once they were alone, Lena signed the paperwork and said, "Why confuse hospital red tape. So much easier to assume the authority of a spouse."

Sitting at a small table with mugs of coffee while three maintenance men sat across the room, Lena defended her lie about being Julian's wife.

"This hospital is not in Limekiln. Who knows what rules and regulations they have? I never want to put people at a disadvantage of defending a stupid rule. They might tell me I can't speak for Julian. They don't know us. Better they think I'm his wife."

"Lena, I'm not arguing."

"Where's Rooney?"

"She called her mother to come and pick her up. Probably gone by now. She never thought when she started the hike looking for Julian that she'd log in miles away from her car and end up at the hospital."

"Cheryl is taking over the wedding cakes. She's watched me for years. I trust her with my rum custard filling and coconut rum frosting." Lena twisted in her chair. "I need to be with Julian."

Alice took her friend's hand and gave it a squeeze.

"This is ridiculous us sitting here while Julian's upstairs," said Lena.

"They'll call you soon."

"You'll catch a cold if you don't get into a hot shower soon," said Lena.

"We're fine. Audrey and I came to the hospital to see how you're doing. But you are right. Audrey and I are stinky. We need to go home to shower. But I don't want you to be alone."

"How will you get home?" asked Lena. "Your truck is still at Beckerman's."

"Good question."

"Please stay until they tell me I can see Julian," said Lena grabbing Alice's hand. "Then call Cheryl. She'll give you a ride. You can tell her everything that's happened."

Alice sipped the tepid black coffee and picked pieces of dried mud from Audrey's fur.

"You know he's going to be okay," said Alice. "I told him about when I made peanut krispies." With a tight jaw, Lena gave a weak smile.

"You are a terrible candy-maker," said Lena, tears filling her eyes before expressing her anger. "If I see Phil, I'll beat him bloody." Lena removed her fur coat and revealed her ample curves with a pink knit top that read *Jingle My Bells*. Without warning, Lena's fist came down on the table. "Taking Julian was Phil's way to get back at me." A sob broke, and Lena's forehead dropped against her arm resting on the table. "It's all my fault."

A certain unease crossed the faces of the three maintenance men across the room. Quietly they rose and left. Audrey pushed in closer to Lena, placing her head against Lena's thigh. Alice stayed silent over her friend's distress. Alice knew Lena sometimes needed to feel the moment and not be cajoled out of coping with anger and fear.

After the busy morning in the cold and scrubbing Audrey in the bathtub, Alice found the hot shower in her own home life-affirming. Under the stream of water, she could only imagine the three elderly guests toweling Audrey downstairs, filling her ears with baby talk. Alice wasn't sure how it happened that Audrey allowed her to shower upstairs while the dog stayed downstairs. She thought it might relate to the chicken hotdog treats Virgil shared. They had become snack buddies.

"Audrey, have a weenie," he said as he popped one into her mouth and popped another into his.

Lena decided to stay at the hospital. Doctors wanted to keep Julian overnight. Both hands had broken bones and his heart beat was still irregular.

As soon as she showered, Alice felt ready for the world. Bobby texted and asked her to observe the interrogation of Gina Pickler, Monday morning at the police station.

Alice felt conflicted. It wasn't in Gina's nature to help a man like Phil, and yet she did. Why? Gina lied to them at the door. She knew Julian was alone and naked in the duck blind. Or was she coerced to protect Phil?

Alice slept little that night. Even Audrey proved to be restless, often rising onto her haunches to listen, a low grumble in her throat.

Every time she woke, Alice questioned, *With Gina in jail and Phil's stash house seized, where will the con man turn?*

Chapter 28

Alice marveled at the police station in their small town of Limekiln. They had a window allowing her to peek into a stark interrogation room. No ornamentation or pictures added interest to the bleak green room. Bobby talked to Gina Pickler, who sat at a table with him on the opposite side. The emptiness of the room made Alice jittery. Not even a paper cup of water for Gina to sip.

"We won't be here long," whispered Alice to her dog, resting at her feet. "Maybe we'll play stick. It's probably too cold for you to snap at soap bubbles."

Alice felt nervous for the cafeteria lady. The police found the guitar and drum stolen from the historical museum in Gina's living room. Claude's file on Phil wasn't with the items, neither was Phil. The police, however, did bag a pair of Phil's shoes.

It was hard for Alice to watch Gina squirm. For years, she thought of her as a respected friend, but her actions could have aided Phil in causing Julian's death. Alice felt a struggle of emotions, wanting to roll back the clock to a time before Phil returned to Limekiln.

With no lead-up to the big question, Bobby hit Gina with the severity of her situation at the go.

"Gina, did you shoot Richie Mills?" asked Bobby, face stern.

"No. NO!" Gina's eyes went wide open with fear. Even the flesh on her face trembled.

"Are you saying Phil was the murderer?"

"No . . . I don't know. He never said." Gina hid her face on her forearm, her straight hair falling forward like a tent covering her eyes. She wore blue pants and a red and blue plaid shirt. The cuffs well worn, stitching broken, threads dangling. In a muffled voice, Gina managed to say, "I don't know who shot Richie. I really don't."

Alice thought it was a good thing she wasn't in the room. At that moment she wanted to give her friend a hug. Because of Lena's past, Alice knew how Phil spotted vulnerability and snake-oiled women. Was Gina trapped by the goodness of her heart or nailed by a deep loneliness, wanting to be special in someone's eyes, anyone's eyes? Even Phil's?

"Was the fire at Lena and Cheryl's cafe set by you?" asked Bobby.

Gina raised her head with tears in her eyes.

"No. I don't like fire. Been burned too many times in the kitchen."

"But the flood at Bait and Books was your doing." Bobby said it as a statement although Alice knew he had no evidence.

"No!" insisted Gina. Her eyes widened. An odd innocence entered her voice. "Well, Phil told me about his plan. He said nobody would be hurt because the Zug family has insurance. It doesn't matter."

"Then, why do it?" asked Bobby, his voice cold.

"Phil said . . . they weren't nice to him." Gina's fingers knotted and stretched as if trying to help craft an explanation.

"So, because he had hurt feelings," Bobby's voice reflected contempt, "he talked you into aiding the destruction of their property."

"I only held a flashlight." Gina shrivaled with confusion.

"But afterwards, you helped to clean up the store," stated Bobby.

"Mrs. Zug called me," said Gina. "I can always use the work, and she was willing to pay good."

More conflict was back to torment Alice. How could Gina not have considered the damage to Neda's shop?

"The meatball thrown into Alice's backyard during the daytime? That was you?"

At first Gina opened her mouth, perhaps to protest, but finally answered, "Yes."

"Why?"

She hesitated. "Phil said all of it was just a poke in someone's eye," said Gina, pleading the innocence of the antic. "No one was supposed to be hurt. The dog would get sick. Phil said he couldn't go out during the daytime because people would see him. He needed me."

There it is, thought Alice, *Gina's motivation. She wanted to be needed.*

"That morning I had to hurry because Mrs. Tricklebank was also at the shop and agreed to deliver books to customers who lived near her. I went to her house first before making my deliveries for Mrs. Zug. No one ever notices me, you see, but if Phil had delivered it, someone might remember him."

Bobby's hand went up, stopping her explanation. "To keep this simple, how about you call people by their first name. Titles sound like phony respect."

Gina sat smaller in her chair. Thrown back on her heels by his accusation of not being respectful. Her face reddened.

"Now, who made the meatball?"

"We both did," said Gina, her voice barely audible. "His hands aren't used to rolling meat into balls."

"He let you handle the poison."

"He insisted I wear gloves," said Gina as if pointing out Phil's concern for her.

"A meatball laced with rat poison," said Bobby. "Alice's dog could have died."

Gina opened her mouth, but closed it. Her eyes stared at the table top. "It's just a dog."

Alice's anger flared, and she thought of Crystal Butterman's distress when Bianca went missing. At the time of the hunt, Audrey veered to the trailer with the green stripe, Gina's trailer, before following the small dog's scent to a dumpster about a mile away. Did Gina consider Crystal needed a poke in the eye? To an owner, a dog wasn't just a dog. Alice looked down at Audrey who was looking up at her with concern in her eyes. Stooping to pet her dog, Alice found comfort as Audrey rolled onto her back for a belly rub.

Had Phil taught Gina how to game a system? *Throw tacks in front of the trailer. That way no one will suspect you. You'll be another suffering victim. The bonus is keeping people and dogs away from your front door.*

Alice rubbed Audrey's feet remembering how her hound pulled her paw back after the pinch of a tack as she tried to sniff for Julian at Gina's trailer. Why didn't Gina's helpful nature of giving second helpings to students in a cafeteria line also extend to neighbors and dogs?

"You robbed the museum when Phil was in jail," said Bobby.

"Yes."

"Broke the window in the backdoor."

"Phil said it was the only way in," said Gina, focusing on the table top.

"Who burned the hay wagon?"

"Phil."

"Who hit Adam? Slashed picture at the high school?"

Alice looked away from her dog to Gina.

Gina paused before she spoke with new authority. "Me. I slashed it. People forget I have keys to the school. Get there early to prepare meals."

"Why'd you do it?"

Gina took a deep breath and looked directly at Bobby, her eyes angry. "I never liked that picture. It was the face – as if the kid painted my portrait. I saw that same sad face in my mirror every day. Every day a reminder of who I was."

"Who stole Baby Jesus from the manger in the town square during the fireworks?"

Alice's head came up, stunned as Bobby closed in. This was the first she heard of the theft at the manger.

"Phil took it. I couldn't, Lieutenant Unzicker. I attend church on Sunday."

"You were home yesterday. Right?" asked Bobby. "You let Phil borrow your car to abduct Julian."

Gina's brow furrowed as she fought back tears. Her hand wiped her cheek.

"I did, but it wasn't to kidnap." Alice watched Gina shift in her chair, her eyes moved as if searching for escape.

"And when you loaned him the car last week, he brought it back dented on the passenger side. Right?" Gina nodded and Bobby continued, "When he couldn't kill Richie in a car accident, he shot him."

Gina's mouth dropped open. She continued to squirm in her chair like a trapped animal.

"No! I don't know about Richie. Honestly. You have to believe me. I don't know."

Bobby leaned forward, his hand touching Gina's, his voice gentle. "We know Phil attempted to kill Julian. I need to know how he *tricked* you into helping." Bobby nodded with encouragement.

Calmer but still confused, Gina said, "I let him use my car, but it wasn't exactly a kidnapping."

"How was it different?" asked Bobby.

"Julian was willing to go with him . . . at first . . . Phil said he wanted to talk about Lena."

"Then he broke Julian's hands with his hammer."

Gina's eyes widened, not knowing where to focus.

Slowly with understanding in his voice, Bobby said, "I think you've been duped, Gina. Are you sure you don't know about Richie's death?" Gina shook her head. "Or about how years ago Phil broke Stephen Zug's arm?" Gina looked horrified, unable to speak. "Or about Phil murdering Charlie Sweet so he could marry Lena?"

"That was an accident," whispered Gina. "Everyone said so." The pulse in her throat fluttered through soft pink skin.

"Pretty clear Phil caused Charlie's accident. Then killed him by striking him in the face with his hammer."

Is the evidence in? Alice guessed not.

Bobby, taking advantage of the moment, pivoted back to Julian, probably to keep Gina off guard to scare the truth out of her. "Gina, I think you helped Phil in his attempt to kill Julian."

Sitting straighter, Gina rallied. "No. It wasn't like that. He only wanted to scare Lena. I promise." Gina's voice pleaded for belief.

"Gina, here's what we're looking at." Bobby leaned forward as if sharing a secret. "Phil dumped Julian naked in a duck blind, doused him with dirty water from the slough, left him tied up in the cold. Broke both of his hands with a hammer. You see what I'm getting at?"

"Don't know anything about it. I was in the car." Years of teaching helped Alice spot her lie.

"Gina, Phil couldn't force Julian down the hill by himself. The hill was slick and Julian's wrists bound. I know you helped. Admit it. You helped."

Alice watched her tired, old friend nod.

"Tell me again," said Bobby in a his softer, more satisfied, voice, "how Phil snatched Julian off the street?"

It took Gina a long time to confess. Her tone that of defeat.

"He called and asked him to meet behind the grocery store when Lena was inside Beckerman's. Phil said Julian was eager to meet up."

Alice understood Julian's eagerness. After the taunting at the house, of course Julian wanted to take Phil on anywhere, anytime.

"He *walked* Julian across the field to my trailer." Gina's body twisted, staring at her lap.

"Before sunrise?"

Gina nodded. "I don't really know what happened. When I saw Julian, his wrists were already tied and his mouth was taped."

"And broken, right? Julian's hands were already broken?"

Gina hung her head. "Phil needed me to help him get Julian to my parked car. We drove out to the duck blind for privacy. I helped Phil take Julian down the hill and then went back to the car."

"Were you there when Phil poured water on him?"

Shame crossed Gina's face. "Yes."

"Why did Phil pour beer?"

"He said it would create doubt about what happened and who did it. Someone might take it as a joke gone bad."

"*Someone* meaning the police?" said Bobby.

Gina nodded

"Gina, Julian told us of Phil having the gun. Was it yours?" asked Bobby, his eyes narrowing.

"Yes. But Phil never used it." The flesh on Gina's face trembled.

"Just threatened Julian with it," said Bobby. "What did you think would happen when you left Julian with Phil in the blind?"

"Phil said it was the only way he could convince Julian to talk to him." Gina's tone offered no emphasis of truth.

"How'd he remove Julian's clothing? When Alice found him, Julian's hands and feet were bound." Bobby paused a moment before adding, "Keep in mind, Julian's in the hospital and talking."

All the air seemed to go out of Gina. In a soft, beaten voice, she said, "I held the gun on Julian. Phil undressed him by cutting his clothes off. I thought that was bad, but Phil said it was necessary so he could get even with his ex." Gina looked up and quickened the pace, her eyes wide. "You know she wasn't very nice to him when they were married, and he loved Lena once. He told me."

Alice's mind filled in what Gina didn't say: the cafeteria lady's life narrowed compared to Lena's. As a baker in her own cafe, Lena seemed to glide through life, marrying four times, and having children. For

Gina there was harder work. Alice guessed Gina hadn't been invited to Trisha's wedding. No recognition or thank you for Mrs. Pickler. Alice recalled Gina's hatred of the slashed school painting

"Where's the other gun?" asked Bobby in the same tone he might have used to ask the time.

"What other gun?" Gina wiped tears away from her cheek with the flat of her hand.

"The gun that killed Richie."

"There's only my gun, and it hasn't been fired." Panic changed Gina's voice. "Phil only used it to convince Julian to walk to the trailer. If there's another gun . . . I never saw it."

Gina's world of macaroni and cheese really didn't include the drama of guns. For some reason she put her hands on the table and stroked the top as if smoothing wrinkles.

Bobby's voice became quiet as he thanked her for being forthcoming with details. His hand touched the back of hers. "Gina, you've been snookered. I don't want an attorney to think of you as an accomplice." He handed her a legal pad and asked her to write out all that happened, listing the *mischief* she did, and the planning and execution of Phil's damaging actions.

Alice knew the necessity of Bobby being hard on Gina, to turn her into a witness against Phil. But she saw childlike hope in Gina's eyes and knew her friend thought if she wrote everything out, she'd be back behind the cafeteria line after Christmas break.

How does Bobby do it? How can he allow her to live with false hope?

Alice left the room with tears in her eyes. She wasn't hardened enough to stay.

Not taking time to throw on her coat, Alice stood outside the police station with Audrey and punched numbers into her phone.

"Gilly," she said to her lawyer, "I'm at the police station with Mrs. Pickler. She's in terrible trouble and needs your help."

"Enough said. Be there in five," said Gilly, in her comforting, charge-forward voice.

Chapter 29

Monday afternoon brought quiet drizzle and sleet as if nature couldn't decide how best to keep people in their homes. Claiming a new chill in the air, Alice's house guests layered on quilted vests. Gladys made hot chocolate and ripped open a bag of sandwich cookies.

Glad all the nonsense is over," said Silvie. "Always thought Phil was a shilly-shallow fella."

"He's a doozy," said Virgil, his head shaking back and forth.

The three called dibs on Audrey's favored couch in front of the television, much to the distress of the dog who pawed at Silvie's knee.

"You sit here all the time," said Silvie. "Go 'way. Shoo. We're watching the TV. Skedaddle."

The hound swallowed a woof and gave a snort of disappointment before lying down by the stairs, apparently watching for one of them to move so she could claim the spot. Alice took a deep breath. *It isn't over. Where is Phil?*

When a text came from Taylor Greer, Phil's niece, Alice suited up Audrey for the cold rain.

"Lieutenant Unzicker said he was going to call Phil's family to tell them what happened to Julian," said Alice to her guests. "The full force is checking out buildings where Phil may be hiding." Alice looked at her phone again. "I received a text from Phil's niece. Wants me to meet her in town."

"When will you be back?" asked Virgil stirring his cocoa with a candy cane before taking a noisy sip. "Old Christmas cartoons come on in an hour."

With a big smile, Alice added, "Won't be long. Be back in plenty of time for cartoons."

As Alice drove with her dog into town, she felt uneasy at the curiously worded message.

Meet me in the back parking lot near the gangway. Important.

Alice knew the location. The gangway was a narrow walkway between two brick buildings that allowed shoppers easy access between the back parking lot and the shops of the town square. At that end of the square the cleaners and the real estate office had closed for the holidays as well as the ice cream shop and the travel office nearby. The location struck Alice as lonely but not isolated.

"Do you think Taylor has an idea of Phil's whereabouts?" Alice asked Audrey. The dog tilted her head as if considering an answer. "Just in case Phil's stolen Taylor's phone and sent the message to me, I've got a weapon."

Before she left, Alice pulled a jar of cayenne pepper from her shelf and stuffed it in her jacket pocket. *He can't hit either of us with his hammer if red pepper is in his eyes*, concluded Alice. *We need this Phil thing settled.*

Tomorrow was the wedding, and people were ready to welcome the holidays by clinking champagne glasses affirming commitment. Gladys particularly looked forward to the celebration, often talking of one more chance to dance the Watusi.

"Do you picture Gladys ever dancing the Watusi?" Alice asked her dog. Audrey apparently had no opinion as she flattened her body on the bench seat.

The three house guests made her smile. Of course, once they left, Alice faced weeks of rearranging her house. Thinking they were helpful, Gladys and Silvie had relocated eating utensils, restacked pots and pans to accommodate a new iron they bought at the hardware store. Gladys, it seemed, was on a campaign to eliminate wrinkles from kitchen towels, and the kitchen provided the perfect spot for an ironing board.

Still they brought life into the house, promising to "hitch" a ride back to Limekiln when Kennedy's new hound Clementine gave birth to puppies.

"Been a long time since we had a puppy," said Silvie. Alice winced at someone of their age being overpowered by a muscular dog, but if the three fed a puppy like they fed Audrey, extra poundage might slow a dog down.

Audrey picked up her head and scooted closer to Alice, placing her jaw on her owner's thigh.

"Too much company for you too?" asked Alice, dropping her hand to the top of Audrey's head. "Too many chicken hot dog treats? Don't kid yourself. I know about Virgil feeding you liverwurst."

Maybe her dog's worry face came with too much tension in the house, wondered Alice. After all, bloodhounds were very sensitive, perhaps intuitive.

Alice parked the pickup in the back lot, and she and Audrey scurried for the protective, clear plastic canopy over the gangway just as the sometimes rain, sometimes sleet fell harder. In the swirling weather, Christmas shoppers abandoned the town square. No one congregated to share stories in the wind and cold of town.

The downside of standing under the canopy was the wind tunnel blasts provided by two buildings on either side of the gangway. Alice found herself turning a shoulder to the wind for protection. Audrey's face wrinkled more with each gust carrying ice pellets. The hound's eyes narrowed with disgust. Alice and Audrey stepped closer to the square and to each other.

The black umbrella entering the gangway wasn't held by Taylor. Lena fought with her umbrella and huddled in her long gray coat with a scarf wound around her neck and face, looking every bit like some-one who stepped off a movie set filming the Russian Revolution. A hat was pulled down about her ears, but long blonde curls lifted in the wind from her shoulders. Her feet in heeled boots stomped, trying to keep warm. As usual Alice wore layered warm clothing - turtle-neck, sweater, brown jacket, jeans - so other than bits of ice hitting her face, she was warm. Audrey too had a warm sheep skin-like jacket for warmth.

"What are you doing here?" asked Alice. "Shouldn't you be with Julian?"

"I could ask you the same," said Lena, collapsing the umbrella and rolling it into a small tube.

"Taylor texted saying she had important information," said Alice. Her hand tapped her pocket with the cayenne as she wondered what was so important that they both had been summoned to the gangway. Why not to Lena's house? Why didn't she call the police?

"Texted me too. But didn't say you would be here." Lena stomped, and Alice moved to stand near her, allowing her height to act as a wind break for her shorter friend. Audrey's nose pulled in close between the two women.

"I thought Julian was coming home today," said Alice.

"He did," answered Lena, while glancing over her shoulder. "Cheryl's with him, and both are loudly protesting. But I told him a message came from Taylor. For the moment, I'm saved from hearing further complaints about the doctor's instructions of no beer."

"I wonder what's so special about this gangway?" asked Alice, "Could be at Beckerman's drinking hot chocolate?"

"Taylor told me to meet her in the parking lot," said Lena, "but I don't know why, other than she said she's here for the day and plans to go home for Christmas."

Alice looked out toward the square and back toward a sparse parking lot behind the buildings. Both women stood not talking for what seemed an eternity until Audrey wiggled with a gurgle in her throat, and Alice heard footsteps behind her. Phil walked under the canopy with Taylor behind him. She wore a puffy black jacket with the hood pulled up against the weather and tied tightly, a little string bow hugged her chin. With no gloves, her hands were red.

Phil had a beat-up leather jacket that came to the top of his hips, jeans with his hammer hanging loosely by his thigh, no hat, no gloves. Taylor and Phil were the same height. Their silhouettes against the rain, interchangeable. Wet footprints against the walkway, also the same size. Taylor's gun hand trembled. Alice didn't need her dog's nose to tell her both had been drinking.

"Knees," demanded Taylor.

"Seriously?" Phil's raspy voice held contempt.

Taylor gestured with the gun. When he knelt on the pavement, his knees cracked.

"Girl, this is nuts." His lip curled as if amused. "What do you think you're doing?"

Judging by Taylor's face, Alice expected her to say, *I don't know*.

Lena took one step toward her niece who took one step back. "Taylor, this isn't you. Put the gun down."

"Yeah, put the gun down," said Phil. "You're not going to *shoot* anybody."

"Shut up!" yelled Taylor. "This is all your fault. Everything is your fault. You messed up Dad's life. He loves you, and you spit on him every chance you get. He's ashamed and embarrassed every time there's a reminder in a police blotter . . . "

"Hey, I never pulled anything in Whittle. That was outta respect for your old man."

"Who do you think you're talking to?" Taylor's bare hands shook, and the muscles of her face drew together as if she might cry. "You want me to name the people you hurt?"

"They were looking for *deals* same as me. Everybody's greedy, want something for nothing. Easy prey," said Phil raising one open hand palm up. "Can I get up now?"

"No."

"Let me ask again," his voice was dark. "What you gonna do? Shoot me in front of witnesses?"

"Taylor, honey. . ." pleaded Lena. "Let's go someplace warm. We can talk this out."

Alice knew talking was good. If they stayed in the gangway, the inevitable conclusion bad.

Phil let out a string of expletives referencing Lena. "No disrespect, *honey*, but you've always had an idiotic way of seeing the world." Phil eyed Lena, shaking his head, then pitched his voice higher with irony. "Yeah, Taylor, put the gun down. Listen to your *old* auntie."

His posture reminded Alice of an animal ready for the first opportunity to strike. She reached into her pocket and loosened the top of the jar of cayenne. She imagined Baer saying, *Swing for the fences.*

With her free hand waving a dismissal of thought, Taylor shook her head, focusing on Phil.

"Come on Taylor," said Phil. "You made your point with the big scary gun. O-oo look, I'm terrified. Now, can I at least stand up?"

"No." Taylor took two more steps backward until she stood square against the brick wall of the cleaners.

Alice thought, *Time to stir the pot.*

"Why'd you shoot Richie Mills?" asked Alice directing her attention to Taylor. "Why not kill Phil in the first place?"

Lena gasped. Phil's face, darkly serious. The younger woman looked stunned and confused.

"What do you mean?" asked Taylor, her voice breathy.

Alice nodded. "Right kind of gun. Your footprints match those prints left at the Mansion."

"See. It wasn't me," said Phil so smug that Alice wished she had the gumption to shoot him herself.

Taylor's eyes darted from Phil to Alice and back to Phil. She swallowed hard, placing both hands on the gun.

"If I had shot Uncle Phil," she said with her throat tight and her voice measured by bone-deep anger, "the police would have looked at our family. Probably at Dad, and he can't take more stress. Don't they always suspect the family? But in shooting Richie, the police were supposed to look at Phil. He has motive. Richie testified against him. Uncle Phil even said as much at our house when Dad had a few neighbors over for beer. Phil said he wanted to get even with Richie for betraying him. With Richie dead, the police could arrest Phil. Send him to jail forever. Dad doesn't mind visiting the prison to see his *little* brother." She glared at Phil.

"How'd you get Richie to the Mansion?" asked Alice.

"First I called him. After Phil played tag with Richie's pickup," said Taylor. "When I met him at the apartment, Richie was mad but mostly scared. I told him he needed to get away. Hide. He said he couldn't ask for help from a lady friend because Phil knew her. It would be the first place he'd look. Richie didn't want her hurt. I suggested he hide at the Mansion. A couple years ago, Auntie Lena had mentioned in a letter the owner died."

The picture of hasty cleaning of Richie's apartment came to Alice's mind. He scooped clutter with his foot into piles for Taylor's arrival, not for a visit from Crystal Butterman.

"I don't *own* a gun," said Phil. He touched his temple with his index finger. "Think, Taylor. You're not thinking. Don't own *a gun*. How were the police supposed to pin the murder on me?"

"You could have stolen this one from Dad."

"Or borrowed Mrs. Pickler's," said Alice, hoping her voice carried the right amount of menace. She wanted Phil to know she knew about his accomplice.

"Gina. Lovely Gina." Phil's voice was syrupy, but his eyes narrowed to slits of hate. "Hey Babycakes," he said to Lena, "Gina's even more naive than you. Wanting to bandage my poor *bruised* soul. Makes her an easy mark."

"I cared for you," said Lena, emotions raw. She took a step forward then back. "She probably cared for you too."

Taylor snarled. "Auntie Lena, I never understood why you were enchanted. Where's his appeal?"

"She was in it for the kicks. Enjoyed being a bad girl." Phil turned to Alice, "Lena ever tell you how we robbed the liquor store?"

"It was shoplifting," Lena fired back. "And hours later, I went back and paid for it all."

"Whatever you say," said Phil with a snicker. "How about when we streaked the interstate?"

"That was long ago," shouted Lena. "I'm different now."

"Sure you are. Not an impulsive bone in your body."

Lena flinched and her fist went to her hip - the same hip with a red heart tattoo, her quick decision to please Julian after hearing of a whimsical painting he enjoyed.

Audrey's baritone bark took everyone by surprise, and they all jumped, looking for an intruder in the rain. Alice saw the dog's shimmy, her tail slapping Alice's thigh. She followed her dog's gaze, but no rescuer walked in the square.

"Well, if you're only going to boo-hoo about the past, I'm getting off my knees." Phil shifted to a hunkered down, squat position, back to the wall opposite Taylor, wrapping his hands around his knees. "My butt's gonna get cold, so do you mind wrapping up this pity fest. What's the plan Taylor? Why witnesses?"

Alice saw Phil was ready to pounce. His body had those little movements like teenaged boys do before one gives the first shove or throws the first punch.

"I want people to know what a bad man you are. You hurt Dad."

"Really? That's where we are? People in this town have a pretty clear picture of who I am. As far as your Dad, he chose his life in small town Whittle, breaking his back raising a family on a bike shop income that should have closed."

"If we're so pathetic to you, why do you keep coming back?" whined Taylor. "Why did you take money from Dad?"

Phil smiled and held out one palm, the hand that was not next to his hammer. "Answered your own question. Who am I to prevent your father from feeling all noble when he doles out cash to me?"

"Money lust," offered Lena, then retreating by lowering her eyes.

A chill hit Alice. Taylor wasn't ready to shoot Phil. And Phil *knew* it. His easy cavalier attitude wasn't leading her anywhere good.

Alice turned to Taylor and said, "We're here as witnesses to Phil's despicable life, yes?" Taylor nodded. "He took money from your family. We know he manipulated Richie to steal for him all those years. And he misrepresented his interest in Gina to use her in taking revenge on Limekiln."

"Me?" Phil's voice notched up in mock outrage. "There's a peach. I was perfectly willing to watch over abandoned real estate until I stumbled onto Gina in the middle of the night. Gina *picked* me. Ultimate do-gooder. Missionary woman like Lena, here."

Lena's face deadened, and she pulled her scarf a little tighter around her throat. Alice expected her to say, *shoot him so we can go for cocoa.*

"Taylor, can we admit you're a whiner?" asked Phil. "It would upset your ol' man if you shot me. You've proved your point. I'm a bad guy . . . but you want me in jail? This Julian thing ain't gonna do it. He came with me willingly. No kidnapping charges, Taylor. The best the police got on me is battery."

Taylor's eyes hardened. Alice jumped into the conversation.

"You're right, you are a bad guy," said Alice. "We know you broke Stephen's Zug's arm."

Phil's smile was wicked as he changed his focus to her. "Old News."

Alice wondered how he would come at her for mentioning

Stephen. Two more turns of the top on the jar of pepper and she could pop it off in a second.

"You brutally went after Stephen when he was a kid," said Alice, squaring her stance, getting ready. "It was a warning to his father to keep his mouth shut about Charlie Sweet."

The smirk left Phil's face. Hatred entered.

Alice expected a strike. Something feral entered Phil's posture. Wrongdoing bred hate. Not that Audrey noticed. Her happy tail wagged as she faced the square. Her body shimmied as if expecting a friend.

"You think I killed Charlie?" One of Phil's hands opened with the absurdity of Alice's conclusion.

"Charlie Sweet's death wasn't an accident. Taylor, you don't have to shoot Phil. He's going away for murdering Lena's husband." Alice ignored the sounds coming from Lena, not sure if her friend gasped or gagged. "Years ago, Phil chased Charlie. His red truck forced Charlie's car off the road and into the trees. But that wasn't enough, was it? Charlie had been injured but wasn't dead. Phil killed him with a hammer blow, figuring a couple more wounds wouldn't be noticed, especially with Buddy Wink leading the investigation. Only Phil didn't figure on Roger Zug being in his field, watching."

Phil's face went cold and stiff.

Lena stepped forward, biting her upper lip, fighting anger and tears. Audrey seemed to pick up on the tension and became animated, twisting and turning with a tail that whipped with enthusiasm. Alice had a more difficult time restraining her dog who found interest in the rain of the town square.

"You got no proof," declared Phil, voice alarmingly quiet. "All circumstantial."

"Roger only knew you through rumors, didn't know you owned that red truck. But, a few years later when he moved to town, he became suspicious. Mentioned to my neighbor Scott Stingini about a red truck leaving the scene. Tried to tell the police what he knew, but by then Officer Wink had left the force, and the case was closed. However, Claude Grouper listened. He'd taken pictures after the accident. Historians are always willing to listen and build files."

"Zug and Grouper are crazy. Nosy like you."

Phil's eyes moved as if calculating Alice's weakness. She pushed Audrey toward the square, out of range of falling cayenne if she threw it . . . out of range of a swinging hammer.

Her conclusions turned Phil prickly. His neck flushed up to his jaw. She expected his hatred to focus on her and not his niece holding the gun. *He's almost there, Baer. If he comes at me, I'll throw the pepper. That should stop him long enough for me to grab Taylor's gun.*

"You weren't teaching Stephen a lesson of respect like you told people," said Alice, her voice harder now. "Nope. You sent a message to his father. You could kill his son at any time . . ."

The two other women stared at Phil, stunned by Alice's accusation. Lena's breathing, close to panting, froze as if she had never seen Phil before.

Taylor's hand wobbled, and she lowered the gun.

In a blink, Phil jumped to his feet and charged the two shorter women. He backhanded Lena sending her flying to the brick wall. At the same time his other hand pulled the hammer attached to his belt. To Alice, time escaped in a breath, her body too sluggish to help Taylor. As she stepped forward to stop Phil with her hand on the pepper, her black and tan hound threw her weight into Alice's thigh. Something hot brushed her cheek as Alice stumbled backward. When Alice's head hit the brick wall, she felt deaf. She thought she saw Phil's body go limp as he raised the hammer to swing at Taylor's head before dropping to the pavement. In that blinding moment, nothing made sense.

Lena sat on the walkway with her mouth open before her scream. Taylor still had her arm raised for protection. Pulling away from Alice, Audrey took new interest in Phil who lay in a pool of blood.

Alice looked toward the square. Where did the bullet come from? No one walked in the square. Gentle rain fell straight. But across the square, a woman dressed in black stood up on top of the music store roof, holding a rifle in both hands, gunstock still pressed into her shoulder.

"Rooney."

Alice and Audrey waited in her pickup after the gangway filled with police and paramedics. She held Audrey close, not able to let her go. Was Audrey's push a clumsy moment in the cold or a dog's intuition? Her hound's eyes closed with Alice's hugs. If she held on tight enough, Alice hoped her own involuntary muscle twitches would stop.

The engine ran and the heat in the pickup was adequate, but Alice's legs couldn't stop trembling.

"It's probably shock," Alice said to her hound. "I'd rather be with you, than out there."

The police cuffed Taylor and took her into custody for the murder of Richie. The paramedics gave Lena an icepack and announced she'd probably have quite a shiner from Phil's wallop. Then they helped her into the ambulance. Alice's own scratch had been treated without anyone commenting on how lucky she was.

In the past, bad guys were secured in cells before Bobby talked to her. Alice wanted to go home, but was afraid to drive. So, she sat petting her dog and cupping the hound's big paws in her hands even though the cold and wet left them several minutes before.

What did Rooney mean when she said her job in the military was to take out the garbage? Her single shot was clean through the drizzle, positioned perfectly through the plastic canopy. One shot to Phil's head. Much too difficult for anyone who hadn't constantly trained in sharpshooting.

The passenger door opened to Rooney, and Alice felt tears pool in her eyes. "I'm so sorry," said Alice.

Rooney gave her a what-for kind of face and pushed Audrey's butt closer to Alice as she climbed into the pickup.

"You okay?" asked Rooney.

"A little shaken."

"You're not going soft on me, Mrs. T.? Shooting is my job." Rooney lifted Alice's curly gray hair back from her face to look at the thin red stripe across her cheek. "I'm sorry for . . . almost killing you."

"Tis but a scratch," said Alice mimicking an actor in *Hamlet*.

"I remember that from senior English. You're going with a quote from *Hamlet*?" teased Rooney. "He died."

Alice gave a weak smile. "The bullet barely broke skin. I'm fine." Her knee jumped, and Alice tensed her muscles to gain control. "I thought I was ready for Phil to attack."

"How did you think you were going to stop him?" asked Rooney, her voice carrying doubt.

Alice dropped her eyes and lowered her chin, feeling scolded. "I brought a jar of cayenne pepper."

Rooney took a deep breath. "Don't mention that to the lieutenant. *Please.*"

"Too embarrassing. That's for sure." said Alice. "Thank you for saving Taylor."

"I didn't expect you to move forward," said Rooney while they both watched the police take pictures of the gangway, Phil's body still in place. "You got a great dog here. How'd Audrey tell I fired and you were in danger?"

"I don't think she really knew. When she's bored and wants me to know it's time to get on with it, she throws herself against my thigh. I was fortunate."

Alice pushed away memories of Audrey's shimmy before the bullet came, a particular action saved for Rooney.

"Maybe," said Rooney. "But too much of a coincidence for me to believe she saved you by a happenstance."

The hound twisted on the seat and touched Rooney, nose to nose.

"I can't think about that now," said Alice, her knee caps trembled. "Will this . . . saving of all of us hurt you?"

Rooney took Alice's hand and gave it a squeeze while trying to prevent the hound from licking her face. "When I first heard Phil was in town, I asked Lieutenant Unzicker how I could help. He told me if anything went down with Phil, it would involve *you*. Asked me to be ready, any way I could. Made me a temporary officer, sort of."

"That's why you've been at my elbow when I turn around?" asked Alice.

"More than you know." Rooney grinned.

"But how did you know about today? Did you see me when I parked? I didn't see anyone on the street."

Rooney's smile crinkled her eyes as one might be amused by an old aunt discovering the wonders of a computer. "That old guy at your house. Virgil gives me a call when you're on the move." Alice's head tilted, considering questions. Rooney continued, The lieutenant talked to Julian, and Julian told the old guy to be on guard. Gave him my phone number. Both told me of their time in the military. Recognized I might be interested in helping."

Alice bit her lip. "I thought you said you weren't a sniper. How did you . . ."

"I'm not a sniper, just good with a rifle. But I am a Marine," she said with pride. "Women can't work hot combat." Rooney turned in her seat to face Alice. "But I'm allowed to provide security for special people or places. Big events need protection. Generals come visiting dangerous places. My unit gets *quiet* deployments. We're sort of a high-wire act. Guys in my unit call me Flyswatter. I don't measure a guy's motivation. Only stop bad behavior. I'm *good* at recognizing bad guys. Learned to profile in the three seconds it took Phil . . . I heard

Stephen scream and his bones break. Guys like Phil are *burned* into my radar. Look, I need to report into the police station. Lots of paper work on this one. You gonna be okay or should I get someone to drive you home?"

With a shiver, Alice told her she'd be fine, and Audrey made another attempt to lick Rooney's face. Alice's shoulders sagged as she stared at Rooney in a new way.

"I've been hoping," said Alice in a rush toward normal, "you and Stephen could finally get together." She fought tears, knowing good intentions comes with a toll, a price to be paid.

"You and my mother." A twinkle lit Rooney's eyes. "And Stephen and me. But we need to get past a few skill-sets. Today felt good, *really good*." Rooney rolled her eyes. "Do you ever see me selling bait?"

Chapter 30

Christmas Eve turned out to be another gray day in the forties, but by evening the air cooled enough to allow a miracle to happen at Nick and Trisha's wedding reception. Following dinner at the country club barn, the guests stood and sang *White Christmas* as groomsmen threw open the barn doors to snow falling like feathers. Huddled against blasts of cold air, guests gasped at the beauty of white flakes against a dark blue sky. The scene was all so perfect with Trisha in a dress of white silk, her bridesmaids dressed in Christmas red, one mother spiffed up in burgundy, the other in navy blue with star-like sparkles. For whatever reason after the singing of *White Christmas*, the guests grasped each other's hands and sang *Auld Lang Syne* as the barn doors closed. No one seemed to mind Gladys' off key voice sounding like a siren or Audrey's alto howl. The band held off the program of dancing, looking to Emily Parker for directions of what to do.

Of course, the perfection of the moment had been organized by John Parker who obviously wasn't going to disappoint his daughter who wanted snow on her wedding day. For a glorious moment of pretty snow, everyone ignored the noise of an engine and wafts of exhaust blowing into the country club. Outside churned a snow machine brought in from Little Devil's Bluff Ski Slope.

Alice hadn't planned to attend the reception. It was one thing to sit in the former crying baby room at the church ceremony with Audrey, but to Alice, Audrey's wet mouth didn't seem appropriate for an elegant wedding reception of over two hundred people. There was sure to be one person allergic or queasy at dog slobber. Then, too, were the lingering memories to dampen Alice's spirit: Gina Pickler sitting in a jail cell and Phil Greer in the county morgue. But the bride's mother in her role as dictator insisted Alice attend with Audrey, placing a table above the dining room in what had been designed to look like a barn loft. From above, Alice watched Nick hold Trisha's hand, making circles with his thumb.

Alice wished Lena and Julian could have attended the wedding and reception, but doctors ordered him to take it easy, and Lena seemed anxious to play nurse to her hero with two broken hands. Lena, however, sporting a black eye, managed to squeeze time to see the wedding cakes on each table and snap pictures of her ingenuity of combining real roses and sugar roses side by side. Alice praised Lena's herculean effort to make the room spectacular.

"I want you to know," she said to Alice, "I took your advice and gave Crystal Butterman the wedding ring. Didn't tell her Phil gave to me. Reminded her she had Zadie's adopted parents to impress. Doesn't hurt to fabricate a little marriage story. Keeps people content." Lena's eyes danced with a naughty glee. "She's moving to *Wisconsin*, for God's sake."

When Alice asked to borrow Julian's car to transport her three house guests to the wedding and reception, Julian said, "You got guts. I'll give you that." He gestured with his head for Lena to hand Alice a thin, oblong box wrapped with a bow, an early Christmas gift.

Julian turned quiet, avoiding eye contact, but managed to say, "Don't open it yet. And don't say I never gave you nothing." The gruff old coot looked embarrassed at having a grateful side, a softer moment entered his eyes.

Alice was touched by his unstated thank you.

In Alice's mind the timeline for the reception went something like first dinner at the country club, second, convince house guests to cut out early before the dancing. Her plans never happened since she and Audrey were sequestered in the loft.

Silvie, Virgil, and Gladys climbed the stairs to the loft for the champagne toast and informed the wait staff they were changing their seats. Silvie's white hair was curlier than usual, trapped under netting shaped like a bucket.

"This is my official wedding hat," said Silvie, giving it a pat. "Stays in my hatbox 'til I need it. Don't have time for shopping anymore."

She wore black pants with a heavily beaded gray top over her Cuddly Duds undershirt.

Virgil looked distinguished in a suit, white shirt, blue tie. His newly cut hair revealed his pink scalp. Gladys's tea pot body wore red pants with a shiny satin jacket with a splish-splash of bold red flowers. On her head perched to one side was a hat.

"It's British," she announced. "Called a fascinator. Found it at the Button Museum."

Over a crown of buttons were loops of black cord and a red feather.

Alice dressed in her normal, dressy look, wide-legged black pants with a streamlined tunic in cream. An understated silver-tone rope hung around her neck. Alice's fingers fiddled with it as an intrusion when it banged against the table as she moved.

Guests commented on Audrey's smart attire. The hound sported a black collar with Lena's gift of a silk poinsettia.

"We can't let you two girls eat alone," said Virgil, pulling out two chairs for his companions and grabbing the loose skin underneath Audrey's jaw.

Once the older folk settled down on chairs in the loft, Rooney and Stephen climbed the stairs, holding hands, and joined them.

Gladys giggled at the champagne. "Bubbles put me in the mood for the Watusi. All jazzy inside. Do you know that dance?" she asked Stephen.

Stephen shook his head. "Can't say I do."

"Might be before your time," said Virgil.

"Oh, I'll dance with you, kiddo, whatever the music," said Silvie. "Unless the band plays a polka. Then you and I are hoppin'. Haven't heard a good polka in years."

That morning the wedding ceremony had been beautiful with John Parker walking Trisha down the aisle in her white silk ball gown with lace covering her shoulders and arms, her hair caught up in a designed tangle of blonde curls cascading down her back. When the minister briefly referred to the misfortunes and tribulations in Limekiln, it was obvious he spoke of more than Phil. He quickly followed up with a message of strength and forgiveness in marriage. John and Emily turned to look at each other with kind smiles. Alice felt Flossy Grueber's blog had lost its sting - at last. Many heads nodded and noses sniffed, including Audrey's whose nose found interest in the corner of the baby room. Several days of tension and fear evaporated with memories of other weddings and the thrill of a couple beginning a new life.

Later when the dancing began at the reception, Rooney proclaimed she couldn't dance, no sense of rhythm. Stephen asked Audrey who was more than pleased to stand on her hind legs with front paws on Stephen's shoulders, her tongue lolling out the side of her mouth. Stephen gripped the dog with his good arm, the shorter one on Audrey's shoulder.

Silvie leaned toward Alice. "Your dog is likeable but a goof."

After a couple one-two-three's, Rooney consented, and she and Stephen went down to the dance floor.

"We want one dance then we're ready to go home," said Silvie. "It's Christmas Eve, and we have church services tomorrow."

The three guests joined the dancers for the Chicken Dance, wiggling and waving. Rooney and Stephen, however, moved to a shadow, where their foreheads touched.

Alice wanted to pocket thanks from a few neighbors for remembrances on a quieter day. As the music turned louder, younger guests hit the dance floor and heat rose up to the loft. Finally Alice's houseguests were more than ready to go home, as was Audrey.

Once at the house, the three older friends went to bed. Alice took Audrey upstairs. Tuckered out with all the new smells of the day, the hound climbed onto the bottom of the bed, rolled onto her back, and snored.

After changing into pajamas, Alice angled and scrunched under covers so as not to disturb her dog. Alice's feet stuck out, and she found she couldn't sleep. Moments from the past week crashed in front of her eyes. If she were not hosting guests, she'd release lingering tension by scrubbing the bathtub. Not wanting to disturb anyone, particularly Audrey who might conclude a walk was in her future, Alice lay in bed tossing, feeling again and again the moment in the gangway when her hound threw her body against her owner's leg, heaving her into a wall and saving her life, yet again.

Realizing Christmas was two minutes away and feeling the need to do *something*, Alice sat up in bed and opened the gift from Julian. A bumper sticker made Alice grin. Her eyes filled with merry tears as she read, *My bloodhound can find your honor student.*

So very like Julian, thought Alice, and she ran her big toe along Audrey's side. *Yes, you can, my big girl.*

Her dog's four legs twitched and moved as if she were dreaming of a good run in an open field. A small, sleepy baritone howl escaped the dog's throat. Alice felt her own body relax, sleep coming at last to take her to join Audrey in the dreamy field of the hunt.

Acknowledgements

Thank you . . .

To Phyllis who gave generously of her time to read the manuscript and offer suggestions even as she was in the middle of writing her own novel.

To long time friends and new: Barb, Carolyn, Peg, Carol, Nancy, Joyce, Linda, and Charlotte for encouragement, support, suggestions, coffee . . . and lunch, too.

To members of the Barrington Writers Workshop who listened, read, and offered suggestions.

To owners of dogs, especially bloodhounds, who answered questions, shared stories, and posted pictures online. Dog faces are always an inspiration.

To Chicago Writers Association for posting publicity suggestions and offering support.

And where would I be without Al's support and patience. He tirelessly reads and rereads, keeps me hydrated with coffee, and puts up with my crazy hours and sudden bursts of focused writing.

Even with this swirl of help and more readings than I can count, sneaky-devil mistakes hide in sentences. These errors are all mine. Sigh!

CPSIA information can be obtained
at www.ICGtesting.com
Printed in the USA
FFOW03n1813230517
35917FF